ISBN 978-1-330-87651-0
PIBN 10108453

1 MONTH OF
FREE
READING

at
www.ForgottenBooks.com

By purchasing this book you are eligible for one month membership to ForgottenBooks.com, giving you unlimited access to our entire collection of over 700,000 titles via our web site and mobile apps.

To claim your free month visit:
www.forgottenbooks.com/free108453

AFTER ICEBERGS

WITH A PAINTER:

A

SUMMER VOYAGE TO LABRADOR AND AROUND NEWFOUNDLAND.

BY

REV. LOUIS L. NOBLE,

AUTHOR OF THE "LIFE OF COLE," "POEMS," ETC.

NEW YORK:
D. APPLETON AND COMPANY,
443 & 445 BROADWAY.
LONDON: 16 LITTLE BRITAIN.
M.DCCC.LXI.

TO

E. D. PALMER,

THE SCULPTOR,

THIS VOLUME IS RESPECTFULLY

𝔇𝔢𝔡𝔦𝔠𝔞𝔱𝔢𝔡.

THE title-page alone would serve for a preface to the present volume. It is the record of a voyage, during the summer of 1859, in company with a distinguished landscape painter, along the north-eastern coast of British America, for the purpose of studying and sketching icebergs.

It was thought, at first, that the shores in the neighborhood of St. Johns, Newfoundland, upon which many bergs are often floated in, would afford all facilities. It was found, however, upon experiment, that they did not. Icebergs were too few for the requisite variety; too scattered to be reached conveniently; and too distant to be minutely examined from land. One needed to be in the midst of them, where he could command views, near or remote, of all sides of them, at all hours of the day and evening.

For that purpose a small vessel was hired to take us to Labrador. Favoring circumstances directed us to Battle Harbor, near Cape St. Louis, in the waters of which icebergs, and all facilities for sketching them, abounded.

To diversify the journey, we returned through the Gulf of St. Lawrence, coasting the west of Newfoundland, and the shores of Cape Breton, and concluding with a ride across the island, and through Nova Scotia to the Bay of Fundy.

If the writer has succeeded in picturing to his reader, with some freshness, what he saw and felt, then will the purpose of the book, made from notes pencilled rapidly, have been accomplished.

L. L. N.

HUDSON, NEW JERSEY,
March, 1861.

CONTENTS.

CHAPTER I.

PAGE

Cool and Novel, ... 1

CHAPTER II.

On the Edge of the Gulf-Stream, ... 5

CHAPTER III.

The Painter's Story, ... 8

CHAPTER IV.

Halifax, ... 15

CHAPTER V.

The Merlin, ... 19

CHAPTER VI.

Sydney.—Cape Breton.—The Ocean, ... 23

CHAPTER VII.

The first Icebergs, ... 27

CHAPTER VIII.

Newfoundland.—St. Johns, ... 30

CHAPTER IX.   PAGE

An English Inn.—The Governor and Bishop.—Signal Hill,   .   .   33

CHAPTER X.

The Ride to Torbay.—The lost Sailor.—The Newfoundland Dog, .   38

CHAPTER XI.

Torbay.—Flakes and Fish-houses.—The Fishing-barge.—The Cliffs.—
   The Retreat to Flat Rock Harbor.—William Waterman, the fisherman, ...   41

CHAPTER XII.

The Whales.—The Iceberg.—The Return, and the Ride to St. Johns
   by Starlight, ...   52

CHAPTER XIII.

St. Mary's Church.—The Ride to Petty Harbor,   .   .   .60

CHAPTER XIV.

Petty Harbor.—The Mountain River.—Cod-liver Oil.—The Evening
   Ride back to St. Johns, ...   65

CHAPTER XV.

The Church Ship.—The Hero of Kars.—The Missionary of Labrador,   71

CHAPTER XVI.

Sunday Evening at the Bishop's.—The Rev. Mr. Wood's Talk about
   Icebergs, ...   74

CHAPTER XVII.

Our Vessel for Labrador.—Wreck of the Argo.—The Fisherman's
   Funeral, ...   76

CHAPTER XVIII.   PAGE

Our First Evening at Sea, ...   80

CHAPTER XIX.

Icebergs of the Open Sea.—The Ocean Chase.—The Retreat to Cat
    Harbor, ...   82

CHAPTER XX.

Cat Harbor.—Evening Service in Church.—The Fisherman's Fire.—The
    Return at Midnight, ...   89

CHAPTER XXI.

After Icebergs again.—Among the Sea-Fowl, ...   93

CHAPTER XXII.

Notre Dame Bay.—Fogo Island and the Three Hundred Isles.—The
    Freedom of the Seas.—The Iceberg of the Sunset, and the Flight
    into Twillingate, ...   96

CHAPTER XXIII.

The Sunday in Twillingate.—The Morning of the Fourth, . .   103

CHAPTER XXIV.

The Iceberg of Twillingate, ...   106

CHAPTER XXV.

The Freedom of the Seas once more.—A Bumper to the Queen and
    President, ...   112

CHAPTER XXVI.

Gull Island.—The Icebergs of Cape St. John, . . .   115

CHAPTER XXVII.

The Splendid Icebergs of Cape St. John, ...   121

CHAPTER XXVIII.   PAGE

The Seal Fields.—Seals and Sealing.—Captain Knight's Shipwreck,   129

CHAPTER XXIX.

Belle .Isle and the Coast.—After-dinner Discussion.—First View of
    Labrador.—Icebergs.—The Ocean and the Sunset,   .   .   135

CHAPTER XXX.

The Midnight Look-out Forward.—A Stormy Night.—The Comedy in
    the Cabin, ...   143

CHAPTER XXXI.

The Cape and Bay of St. Louis.—The Iceberg.—Cariboo Island.—
    Battle Harbor and Island.—The Anchorage.—The Missionaries,   149

CHAPTER XXXII.

Battle Island and its Scenery, ...   155

CHAPTER XXXIII.

Mosses, Odors, and Flowers.—A Dinner Party,   .   .   .   161

CHAPTER XXXIV.

Our Boat for the Icebergs.—After the Alpine Berg.—Study of its
    Western Face, ...   165

CHAPTER XXXV.

The Alpine Berg.—Studies of its Southern Front.—Frightful Explosion
    and Fall of Ice.—Studies of the Western Side.—Our Play with the
    Moose Horns.—Splendor of the Berg at Sunset,   .   .   169

CHAPTER XXXVI.

Ramble among the Flowers of Battle Island.—A Visit to the Fisher-
    men.—Walk among the Hills of Cariboo,   .   .   .   179

CHAPTER XXXVII. PAGE

After the Bay St. Louis Iceberg.—Windsor Castle Iceberg.—Founders
Suddenly.—A Brilliant Spectacle, ... 184

CHAPTER XXXVIII.

Sunday in Labrador.—Evening Walk to the Graveyard.—The Rocky
Ocean Shore, ... 188

CHAPTER XXXIX.

The Sail to Fox Harbor.—A Day with the Esquimaux, and our Return, 192

CHAPTER XL.

A Morning Ramble over Cariboo.—Excursion on the Bay, and the Tea-
drinking at the Solitary Fisherman's, ... 196

CHAPTER XLI.

Painting the Cavern of Great Island, and our Sail Homeward in a Gale, 200

CHAPTER XLII.

After the Iceberg of Belle Isle.—The Retreat to Cartwright's Tickle.—
Bridget Kennedy's Cottage, and the Lonely Stroll over Cariboo, 204

CHAPTER XLIII.

The Iceberg of the Figure-head.—The Glory and the Music of the Sea
at Evening, ... 210

CHAPTER XLIV.

Cape St. Charles.—The Rip Van Winkle Berg.—The Great Castle
Berg.—Studies of its Different Fronts, ... 214

CHAPTER XLV.

The Sail for St. Charles Mountain.—The Salmon Fishers.—The Cavern
of St. Charles Mountain.—Burton's Cottage.—Magnificent Scene

from St. Charles Mountain.—The Painting of the Rip Van Winkle
Berg.—The Ice-Vase, and the Return by Moonlight,   .   .   219

CHAPTER XLVI.

After our Last Iceberg.—The Isles.—Twilight Beauties of Icebergs.—
Midnight Illumination, ...   228

CHAPTER XLVII.

Farewell to Battle Harbor.—The Straits of Belle Isle.—Labrador Landscapes.—The Wreck of the Fishermen,   .   .   .   236

CHAPTER XLVIII.

Sketching the Passing Bergs.—The Story of an Iceberg,   .   .   241

CHAPTER XLIX.

Drifting in the Straits.—Retreat to Temple Bay.—Picturesque Scenery.
—Voyager's Saturday Night, ...   264

CHAPTER L.

Sunday in Temple Bay.—Religious Services.—The Fisherman's Dinner
and Conversation.—Chateau.—The Wreck.—Winters in Labrador.
—Icebergs in the Winter.—The French Officers' Frolic with an
Iceberg.—Theory of Icebergs.—Currents of the Strait.—The Red
Indians.—The Return to the Vessel, ...   267

CHAPTER LI.

Evening Walk to Temple Bay Mountain.—The Little Iceberg.—
Troubles of the Night, and Pleasures of the Morning.—Up the
Straits.—The Pinnacle of the Last Iceberg.—Gulf of St.
Lawrence, ...   274

CHAPTER LII.

Coast Scenery.—Farewell to Labrador, ...   279

CHAPTER LIII. PAGE

Western Newfoundland.—The Bay, the Islands, and the Highlands of
St. John.—Ingornachoix Bay, ... 284

CHAPTER LIV.

Slow Sailing by the Bay of Islands.—The River Humber.—St. George's
River, Cape, and Bay.—A Brilliant Sunset, . . . 287

CHAPTER LV.

Foul Weather.—Cape Anguille.—The Clearing Off.—The Frolic of the
Porpoises.—The New Cooks.—The Ship's Cat, . . 290

CHAPTER LVI.

St. Paul's Island.—Cape North.—Coast of Cape Breton.—Sydney
Light and Harbor.—The End of our Voyage to Labrador, and
around Newfoundland, ... 298

CHAPTER LVII.

Farewell to Captain Knight.—On our way across Cape Breton.—A
Merry Ride, and the Rustic Lover, ... 301

CHAPTER LVIII.

Evening Ride to Mrs. Kelly's Tavern.—The Supper and the Lodging, 306

CHAPTER LIX.

Sunday at David Murdoch's.—Scenery of Bras d'Or, . . . 314

CHAPTER LX.

Off for the Strait of Canso.—St. Peters, and the Country.—David Murdoch's Horses, and his Driving.—Plaster Cove, . . 318

CHAPTER LXI.

Adieu to David and Cape Breton.—The Strait of Canso.—Our Nova
Scotia Coach.—St. George's Bay.—The Ride into Antigonish, . 322

CHAPTER LXII.   PAGE

New Glasgow.—The Ride to Truro.—Railway Ride to Halifax.—Parting with the Painter, ... 326

CHAPTER LXIII.

Coach Ride from Halifax to Windsor.—The Prince Edward's Man, and
the Gentleman from Newfoundland, ... 329

CHAPTER LXIV.

Windsor.—The Avon, and the Tide.—Steamer for St. Johns, New
Brunswick.—Mines Basin.—Coast Scenery.—The Scene of Evan-
geline.—Parsboro.—The Bay of Fundy.—Nova Scotia and New
Brunswick Shores.—St. Johns.—The Maine Coast.—Island of
Grand Manan, ... 332

ILLUSTRATIONS.

————•••————

PAGE

No. 1.—VIGNETTE—ICEBERGS AT SUNSET, . . 1

No. 2.—A LARGE ICEBERG IN THE FORENOON LIGHT

NEAR THE INTEGRITY, ... 119

No. 3.—AN ARCHED ICEBERG IN THE AFTERNOON LIGHT, 136

No. 4.—ICE FALLING FROM A LOFTY BERG, . . 173

No. 5.—ICEBERG IN THE MORNING MIST—WHALE-BOAT, 214

No. 6.—ICEBERG IN THE STRAIT OF BELLE ISLE, . . 241

AFTER ICEBERGS WITH A PAINTER.

CHAPTER I.

COOL AND NOVEL.

"AFTER icebergs!" exclaims a prudent, but imaginary person, as I pencil the title on the front leaf of my note-book.

"Why, after deer and trout among the Adirondack Mountains with John Cheeney, the Leather-stocking of those wilds, who kills his moose and panther with a pistol; or after salmon on the Jaques Cartier and Saguenay, is thought to be quite enough for your summer tourist.

"After buffalo is almost too much for any not at home in the great unfenced, Uncle Sam's continental parks, where he pastures his herds, and waters them in the Platte and Colorado, and walls out the Pacific with the Rocky Mountains. He is rather a fast hunter who indulges in the chase in those fair fields. It is no boy's play to commit yourself to mule and horse, the yawls of the prairie, riding yourself sore and thirsty over the gracefully rolling, never-breaking swells, the green seas sparkling with dewy flowers, but never coming ashore. The ocean done up in solid land is weary voyaging to one whose youthful footsteps were over the fields, to the sound of sabbath bells.

"After ostriches, with the ship of the desert, although rather a hot chase for John and Jonathan over broad sands, yellow with the sunshine of centuries, and the bird speeding on legs swift as the spokes of the rapid wheels, is, nevertheless, a pleasure enjoyed now and then.

"But after icebergs is certainly a cool, if not a novel and perilous adventure. A few climb to the ices of the Andes; but after the ices of Greenland, except by leave of government or your merchant prince, is entirely another thing.

"You will do well to recollect, that nature works in other ways in the high north than in the high Cordilleras and Alps, and especially in the latter, where she carefully slides her mer-de-glace into the warm valley, and gently melts it off, letting it run merrily and freely to the sea, every crystal fetter broken into silvery foam. But in Greenland she heaves her mile-wide glacier, in all its flinty hardness, into the great deep bodily, and sends it, both a glory and a terror, to flourish or perish as the currents of the solemn main move it to wintry or to summer climes. After icebergs ! Weigh well the perils and the pleasures of this new summer hunting."

" We have weighed them, I confess, not very carefully ; only ' hefting' them a little, just enough to help us to a guess that both are somewhat heavier than the ordinary delights and dangers of sporting nearer home. But, Prudens, my good friend, consider the ancient saw, ' Nothing venture nothing have.' Not in the least weary of the old, we would yet have something new, altogether new. You shall seek the beauties of scales and of plumage, and the graces of motion and the wild music of voices, among the creatures of the brooks and woodlands. Our game, for once, is the wandering alp of the waves ; our wilderness, the ocean ; our steed, the winged vessel ; our arms, the pencil and the pen ; our game-bags, the portfolio, painting-box, and note-book, all harmless instruments, you perceive, with mild report. It is seldom that they are heard at any distance, although, at intervals, the sound has gone out as far as the guns of the battle-field.

"Should we have the sport we anticipate, you may see the rarest specimen of our luck preserved in oil and colors, a method peculiar to those few, who intend their articles less for the market than for immortality, as men call the dim glimmering of things in the dusky reaches of the past.

"But you shall hear from us, from time to time, if possible, how we speed in our grand hunt, and how the pleasures and the risks make the scale of our experience vibrate. Within a few minutes, we shall be on our way to Boston, darting across grassy New England, regardless as the riders of the steeple-chase of cliff and gulf, fence, wall and river, with a velocity of wheels that would set the coach on fire, did not ingenuity stand over the axles putting out the flame with oil.

"This evening, we meet a choice few in one of those bowery spots of Brookline, where intelligence dwells with taste and virtue, and talk of our excursion.

"To-morrow, amid leave-takings, smiles and tears, and the waving of handkerchiefs, of which we shall be only quiet spectators, with the odor of our first sea-dinner seasoning the brief excitement of the scene, and all handsomely rounded off with the quick thunder of the parting gun, we sail, at noon, in the America."

CHAPTER II.

FRIDAY MORNING, *June* 17, 1859. Here we are on the edge of the Gulf-Stream, loitering in a fog that would seem to drape the whole Atlantic in its chilly, dismal shroud. We are as impatient as children before the drop-curtain of a country show, and in momentary expectation that this unlucky mist will rise and exhibit Halifax, where we leave the steamer, and take a small coasting-vessel for Cape Breton and Newfoundland.

As we anticipated, both of us have been sea-sick continually. I had hoped that we should have the pleasure of one dinner at least, with that good appetite so common upon coming off into the salt air. But before the soup was fairly off there came over me the old qualm,

the herald of those dreadful impulses that drive the unhappy victim either to the side of the vessel, or down into
its interior, where he lays himself out, pale and trembling,
on his appointed shelf, and awaits in gloomy silence the
final issue.   It is needless to record, that, with that unlucky attempt to enjoy the luxuries of the table, perished,
not only the power, but the wish to eat.

Yesterday, when I came on deck, I found C—— con-
versing with Agassiz.   Although so familiar with the Alpine glaciers, and all that appertains to them, he had never
seen an iceberg, and almost envied us the delight and excitement of hunting them.   But not even the presence
and the fine talk of the great naturalist could lay the
spirit of sea-sickness.   Like a very adder lurking under
the doorstone of appetite, it refused to hear the voice of
the charmer.   Out it glided, repulsive reptile ! and away
we stole, creeping down into our state-room, there to burrow in damp sheets, taciturn and melancholy "wretches,
with thoughts concentred all in self."   An occasional
remark, either sad or laughable, broke the sameness of
the literally rolling hours.   By what particular process
of mind, I shall not trouble myself to explain, the Painter, who occupied the lower berth, all at once gave signs
that he had come upon the borders of a capital story, and
with the spirit to carry even a dull listener to the further

side of it, and keep him thoroughly amused. It was a traveller's tale, a story of his own first ride over the mountains of New Granada, accompanied by a friend, on his way to the Andes.

CHAPTER III.

TWENTY days, and most of them days of intense heat and sea-sickness, were spent on a brig from New York to the mouth of the Magdalena. In twenty minutes all that tedious voyage was sailed over again, and he was in the best humor possible for the next nine days in a steamboat up the river, a mighty stream, whose forests appear like hills of verdure ranging along its almost endless banks.

After the steamboat, came a tiresome time in a canoe, followed by a dark and fireless night in the great woods, where they were stung by the ants, and startled by the hootings and howlings, and all the strange voices and noises of a tropical forest.

Then the tale kept pace with the mules all day, jogging

on slowly, an all-day story that pictured to the listener's mind all the passing scenery and incidents, the people and the travellers themselves, even the ears of the self-willed, ever-curious mules. Towards sunset, the way-farers found themselves journeying along the slope of a mountain, willing to turn in for the night at almost any dwelling that appeared at the road-side. The guide and the baggage were behind, and suggested the propriety of an early halt. But each place, to which they looked forward, seemed sufficiently repulsive, upon coming up, to make them venture on to the next. They ventured, without knowing it, beyond the very last, and got benighted where it was difficult enough in the broad day. After a weary ride up and up, until it did appear that they would never go down again in that direction, they stopped and consulted, but finally concluded to continue on, although the darkness was almost total, trusting to the mules to keep the path. At length it was evident that they were at the top of the mountain, and passing over upon its opposite side. Very soon, the road, a mere bridle-path, became steep and rugged, leading along the edges of pre-cipices, and down rocky, zigzag steps, that nothing but the bold, sure-footed mule would or could descend. The fact was, they were going down a fearfully dangerous mountain-road, on one of the darkest nights. And, won-

1*

derful to tell, they went down safely, coming out of the
forest into a level vale beset with thickets and vine-cov-
ered trees, a horrible perplexity, in which they became
heated, scratched, and vexed beyond all endurance. At
last, they lost the way and came to a dead halt. Here.
C—— got off, and leaving the mule with F——, plunged
into the bushes to feel for the path, pausing occasionally
to shout and to wait for an answer. No path, however,
could be found. In his discouragement, he climbed a
tree with the hope of seeing a light. He climbed it to the
very top, and gazed around in all directions into the wide,
unbroken night. There was a star or two in the black
vault, but no gleam of human dwelling to be seen below.

Extremes do indeed meet, even the dreadful and the
ridiculous. And so it was with C—— in the tree-top.
From almost desperation, he passed into a frolicsome
mood, and began to talk and shout, at the top of his voice,
in about the only Spanish he could then speak, that he
would give cinco pesos, cinco pesos,—five dollars, five dollars, to any one that would come and help them. From
five he rose to ten. But being scant of Spanish, he could
express the ten in no other way than by doubling the
cinco—cinco cinco pesos, cinco cinco pesos. Fruitless
effort! A thousand pounds would have evoked no
friendly voice from the inhospitable solitude.

The airing, though, was refreshing, and he clambered down and attempted his way back, shouting as usual, but now, to his surprise, getting no reply. What could it mean ? Where was F——? Had he got tired of waiting, and gone off ? With redoubled energy C—— pushed on through the interminable brush to see. He was in a perfect blaze of heat, and dripping with perspiration. A thousand vines tripped him, a thousand branches whipped him in the face. When he stopped to listen, his ears rung with the beating of his own heart, and he made the night ring too with his loud hallooing. But no one answered, and no mules could be found. Nothing was left but to push forward, and he did it, with a still increasing energy. Instantly, with a crack and crash he pitched headlong down quite a high bank into a broad brook. For a moment he was frightened, but finding himself sound, and safely seated on the soft bottom of the brook, he concluded to enjoy himself, moving up and down, with the warm water nearly to his neck, till he had enough of it ; when he got up, and felt his way to the opposite bank, which, unfortunately for him, was some seven or eight feet of steep, wet clay. Again and again did he crawl nearly to the top, and slip back into the water—a treadmill operation that was no joke. A successful attempt at scaling this muddy barrier was made, at length, through the kindly intervention of some vines.

But how was all that ? Where was he ? He never crossed a stream in going to the tree. He must be lost. He must have become turned at the tree, and gone in a wrong direction. And yet he could not relinquish the notion that all was right. He decided to continue forward, pausing more frequently to halloo. To his exceeding joy, he presently heard a faint, and no very distant reply. He quickly heard it again—close at hand—" C——, come here !—come here ! " He hastened forward. F—— was sitting on the mule. He said, in a low tone of voice, " Come here, and help me off. I am very sick." He was alarmingly sick. C—— helped him down, and laid him on the ground. The only thing to be done was to make a rough bed of the saddles and blankets, secure the mules, and wait for daylight. While engaged in this, one of the mules suddenly broke away, and with a perilous flourish of heels about C——'s head, dashed off through the thickets, and was seen no more. To crown their troubles, a ferocious kind of ant attacked them at all points, and kept up their assault during the remainder of the miserable night. They had made their bed upon a large ant-hill. In the morning, there they were, they knew not where, with but one mule, trappings for two, and F—— too indisposed to proceed. C—— mounted the mule and set off for relief. A short ride brought him out upon the path, which soon led down to the border of a wide marsh. The crossing of the marsh was terrible. The poor animal sank into the mire to the girth, reared, plunged and rolled, plastering himself and rider all over and over again with the foulest mud. When they reached the solid ground, and trotted along towards some natives coming abroad to their labor, the appearance of our traveller, in quest of the sublime and beautiful, was certainly not imposing. He told his story to the staring Indians in the best way his ingenuity could invent, none of which they could be made to comprehend. He inquired the way to the town, the very name of which they seemed never to have heard. He asked the distance to any place,—the nearest,—no matter what. It was just as far as he was pleased to make it.

"Was it two leagues?"

"Si, Señor."

"Was it five leagues?"

"Si, Señor."

"Was it eight, nine, ten leagues?"

"Si, Señor."

"For how much money would they guide him to the town?"

Ah ! that was a different thing ; they had more intelligence on that subject. They would guide him for a great deal. In fact, they would do it for about ten times its value. He spurred his muddy mule, galloped out of sight and hearing, more amused than vexed, and went ahead at a venture. The venture was lucky. In the course of the morning he made his entrance into the city, succeeded in finding out the residence of the person to whom he had letters of introduction, presented himself to the gentleman of the house, an American, and had both a welcome and a breakfast. Before the day was past, F—— and himself were comfortably settled, and, with their kind host, were making merry over their first ride on the mountains of South America. I am sure I was made merry at the quiet recital. Lying as I was in my berth, rolled in cloak and blanket, and looking neither at the face nor motions of the speaker, but only at the blank beams and boards close above, I laughed till the tears ran copiously, and I forgot that I was miserable and sea-sick.

CHAPTER IV.

WE have now been lying for hours off Halifax. The fog appears to be in a profound slumber. Whistle, bell and big guns have no power to wake it up. The waves themselves have gone to sleep under the fleecy covering. Old Ocean lazily breathes and dreams. The top-mast, lofty and slim, marks and flourishes on the misty sky, as an idler marks the sand with his cane. Pricked on by our impatience, back and forth we step the deck, about as purposeless as leopards step their cage. They are letting off the steam. It is flowing up from the great fountains, a deep and solemn voice, a grand ventriloquism, that muffles in its breadth and fulness all the smaller sounds, as the mighty roar dampens the noisy dashings of the cataract. What a sublime translation of human skill and genius is an engine, this stupendous creature of iron! How splendid are its polished limbs! What power in all those easy motions! What execution in those still and oily manœuvres!

Among the ladies there is one of more than ordinary beauty. Luxuriant, dark hair, a fair complexion with the bloom of health, a head and neck that would attract a sculptor, and surpassingly fine, black eyes. There is a power in beauty. Why has not God given it to us all? You shall answer me that in heaven. There is indeed a power in beauty. It goes forth from this young woman on all sides, like rays from some central light. I have called her a New England girl, but she turns out to be Welsh.

How like magic is the work of this fog! Instantly almost it is pulled apart like a fleece of wool, and lo! the heavens, the ocean, and the rugged shores. A pilot comes aboard from a fishing-boat, looking as rough and craggy as if he had been, toad-like, blasted out of the rocks of his flinty country, so brown and warty is his skin, so shaggy are his beard and hair, so sail-like and tarry is his raiment. The ancient mariner for all the world! His skinny hand touches no common mortal. His glittering eye looks right on, as he moves with silent importance to the place where shine the gilded buttons of the captain.

This is a wild northern scene. Hills, bony with rock and bristling with pointed firs, slope down to the sea. But yet how beautiful is any land looking off upon the barren deeps of ocean. Distant is the city on a hill-side, glittering at a thousand points, while on either hand, as we move in at the entrance of the harbor, are the pleasant woods and the white dwellings, country steeples and cultivated grounds. As the comfortless mist rolls away, and the golden light follows after, warming the wet and chilly landscape, I feel that there are bliss and beauty in Nova Scotia.

Grandly as we parade ourselves, in the presence of the country and the town, I prefer the more modest, back-street entrance of the railroad. The fact is, I am afraid of your great steamer on the main, and for the reason given by a friend of mine : if you have a smash-up on the land, why, there you are ; if, on the sea, where are you ?

I have been talking with the fair lady of Wales. She was all spirit. " There was much," she said, " that was fine, in America ; but Wales was most beautiful of all. Had I ever been in Wales ? " One could well have felt sorry he was not then on his way to Wales. We parted where we met, probably to meet no more, and I went forward to gaze upon the crowded wharf, which we were then approaching. A few hasty adieus to some newly-formed acquaintances, and we passed ashore to seek the steamer for Cape Breton. It was waiting for us just behind the storehouse where we landed, and soon followed the America with a speed not exactly in proportion to the noise and effort.

CHAPTER V.

BE it known that the Merlin, the name in which our vessel delights, is a small propeller, with a screw wheel, and a crazy mess of machinery in the middle, which go far towards making one deaf and dumb by day, but very wakeful and talkative by night ; so thoroughly are the rumbling, thumping and clanking disseminated through all those parts appointed for the passengers. The Merlin has not only her peculiar noises, but her own peculiar ways and motions ; motions half wallowing and half progressive ; a compound motion very difficult to describe, at the time, mainly on account of a disagreeable confusion in the brain and stomach.

The arrangements in the Merlin for going to repose are better than those for quitting it. No chestnut lies more snugly in the burr than your passenger in his berth. If he happen to be short and slender, it is sure to fit him all the better. But when he gets out of it, he is pushed forward into company immediately, and washes in the one bowl, and looks at the one glass. On board the Merlin, one feels disposed to give the harshest words of his vocabulary a frequent airing. He sees how it is, and he says to himself: I have the secret of this Merlin ; she is intended to put a stop to travel ; to hinder people from leaving Halifax for Sydney and St. Johns. Wait you eight and forty hours after this ungenerous soliloquy, and speak out then. What do you say ? The Merlin is the thing !

Away in this dusky corner of the world Peril spins her web. High and wide and deep she stretches her subtle lines : cliffs, reefs and banks, ice, currents, mists and winds. But the Merlin is no moth, no feeble insect to get entangled in this terrible snare. Dark-winged dragon-fly of the sea, she cuts right through them all. Your grand ocean steamer, with commander of repute, plays the tragic actress quite too frequently in the presence of these dread capes. But the Merlin, with Captain Sampson's tread upon the deck, in the night and in the light, with his look ahead and his eye aloft, and his plummet in the deep sea, trips along her billowy path as lightly as a lady trips among her flowers. A blessing upon Captain Sampson who sails the little Merlin from Nova Scotia to Newfoundland. He deserves to sail an Adriatic.

Here we are again in that same bad fog, that smothered much of our pleasure, and some of our good luck, in the America. It is gloomy midnight, and the sea is up. A pale, blue flame crowns the smoke-stack, and sheds a dreary light upon the sooty, brown sails. The breeze plays its wild music in the tight rigging, while the swells beat the bass on the hollow bow. To a landsman, how frightfully the Merlin rolls! But we are dashing along through this awful wilderness, right steadily. Every hour carries us ten miles nearer port. Ye wandering barks, on this dark, uncertain highway, do hear the mournful clang of our bell, and turn out in time as the law of nature directs! Ye patient, watchful mariners that keep the look-out forward, pierce the black mist with your keen sight, and spy the iceberg, that white sepulchre of the careless sailor. Just here there is a mountain in the deep, and we are crossing its summit, which accounts for the sharp, rough sea, the captain tells me. The vessel now turns into the wind, the loose sails roar and crack, and bound in their strong harness, like frightened horses; loud voices cut through the uproar, rapid footsteps thump, and rattling ropes lash the deck. Then there is a momentary lull : they heave the lead. The mountain top is under us, say, five hundred feet. All is right. Captain Sampson puts off into wider waters, and I, chilly and damp, creep into my berth, full of hope and sleep.

CHAPTER VI.

MONDAY, *June* 19, 1859. We are still rising and sinking on the misty ocean, and somewhere on those great currents flowing from the Gulf of St. Lawrence.

Yesterday, at an early hour, we were entering Sydney Harbor, Cape Breton, with a tide from sea, and a flood of brightness from the sun. The lively waters, the grassy fields dotted with white dwellings, and the dark green woodlands were bathed in splendor. A few clouds, that might have floated away from the cotton-fields of Alabama, kept Sunday in the quiet heavens. We went ashore with some thought of attending church, but found the time would not permit. A short walk to some Indian huts, with the smoke curling up from their peaks' like the pictures of volcanoes, a cup of tea of our own making, some toast and fresh eggs in the village tavern, with the comfort of sitting to enjoy them at a steady table on firm land, gave an agreeable seasoning to the hour we lingered in Sydney, and braced us for the long stretch across to Newfoundland.

As you enter Sydney Bay, you see northward some remarkable cliffs, fan-like in shape as they rise from the sea. In the clear and brilliant morning air, they had a roseate and almost flame-like hue, which made them appear very beautiful. I thought of them as some gigantic sea-shells placed upon the brim of the blue main. When they set in the waves, along in the afternoon, the picturesque coast of Cape Breton was lost to view, and we became, to all appearance, a fixture in the centre of the circle made by the sky and the sea. How wearisome it grew! Always moving forward,—yet never getting further from the line behind,—never getting nearer to the line before,—ever in the centre of the circle. The azure dome was over us, its pearl-colored eaves all around us. Oh! that some power would lift its edge, all dripping with the brine of centuries, out of the ocean, and let the eye peep under! But all is changeless. We were under the centre of the dome, and on the hub of the great wheel, run out upon its long spokes as rapidly and persistently as we would. Our stiff ship was dashing, breast-deep, through the green and purple banks that old Neptune heaved up across our path.   Bank after bank he rolled up before us, and our strong bows burst them all, striking foam, snowy foam, out of them by day, and liquid jewelry out of them by night.   The circle was still around us, the tip of the dome above.   We were leaving half a world of things, and approaching half a world of things, and yet we were that same fixture.   Our brave motions, after all, turned out to be a kind of writhing on a point, in the middle of the mighty ring, under the key-stone of the marvellous vault.   The comfort of the weary time was, that we sailed away from the morning, passed under the noon, and came up with, and cut through the evening.

When we caught up with the evening yesterday, and saw the sun set fire to, and burn off that everlasting ring, we were sitting quietly on deck, touched with the sweet solemnities of the hallowed hour.   The night, with all that it would bring us, was coming out of the east, moving up its stupendous shadow over the ocean ; the day, with all it had been to us, was leaving us, going off into the west over the great continent.   We were crossing the twilight, that narrow, lonesome, neutral ground, where gloom and splendor interlock and wrestle.   The little petrel piped his feeble notes, and flew close up, following under the very feathers of the ship, now skimming the glassy hollow of the swells, and then tiptoe on the crest.

2

The wind was strengthening, tuning every cord and straining every sail, winnowing the fiery chaff, and sowing the sparkling grain forward on the furrowed waters. We had a vessel full of wind; and so vessel, wind and sparks together, went away across the sea as if they were seeking some grand rendezvous. Far and wide the waves all hastened in the same direction, rolling, leaping, crumbling into foam, bristling the snowy feathers on neck and breast as they skipped and flew upon each other in their play and passion. And so we all sped forward with one will, and with one step, keeping time to the music of the mighty band : clouds, winds and billows, seabirds, sails and sparkling smoke, and Merlin with her men ; all moving forward, as some grand army moves onward to a battle-field. When there is really nothing to describe, why should not one record the conceits and fancies born of an evening at sea ? So I thought, last evening, when I was a little sea-sick, and sick of the monotony of the scene, and a little home-sick, and felt that this was pleasure rather dearly bought. Still if one would see the planet upon which he has taken his passage round the sun, and through the spaces of the universe, he must be brave and patient, hopeful and good-tempered. Be this, or turn back, at the first view of salt-water, and go home to toil, to contentment and self-possession.

CHAPTER VII.

THE FIRST ICEBERGS.

NEWFOUNDLAND seems to be wreathed with fogs forever. As a dwelling-place, this world certainly appears
far from complete,—an argument for a better country.
But yonder is the blue sky peeping through the mist, an
intimation of that better country. A solitary bird sits
upon a stick floating by, looking back curiously as it
grows less and less. Now it merely dots the gleaming
wave, and now it is quite wiped away. Thus float off
into the past the winged pleasures of the hour.

Again we are at blindman's-buff in the fog. The
whistle and the bell remind us of the perils of this play.
The gloom of evening deepens, and we go below with the
hope of rounding Cape Race, and of wheeling down the
northern sea direct for port, before daylight. *Down* the
northern sea !—This calling north *down* instead of *up*,

appears to me to be reversing the right order of things. It is *against* the stream, which, inshore, sets from Baffin's Bay south ; and, in respect of latitude, it is *up-hill :* the nearer the pole, the higher the latitude. And besides, it is *up* on the map, and was *up* all through my boyhood, when geography was a favorite study. But as down seems to be the direction settled upon in common parlance, *down* it shall be in all these pages.

Icebergs ! Icebergs !—The cry brought us upon deck at sunrise. There they were, two of them, a large one and a smaller : the latter pitched upon the dark and misty desert of the sea like an Arab's tent ; and the larger like a domed mosque in marble of a greenish white. The vaporous atmosphere veiled its sharp outlines, and gave it a softened, dreamy and mysterious character. Distant and dim, it was yet very grand and impressive. Enthroned on the deep in lonely majesty, the dread of mariners, and the wonder of the traveller, it was one of those imperial creations of nature that awaken powerful emotions, and illumine the imagination. Wonderful structure ! Fashioned by those fingers that wrought the glittering fabrics of the upper deep, and launched upon those adamantine ways into Arctic seas, how beautiful, how strong and terrible ! A glacier slipped into the ocean, and henceforth a wandering cape, a restless headland, a revolving island, to compromise the security of the world's broad highway. No chart, no sounding, no knowledge of latitude avails to fix thy whereabout, thou roving Ishmael of the sea. No look-out, and no friendly hail or authoritative warning can cope with thy secrecy or thy silence. Mist and darkness are thy work-day raiment. Though the watchman lay his ear to the water, he may not hear thy coming footsteps.

We gazed at the great ark of nature's building with steady, silent eyes. Motionless and solemn as a tomb, it seemed to look back over the waves as we sped forward into its grand presence. The captain changed the course of the steamer a few points so as to pass it as closely as possible. C—— was quietly making preparation to sketch it. The interest was momentarily increasing. We were on our way to hunt icebergs, and had unexpectedly come up with the game. We fancied it was growing colder, and felt delighted at the chilly air, as if it had been so much breath fresh from the living ice. To our regret, I may say, to our grief, the fog suddenly closed the view. No drop-curtain could have shut out the spectacle more quickly and more completely. The steamer was at once put on her true course, and the icebergs were left to pursue their solitary way along the misty Atlantic.

CHAPTER VIII.

WHEN the mist dispersed, the rocky shores of New-foundland were close upon our left,—lofty cliffs, red and gray, terribly beaten by the waves of the broad ocean. We amused ourselves, as we passed abreast the bays and headlands and rugged islands, with gazing at the wild scene, and searching out the beauty timidly reposing among the bleak and desolate. On the whole, Newfound-land, to the voyager from the States, is a lean and bony land, in thin, ragged clothes, with the smallest amount of ornament. Along the sides of the dull, brown mountains there is a suspicion of verdure, spotted and striped here and there with meagre woods of birch and fir. The glory of this hard region is its coast : a wonderful perplexity of fiords, bays and creeks, islands, peninsulas and capes, endlessly picturesque, and very often magnificently grand. Nothing can well exceed the headlands and precipices,

honey-combed, shattered, and hollowed out into vast caverns, and given up to the thunders and the fury of the
deep-sea billows. Read the Pirate of Scott again, and
Sumburg Head will picture for you numbers of heads, of
which it is not important to mention the name. The
brooks that flow from the highlands, and fall over cliffs
of great elevation into the very surf, and that would be
counted features of grandeur in some countries, are here
the merest trifles, a kind of jewelry on the hem of the
landscape.

The harbor of St. Johns is certainly one of the most
remarkable for bold and effective scenery on the Atlantic
shore. The pictures of it, which of late abound, and are
quite truthful as miniature portraits, fail entirely to suggest the grand expression and strong character of the
coast. We were moving spiritedly forward over a bright
and lively sea, watching the stern headlands receding in
the south, and starting out to view in the north, when we
passed Cape Spear, a lofty promontory, crowned with a
light-house and a signal-shaft, upon which was floating the
meteor-flag of England, and at once found ourselves
abreast the bay in front of St. Johns. Not a vestige,
though, of any thing like a city was in sight, except another flag flitting on a distant pinnacle of rock. Like a
mighty Coliseum, the sea-wall half encircled the deep

water of this outer bay, into which the full power of the
ocean let itself under every wind except the westerly.
Right towards the coast where it gathered itself up into
the greatest massiveness, and tied itself into a very Gor-
dian knot, we cut across, curious to behold when and
where the rugged adamant was going to split and let us
through. At length it opened, and we looked through,
and presently glided through a kind of mountain-pass,
with all the lonely grandeur of the Franconia Notch.
Above us, and close above, the rugged, brown cliffs rose
to a fine height, armed at certain points with cannon, and
before us, to all appearance, opened out a most beautiful
mountain lake, with a little city looking down from the
mountain side, and a swamp of shipping along its shores.
We were in the harbor, and before St. Johns. As we
bade adieu to the sea, and hailed the land with our
plucky little gun, the echoes rolled among the hills, and
rattled along the rocky galleries of the mountains in the
finest style. We were quite delighted. So fresh and
novel was the prospect, so unexpected were the peculiar
sentiment and character of the scene, one could hardly
realize that it was old to the experience of tens of thousands. I could scarcely help feeling, there was stupidity
somewhere, that more had not been said about what had
been seen by so many for so long a time.

CHAPTER IX.

WEDNESDAY, *June* 22, 1859.—We are at Warrington's, a genuine English inn, with nice rooms and a home-like quiet, where the finest salmon, with other luxuries, can be had at moderate prices. Every thing is English but ourselves. I feel that the Yankee in me is about as prominent as the bowsprit of the Great Republic, the queen ship of the metropolis of yankeedom, the renowned port from which we sailed, and through the scholarly air of which my thoughts wing their flight home.

Among other qualities foremost at this moment, (and for which I discover the Bull family is certainly pre-eminent,) is appetite, the measure of which, at table, is time, not quantity. My chief solicitude at breakfast, dinner, tea and supper, is not so much about *what* I am to eat, as about *how* I shall eat, so as not to distinguish myself.

2*

C——, who is looked upon as one of the immortals, and I, in his wake, perhaps as his private chaplain, may be regarded as representative people from the States. We would, therefore, avoid signalizing ourselves at the trencher. The method adopted on these frequent occasions, is to be on hand early, to expend small energy in useless conversation, and to retire modestly, though late, from the entertainment. It is surprising how well we acquit ourselves without exciting admiration. I am hopeful that the impression in the house is, that we are small eaters and talkers, persons slightly diffident, who eat chiefly in order to live, and prosper on our voyage. Under this cover, it is wonderful what an amount of spoil we bear away, over which merriment applauds in the privacy of our rooms.

When the gray morning light stole at the same time into my chamber and my dreams, it was raining heavily, a seasonable hindrance to early excursions, affording ample time to arrange those plans which we are now carrying out. In company with Mr. Newman, our consul, to whom we are indebted for unremitting attentions and hospitalities, we first called on the Bishop of Newfoundland.

The visitation of his large diocese, which embraces both the island and Labrador, together with the distant

isle of Bermuda, has given him a thorough knowledge of
the shores and ices of these northern seas. An hour's
conversation, illustrated with maps and drawings, seems
to have put us in possession of nearly all the facts uecessary in order to a pleasant and successful expedition. At
the close of our interview, during which the Bishop
informed us that he was just setting off upon an extensive coast visitation, he very kindly invited us to join his
party for the summer, and take our passage in the Hawk,
his " Church Ship." It was a most tempting offer, and
would have been accepted with delight had the voyage
been shorter. There was no certainty of the vessel's return before September, a time too long for my purposes.
To be left in any port, in those out-of-the-way waters,
with the expectation of a chance return, was not to be
thought of. We declined the generous offer of the
Bishop, but with real regret. To have made the tour of
Newfoundland and Labrador, with a Christian gentleman
and scholar so accomplished, would have been a privilege
indeed. From the house of the Bishop, a neat residence
near his cathedral, we climbed the hill upon which stands
the palace of the Governor, Sir Alexander Bannerman,
commanding a fine prospect of the town and harbor, the
ocean and adjacent country. As we passed up the broad
avenue, shaded by the poplar, birch and fir, instead of

those patricians of the wood, the maple, oak and elm ; the flag, waving in the cool sea-breeze, and the brown-coated soldier, pacing to and fro, reminded one of the presence of English power. His Excellency, a stately and venerable man, to whom we had come purposely to pay our respects, received us in a spacious room with antique furniture. During the conversation, he expressed much pleasure that a painter of distinction had come to visit the scenery of Newfoundland, and kindly offered such assistance as would facilitate sketching in the neighborhood. A soldier should watch for icebergs, on Signal Hill, a lofty peak that overlooks the sea ; a boat should be at his command, the moment one was needed. Upon leaving, he gave us for perusal Sir Richard Bonnycastle's Newfoundland. From the western front of the house, we overlooked a broad vale, dotted with farmhouses, and, in its June dress of grass and dandelions, quite New-England-like. We continued our walk to Quidy Viddy, a pretty lake, and returned in time to call upon Mr. Ambrose Shea, Speaker of the Assembly, to whom C—— had letters of introduction.

After dinner we set off for Signal Hill, the grand observatory of the country, both by nature and art. Before we were half-way up, we found that June was June, even in Newfoundland. But there is something in a mountain ramble that pays for all warmth and fatigue. Little rills rattled by, paths wound among rocky notches and grassy chasms, and led out to dizzy "over-looks" and "short-offs." The town with its thousand smokes sat in a kind of amphitheatre, and seemed to enjoy the spectacle of sails and colors in the harbor. Below us were the fishing-flakes, a kind of thousand-legged shelves, made of poles, and covered with spruce boughs, for drying fish, the local term for cod, and placed like terraces or large steps one above another on the rocky slopes. We struck into a fine military road, and passed spacious stone barracks, soldiers and soldiers' families, goats and little gardens.

From the observatory, situated on the craggy pinnacle, both the rugged interior and the expanse of ocean were before us. Far off at sea a cloud of canvas was shining in the afternoon sun, a kind of golden white, · while down the northern coast, distant several miles, was an iceberg. It was glittering in the sunshine like a mighty crystal. The work and play of to-morrow were resolved upon immediately, and we descended at our leisure, plucking the wild flowers among the moss and herbage, and gazing quietly at the hues and features of the extended prospect.

CHAPTER X.

THURSDAY, *June* 23. We were stirring betimes, making preparations for our first venture after an iceberg. Unluckily, it was a Romish holiday, and every vehicle in town seemed to be busy carrying people about, by the time we thought it necessary to engage one for ourselves. We succeeded at length in securing a hard-riding wagon, driven by a young Englishman, and were soon on our way, trundling along at a good pace over the smooth road leading from St. Johns to Torbay, the nearest water to our berg, and distant some eight or nine miles. The morning was fine, the sunshine cheering, the air cool and bracing, and all went promisingly. The adjacent country is an elevated kind of barren, clothed with brushwood, spruce and birch, crossed by numerous little trout brooks, and spotted with ponds and wet meadows, with here and there a lonely-looking hut.   But there were the songs of birds, the tinkling of cow-bells, and the odor of evergreens and flowers.   A characteristic of the coast is its elevation above the country lying behind.   Instead of descending, the lands rise, as you approach the ocean, into craggy domes, walls and towers, breaking off precipitously, and affording from the eminences of our road prospects of sparkling sea.   Our hearts were full of music, and our minds and conversation were a kind of reflection of the solitary scene.   For months, our young man tells us, the snow lies so deeply along this fine road as to render it impassable for sleighs, except when sufficiently hard to bear a horse.   The snow-shoe is then in general use.   One of the pests of early summer is the black fly, as we have already experienced.   A few years ago, a sailor ran away from his vessel, at St. Johns, and took to these bushy wilds, in which, at length, he got lost, and finally perished from the bites of this pestilent fly.   He was found accidentally, and in a state of insensibility, being covered with them, and so nearly devoured that he died within a few hours after his discovery.

Speaking of the Newfoundland dog, he told us that one of pure, original blood, was scarcely to be found.   I had supposed, and had good reason for it, from what I had read in the papers, about the time of the visit to St.

Johns, upon the laying of the Atlantic Cable, that any person could for a small sum purchase numbers of the finest dogs. I think a certain correspondent of some New York daily, told us that several gentlemen supplied themselves with these animals upon their departure. If such was the case, then they took away with them about the last of the real breed, and must have paid for them such prices as they would not like to own. Scarcely a splendid dog is now to be seen, and five, ten, and even twenty pounds sterling might be refused for him. We have not seen the first animal that compares with those which trot up and down Broadway nearly every week; and they are not the pure-blooded creature, either, by a good deal. It is to be regretted, that dogs of such strength, beauty and sagacity should have been permitted to become almost extinct in their native country.

CHAPTER XI.

TORBAY.—FLAKES AND FISH-HOUSES.—THE FISHING BARGE.—THE CLIFFS.—THE RETREAT TO FLAT ROCK HARBOR.—WILLIAM WATERMAN, THE FISHERMAN.

TORBAY, finely described in a recent novel by the Rev. R. T. S. Lowell, is an arm of the sea, a short, strong arm with a slim hand and finger, reaching into the rocky land, and touching the waterfalls and rapids of a pretty brook. Here is a little village, with Romish and Protestant steeples, and the dwellings of fishermen, with the universal appendages of fishing-houses, boats and flakes. One seldom looks upon a hamlet so picturesque and wild. The rocks slope steeply down to the wonderfully clear water. Thousands of poles support half-acres of the spruce-bough shelf, beneath which is a dark, cool region, crossed with footpaths, and not unfrequently sprinkled and washed by the surf,—a most kindly office on the part of the sea, you will allow, when once you have scented the fish-offal perpetually dropping from the evergreen fish-house above. These little buildings on the flakes are conspicuous features, and look as fresh and wild as if they had just wandered away from the woodlands.

There they stand, on the edge of the lofty pole-shelf, or upon the extreme end of that part of it which runs off frequently over the water like a wharf, an assemblage of huts and halls, bowers and arbors, a curious huddle made of poles and sweet-smelling branches and sheets of birch-bark. A kind of evening haunts these rooms of spruce, at noonday, while at night a hanging lamp, like those we see in old pictures of crypts and dungeons, is to the stranger only a kind of buoy by which he is to steer his way through the darkness. To come off then without pitching headlong, and soiling your hands and coat, is the merest chance. Strange ! one is continually allured into these piscatory bowers whenever he comes near them. In spite of the chilly, salt air, and the repulsive smells about the tables where they dress the fish, I have a fancy for these queer structures. Their front door opens upon the sea, and their steps are a mammoth ladder, leading down to the swells and the boats. There is a charm also about fine fishes, fresh from the net and the hook,—the salmon, for example, whose pink and yellow flesh has given a name to one of the most delicate hues of Art or Nature.

But where was the iceberg? We were not a little disappointed when all Torbay was before us, and nothing but dark water to be seen. To our surprise, no one had ever seen or heard of it. It must lie off 'Flat Rock Harbor, a little bay below, to the north. We agreed with the supposition that the berg must lie below, and made speedy preparations to pursue, by securing the only boat to be had in the village,—a substantial fishing-barge, laden rather heavily in the stern with at least a cord of cod-seine, but manned by six stalwart men, a motive power, as it turned out, none too large for the occasion. We embarked at the foot of a fish-house ladder, being carefully handed down by the kind-hearted men, and took our seats forward on the little bow-deck. All ready, they pulled away at their long, ponderous oars, with the skill and deliberation of life-long practice, and we moved out upon the broad, glassy swells of the bay towards the open sea, not indeed with the rapidity of a Yankee club-boat, but with a most agreeable steadiness, and a speed happily fitted for a review of the shores, which, under the afternoon sun, were made brilliant with lights and shadows.

We were presently met by a breeze, which increased

the swell, and made it easier to fall in close under the northern shore, a line of stupendous precipices, to which the ocean goes deep home. The ride beneath these mighty cliffs was by far the finest boat-ride of my life. While they do not equal the rocks of the Saguenay, yet, with all their appendages of extent, structure, complexion and adjacent sea, they are sufficiently lofty to produce an almost appalling sense of sublimity. The surges lave them at a great height, sliding from angle to angle, and fretting into foam as they slip obliquely along the face of the vast walls. They descend as deeply as two hundred feet, and rise perpendicularly two, three, and four hundred feet from the water. Their stratifications are up and down, and of different shades of light and dark, a ribbed and striped appearance that increases the the effect of height, and gives variety and spirit to the surface.

At one point, where the rocks advance from the main front, and form a kind of headland, the strata, six and eight feet thick, assume the form of a pyramid, from a broad base of a hundred yards or more running up to meet in a point. The heart of this vast cone has partly fallen out, and left the resemblance of an enormous tent with cavernous recesses and halls, in which the shades of evening were already lurking, and the surf was sounding mournfully.. Occasionally it was musical, pealing forth like the low tones of a great organ with awful solemnity. Now and then, the gloomy silence of a minute was broken by the crash of a billow far within, when the reverberations were like the slamming of great doors.

After passing this grand specimen of the architecture of the sea, there appeared long rocky reaches, like Egyptian temples, old dead cliffs of yellowish gray, checked off by lines and seams into squares, and having the resemblance, where they have fallen out into the ocean, of doors and windows opening in upon the fresher stone. Presently we came to a break, where there were grassy slopes and crags intermingled, and a flock of goats skipping about, or ruminating in the warm sunshine. A knot of kids—the reckless little creatures!—were sporting along the edge of the precipice in a manner almost painful to witness. The pleasure of leaping from point to point, where a single mis-step would have dropped them hundreds of feet, seemed to be in proportion to the danger. The sight of some women, who were after the goats, reminded the boatmen of an accident which occurred here only a few days before : a lad playing about the steep, fell into the sea, and was drowned.

We were now close upon the point just behind which we expected to behold the iceberg. The surf was sweeping the black reef, that flanked the small .cape, in the finest style,—a beautiful dance of breakers of dazzling white and green. As every stroke of the oars shot us forward, and enlarged our view of the field in which the ice was reposing, our hearts fairly throbbed with an excitement of expectation. "There it is !" one exclaimed. An instant revealed the mistake. It was only the next headland in a fog, which unwelcome mist was now coming down upon us from the broad waters, and covering the very tract where the berg was expected to be seen. Further and further out the long, strong sweep of the great oars carried us, until the depth of the bay between us and the next headland was in full view. It may appear almost too trifling a matter over which to have had any feeling worth mentioning or remembering, but I shall not soon forget the disappointment, when from the deck of our barge, as it rose and sank on the large swells, we stood up and looked around, and saw that if the iceberg, over which our very hearts had been beating with delight for twenty-four hours, was anywhere, it was somewhere in the depths of that untoward fog. It might as well have been in the depths of the ocean.

While the pale cloud slept there, there was nothing left for us but to wait patiently where we were, or retreat. We chose the latter. C—— gave the word to pull for the settlement, at the head of the little bay just mentioned, and so they rounded the breakers on the reef, and we turned away for the second time, when the game, as we had thought, was fairly ours. Even the hardy fishermen, no lovers of "islands-of-ice," as they call the bergs, felt for us, as they read in our looks the disappointment, not to say a little vexation. While on our passage in, we filled a half-hour with questions and discussions about that iceberg.

"We certainly saw it yesterday evening; and a soldier of Signal Hill told us that it had been close in at Torbay for several days. And you, my man there, say that you had a glimpse of it last evening. How happens it to be away just now? Where do you think it is?"

"Indeed, sir, he must be out in the fog, a mile or over. De'il a bit can a man look after a thing in a fog more nor into a snow-bank. Maybe, sir, he's foundered; or he might be gone off to sea altogether, as they sometimes does."

"Well, this is rather remarkable. Huge as these bergs are, they escape very easily under their old cover. No sooner do we think we have them, than they are gone. No jackal was ever more faithful to his lion, no pilot-fish to his shark, than the fog to its berg. We will run in

yonder and inquire about it. We may get the exact
bearing, and reach it yet, even in the fog."

The wind and sea being in our favor, we soon reached
a fishery-ladder, which we now knew very well how to
climb, and wound our " dim and perilous way " through
the evergreen labyrinth of fish-bowers, emerging on the
solid rock, and taking the path to the fisherman's house.
Here lives and works and wears himself out, William
Waterman, a deep-voiced, broad-chested, round-shoul-
dered wight, dressed, not in cloth of gold, but of oil, with
the foxy remnant of a last winter's fur cap clinging to his
large, bony head, a little in the style of a piece of turf to
a stone. You seldom look into a more kindly, patient
face, or into an eye that more directly lets up the light
out of a large, warm heart. His countenance is one sober
shadow of honest brown, occasionally lighted by a true
and guileless smile. William Waterman has seen the
" island-of-ice." " It lies off there, two miles or more,
grounded on a bank, in forty fathoms water."

It was nearly six o'clock ; and yet, as there were
signs of the fog clearing away, we thought it prudent to
wait. A dull, long hour passed by, and still the sun was
high in the north-west. That heavy cod-seine, a hundred
fathoms long, sank the stern of our barge rather deeply,
and made it row heavily. For all that, there was time

enough yet, if we could only use it. The fog still came in masses from the sea, sweeping across the promontory between us and Torbay, and fading into air nearly as soon as it was over the land. In the mean time, we sat upon the rocks—upon the wood-pile—stood around and talked —looked out into the endless mist—looked at the fisher- men's houses—their children—their fowls and dogs. A couple of young women, that might have been teachers of the village school, had there been a school, belles of the place, rather neatly dressed, and with hair nicely combed, tripped shyly by, each with an arm about the other's waist, and very merry until abreast of us, when they were' as silent and downcast as if they had been passing by their sovereign queen, or the Great Mogul. Their curiosity and timidity combined were quite amus- ing. We speculated upon the astonishment that would have seized upon their simple, innocent hearts, had they beheld, instead of us, a bevy of our city fashionables in full bloom.

At length we accepted an invitation to walk into the house, and sat, not under the good-man's roof, but under his chimney, a species of large funnel, into which nearly one end of the house resolved itself. Here we sat upon some box-like benches before a wood fire, and warmed ourselves, chatting with the family. While we were

3

making ourselves comfortable and agreeable, we made the
novel, and rather funny discovery of a hen sitting on her
nest just under the bench, with her red comb at our
fingers' ends.   A large griddle hung suspended in the
more smoky regions of the chimney, ready to be lowered
for the baking of cakes or frying fish.   Having tarred my
hand, the fisherman's wife, kind woman, insisted upon
washing it herself.   After rubbing it with a little grease,
she first scratched it with her finger-nail, and then finished with soap and water and a good wiping with a
a coarse towel.   I begged that she would spare herself
the trouble, and allow me to help myself.   But it was no
trouble at all for her, and the greatest pleasure.   And
what should I know about washing off tar ?

They were members of the Church of England, and
seemed pleased when they found that I was a clergyman
of the Episcopal Church.   They had a pastor, who visited
them and others in the village occasionally, and held
divine service on Sunday at Torbay, where they attended,
going in boats in summer, and over the hills on snow-
shoes in the winter.   The woman told me, in an under-
tone, that the family relations were not all agreed in
their religious faith, and that they could not stop there
any longer, but had gone to "America," which they liked
much better,   It was a hard country, any way, no mat-

ter whether one were Protestant or Papist. Three months were all their summer, and nearly all their time for getting ready for the long, cold winter. To be sure, they had codfish and potatoes, flour and butter, tea and sugar; but then it took a deal of hard work to make ends meet. The winter was not as cold as we thought, perhaps; but then it was so long and snowy! The snow lay five, six, and seven feet deep. Wood was a great trouble. There was a plenty of it, but they could not keep cattle or horses to draw it home. Dogs were their only teams, and they could fetch but small loads at a time. In the mean while, a chubby little boy, with cheeks like a red apple, had ventured from behind his young mother, where he had kept dodging as she moved about the house, and edged himself up near enough to be patted on the head, and rewarded for his little liberties with a half-dime.

CHAPTER XII.

THE WHALES.—THE ICEBERG.—THE RETURN, AND THE RIDE TO
ST. JOHNS BY STARLIGHT.

THE sunshine was now streaming in at a bit of a window, and I went out to see what prospect of success. C——, who had left some little time before, was nowhere to be seen. The fog seemed to be in sufficient motion to disclose the berg down some of the avenues of clear air that were opened occasionally. They all ended, however, with fog instead of ice. I made it convenient to walk to the boat, and pocket a few cakes, brought along as a kind of scattering lunch. C—— was descried, at length, climbing the broad, rocky ridge the eastern point of which we had doubled on our passage from Torbay. Making haste up the crags by a short cut, I joined him on the verge of the promontory, pretty well heated and out of breath.

The effort was richly rewarded. The mist was dispersing in the sunny air around us ; the ocean was clearing off ; the surge was breaking with a pleasant sound below. At the foot of the precipice were four or five whales, from thirty to fifty feet in length, apparently. We could have tossed a pebble upon them. At times abreast, and then in single file, round and round they went, now rising with a puff followed by a wisp of vapor, then plunging into the deep again. There was something in their large movements very imposing, and yet very graceless. There seemed to be no muscular effort, no exertion of any force from within, and no more flexibility in their motions than if they had been built of timber. They appeared to move very much as a wooden whale might be supposed to move down a mighty rapid, rolling and plunging and borne along irresistibly by the current. As they rose, we could see their mouths occasionally, and the lighter colors of the skin below. As they went under, their huge, black tails, great winged things not unlike the screw-wheel of a propeller, tipped up above the waves. Now and then one would give the water a good round slap, the noise of which smote sharply upon the ear, like the crack of a pistol in an alley. It was a novel sight to watch them in their play, or labor rather ; for they were feeding upon the capelin, pretty little fishes that swarm along these shores at this particular season.

We could track them beneath the surface about as well as upon it. In the sunshine, and in contrast with the fog, the sea was a very dark blue or deep purple. Above the whales the water was green, a darker green as they descended, a lighter green as they came up. Large oval spots of changeable green water, moving silently and shadow-like along, in strong contrast with the surrounding dark, marked the places where the monsters were gliding below. When their broad, blackish backs were above the waves, there was frequently a ring or ruffle of snowy surf, formed by the breaking of the swell, around the edges of the fish. The review of whales, the only review we had witnessed in Her Majesty's dominions, was, on the whole, an imposing spectacle. We turned from it to witness another, of a more brilliant character.

To the north and east, the ocean, dark and sparkling, was, by the magic action of the wind, entirely clear of fog; and there, about two miles distant, stood revealed the iceberg in all its cold and solitary glory. It was of a greenish white, and of the Greek-temple form, seeming to be over a hundred feet high. We gazed some minutes with silent delight on the splendid and impressive object, and then hastened down to the boat, and pulled away with all speed to reach it, if possible, before the fog should cover it again, and in time for C—— to paint it. The moderation of the oarsmen and the slowness of our progress were quite provoking. I watched the sun, the distant fog, the wind and waves, the increasing motion of the boat, and the seemingly retreating berg. A good half-hour's toil had carried us into broad waters, and yet, to all appearance, very little nearer. The wind was freshening from the south, the sea was rising, thin mists—a species of scout from the main body of fog lying off in the east—were scudding across our track. James Goss, our captain, threw out a hint of a little difficulty in getting back. But Yankee energy was indomitable : C—— quietly arranged his painting-apparatus ; and I, wrapped in my cloak more snugly, crept out forward on the little deck,—a sort of look-out. To be honest, I began to wish ourselves on our way back, as the black, angry-looking swells chased us up, and flung the foam upon the bow and stern. All at once, huge squadrons of fog swept in, and swamped the whole of us, boat and berg, in their thin, white obscurity. For a moment we thought ourselves foiled again. But still the word was On ! And on they pulled, the hard-handed fishermen, now flushed and moist with rowing. Again the ice was visible, but dimly, in his misty drapery. There was no time to be lost. Now, or not at all. And so C—— began. For half an hour, pausing occasionally for passing flocks of fog, he plied the brush with a rapidity not usual, and under disadvantages that would have mastered a less experienced hand.

We were getting close down upon the berg, and in fearfully rough water. In their curiosity to catch glimpses of the advancing sketch, the men pulled with little regularity, and trimmed the boat very badly. We were rolling frightfully to a landsman. C—— begged of them to keep their seats, and hold the barge just there as near as possible. To amuse them, I passed an opera-glass around among them, with which they examined the iceberg and the coast. They turned out to be excellent good fellows, and entered into the spirit of the thing in a way that pleased us. I am sure they would have held on willingly till dark, if . C—— had only said the word, so much interest did they feel in the attempt to paint the "island-of-ice." The hope was to linger about it until sunset, for its colors, lights and shadows. That, however, was suddenly extinguished. Heavy fog came on, and we retreated, not with the satisfaction of a conquest, nor with the disappointment of a defeat, but cheered with the hope of complete success, perhaps the next day, when C—— thought that we could return upon our game in a little steamer, and so secure it beyond the possibility of escape.

The seine was now hauled from the stern to the centre of the barge ; and the men pulled away for Torbay, a long six miles, rough and chilly. For my part, I was trembling with cold, and found it necessary to lend a hand at the oars, an exercise which soon made the weather feel several degrees warmer, and rendered me quite comfortable. After a little, the wind lulled, the fog dispersed again, and the iceberg seemed to contemplate our slow departure with complacent serenity. We regretted that the hour forbade a return. It would have been pleasant to play around that Parthenon of the sea in the twilight. The best that was left us, was to look back and watch the effects of light, which were wonderfully fine, and had the charm of entire novelty. The last view was the very finest. All the east front was a most tender blue ; the fissures on the southern face, from which we were rowing directly away, were glittering green ; the western front glowed in the yellow sunlight ; around were the dark waters, and above, one of the most beautiful of skies.

We fell under the land presently, and passed near the northern cape of Flat-Rock Bay, a grand headland of red sandstone, a vast and dome-like pile, fleeced at the summit with green turf and shrubs of fir. The sun, at last, was really setting. There was the old magnificence of the king of day,—airy deeps of ineffable blue and pearl,

3*

stained with scarlets and crimsons, and striped with
living gold. A blaze of white light, deepening into the
richest orange, crowned the distant ridge behind which
the sun was vanishing. A vapory splendor, rose-color
and purple, was dissolving in the atmosphere ; and every
wave of the ocean, a dark violet, nearly black, was "a
flash of golden fire." Bathed with this almost supernatural glory, the headland, in itself richly complexioned with
red, brown and green, was at once a spectacle of singular
grandeur and solemnity. I have no remembrance of more
brilliant effects of light and color. The view filled us
with emotions of delight. We shot from beneath the
great cliff into Flat-Rock Bay, rounding, at length, the
breakers and the cape into the smoother waters of Torbay. As the oars dipped regularly into the polished
swells, reflecting the heavens and the wonderful shores,
all lapsed into silence. In the gloom of evening the
rocks assumed an unusual height and sublimity. Gliding
quietly below them, we were saluted, every now and then,
by the billows thundering in some adjacent cavern. The
song of the sea in its old halls rung out in a style quite
unearthly. The slamming of the mighty doors seemed
far off in the chambers of the cliff, and the echoes trembled themselves away, muffled into stillness by the
stupendous masses.

Thus ended our first real hunting of an iceberg. When we landed, we were thoroughly chilled. Our man was waiting with his wagon, and so was a little supper in a house near by, 'which we enjoyed with an appetite that assumed several phases of keenness as we proceeded. There was a tower of cold roast beef, flanked by bread and butter and bowls of hot tea. The whole was carried silently, without remark, at the point of knife and fork. We were a forlorn-hope of two, and fell to, winning the victory in the very breach. We drove back over the fine gravel road at a round trot, watching the last edge of day in the north-west and north, where it no sooner fades than it buds again to bloom into morning. We lived the new iceberg experience all over again, and planned for the morrow. The stars gradually came out of the cool, clear heavens, until they filled them with their sparkling multitudes. For every star we seemed to have a lively and pleasurable thought, which came out and ran among our talk, a thread of light. When we looked at the hour, as we sat fresh and wakeful, warming at our English inn, in St. Johns, it was after midnight.

CHAPTER XIII.

FRIDAY, *June* 24. Daylight, with the street noises, surprised me in the very midst of the sweetest slumbers. I had already learned that the summer daybreak, in these more northern latitudes, was far enough ahead of breakfast, and so I flattered myself back into one of those light and dreamy sleeps that last, or seem to last, for several long and pleasant hours. When the bell aroused me, the day appeared old and glittering enough for noon. But it was only in good time for us, a little worn with the excitement and toils of the day before, and in trim to enjoy a good solid breakfast. All thought of revisiting the iceberg of Torbay was postponed, at least for the present, and the day given up to previous invitations.

At eleven o'clock, I attended the consecration of St. Mary's, a fine new church on the South Side, as the street on the opposite shore of the harbor is called. As I walked across the bridge, conducting to that side, the sacred edifice, together with other buildings in the neighborhood, adorned with numerous English flags, presented, in contrast with the craggy mountain above, a lively and picturesque appearance. I may mention, by the way, that St. Johns might well be denominated the city of flags. They are flying everywhere thick as butterflies and poppies in a Yankee garden.

I was made acquainted with a number of clergymen, some of them Cambridge and Oxford men, and invited to take a part in the services. The sermon, preached by Archdeacon Lower, was remarkable for its plainness, simplicity and earnestness, a characteristic of all the sermons I have heard from the clergy of Bishop Field, himself a preacher of singular simplicity and earnestness. I could not avoid drawing the contrast between the simple, practical character of this gospel preaching by accomplished scholars, and the florid, pompous style of many half-educated men in my own country. While the latter may, at times, stir a popular audience more sensibly with the fire that crackles among their brushwood of words, the former are infinitely superior as sound, healthy, evangelical teachers.

On my return to the inn, I found C—— in his room,

busily painting a duplicate of the berg of Torbay. Soon after dinner we set off, in company with Mr. Shea, for Petty Harbor, a small fishing port, nine or ten miles to the south. The road—one of the finest I ever saw, an old-fashioned English gravel road, smooth and hard almost as iron, a very luxury for the wheels of a springless wagon—keeps up the bank of a small river, a good-sized trout stream, flowing from the inland valley into the harbor of St. Johns. Contrasted with the bold regions that front the ocean, these valleys are soft and fertile. We passed smooth meadows, and sloping plough-lands, and green pastures, and houses peeping out of pretty groves. One might have called it a Canadian or New Hampshire vale. At no great distance from the town, we crossed the stream over such a bridge as one would be glad to find more frequently upon the streams at home, and gradually ascended to a shrubby, sterile country, with broad views inland.

From the long, low hills of the western horizon, at no great distance, Mr. Shea informed us that there were prospects of Trinity Bay, of great beauty. Our road, at length, carried us up among the bleak coast hills, winding among them in a most agreeable manner, and bringing to view numbers of small lakes, liquid gems set in black and craggy banks, and which are all to be united by cuttings through the rocks, and then conducted to St. Johns, thus forming one of the completest reservoirs.

The flowers by the wayside, mostly small and pale, touched the air with delicate perfume. I looked for the bees, but there were none abroad ; neither was there to be heard the hum of insects nor warbling of birds. Now and then a lonely bird piped a feeble strain. We continued winding among the thinly-wooded hills, our wheels ringing along the narrow gravel road for an hour. At last we reached the height of land, and overlooked the ocean. Here we rested a few moments, rose from the seats, and looked around upon the majestic scene. Far out upon the blue were many sails, white in the bright sunshine as the wings of doves. The fishing boats, little schooners with raking masts, which swarm in these seas, were scudding under their tan-colored canvas, in all directions, looking like so many winged flies far down upon the spangled plain, a most lively and agreeable contrast to the desolate highlands, where you behold no dwelling, or field, or sign of human work, except the road, which, I cannot help repeating, lies among the rough hills, and rocky masses, as cleanly cut, and smooth as a road in a gentleman's park. What a token of greatness and refinement is the perfect road ! No nation makes such roads as these, in a land bristling with rugged difficulties, that has not wound its way up to the summit of power and cultivation. The savage contents himself with a path that is engineered and beaten by the wild beast.

The praise which an American, used to the rough roads of home, is continually disposed to lavish upon these admirable English roads of rugged Newfoundland, must by no manner of means be shared by the carriages that travel them, things at least one hundred years behind the time. Such vehicles, on such roads, fit about as well as a horseman on one of our city avenues dressed in the iron clothes of a crusader. No Yankee rides in them who does not have his laugh at their absurd strength and clumsiness. They are evidently intended to descend from father to son ; and they are just as certain to do it as they are to descend the hills, from which no common horse and harness can prevent them, when tolerably loaded. If the intelligence which designs, and executes, and orders these wagons about, was not British intelligence, one would not have a word to say. As it is, a little ridicule is at least an innocent pastime. Take off the box, the pleasure-box, and put upon the stalwart machine any thing you choose, stones, saw-logs, fire-engine, cannon, and all will go safely. When you return, put on your pleasure-box again, and you are ready for an airing, wife and daughters.

CHAPTER XIV.

To venture a geological remark: All these coast
highlands correspond with the summits of the Alleghanies,
and with those regions of the Cordilleras, C—— tells me,
which are just below the snow-line. From the sea-line
up to the peak, they correspond with our mountains
above the upper belt of woods. Their icy pinnacles and
eternal snows are floating below in the form of icebergs.
Imagine all the mid-mountain region in the deep, and
you have the Andes here.

We descended in a zigzag way into a deep gorge, one
of those cuts through the shore mountains from inland
regions to the sea, which occasionally become fiords or
narrow bays. Along the rocky steps, resembling galleries, were patches of grass and beds of flowering mosses,

with springs bubbling up in the spongy turf, and spinning themselves out into snowy threads from the points and edges of the crags. At the bottom is the little village of Petty Harbor, where the river, a roaring torrent, meets the salt tide. We alighted at a cottage, Swiss-like among the rocks, before we were quite down, and were pleased to hear Mr. Shea, whose guests we were, making arrangements with a nice-looking woman for an abundant supper, on our return. Mr. S., in company with several persons who now joined us from St. Johns, then proceeded to show us the lions of the place, or lion rather, for every thing and everybody are run up into, and knit into one body, the fishery.

In the first place, we were struck with the general appearance of things. The fishing flakes completely floor the river, and ascend in terraces for a short distance up the sides of the vale. Beneath these wide, evergreen floors, upon which was fish in all states, fresh from the knife, and dry enough for packing, ran the river, a brawling stream at low tide, and deeper, silent water when the tide was in. We could look up the dark stream, and see it dancing in the mountain sunshine, and down through the dim forest of slender props, and catch glances of the glittering sea. Boats were gliding up out of the daylight into the half-darkness, slowly sculled by brown fishermen,

and freighted with the browner cod, laced occasionally
with a salmon. In this wide and noiseless shade, these
cool, Lethean realms, sitting upon some well-washed
boulder, one might easily forget the heat and uproar of
all cities, and become absorbed in the contemplation of
merely present and momentary things. If one doubts it,
let him immerse himself for half an hour, in those still
and gloomy shadows, strongly seasoned with "ancient
and fish-like smells." Should he be able to reflect upon
the absent, or engage his thoughts upon any thing except
that which most immediately affects his senses, he will
possess a power of abstraction which a philosopher and a
Brahmin might envy.

In the course of our walk we visited a cod-liver oil
manufactory. The process of making this article is
quite simple. The livers, fresh from the fish, and nearly
white, are cleanly washed, and thrown into a cauldron
heated by steam instead of fire, where they gradually
dissolve into oil, which is dipped out hot and strained,
first through conical felt bags, and then through those
made of white moleskin, from which it runs pure and
sweet as table-oil. Wine-glasses were at hand, from
which we tasted it, and found it entirely agreeable. In
this state it is barrelled for market, and sold at an aver-
age price of one dollar and fifty cents per gallon. By

what process it is transmuted into that horrid stuff which is sold at a high price, in small bottles, perhaps the druggist can inform us. When I mentioned the character of cod-liver oil in New York, a gentleman present, qualified to decide, did not hesitate to say that it was adulterated with some cheap, base oil. Near by a fish-house, there is ordinarily seen a row of hogsheads open to the sun, and breathing smells that none but a fisherman can abide. A near approach discovers these casks to be filled with cod livers in a state of fermentation. After a few days in the sun, these corpulent and sweaty vessels yield a rancid, nauseous fluid, of a nut-brown hue, at a much less cost than the refined oil of the manufactory, and which, I imagine, must have a flavor not unlike that which the invalid finds lurking in those genteel flasks on the apothecary's shelves. After all, our common whale-oil, I suspect, after some cleansing and bleaching, and slight seasoning with the pure, is bad enough for sick people.

The catch, as the fisher terms the number of fish taken, was small that day, and we encountered, here and there, knots of idle men, smoking, chewing, whittling and talking. For the most part, they were a russet, tangle-haired and shaggy-bearded set, shy and grum at first, but presently talkative enough, and intelligent upon all

matters in their own little world. Fish were so glutted
with capelin that they would not bite well. The seines
did better. Among the dwellings that we passed or entered, was one of a young English woman, of such exceeding neatness, that the painter could not forget it. That
fine-looking, healthy, young English woman, with her bit
of a house just as neat as wax, was often spoken of.

Upon our return to the cottage on the hill-side, where
we at first alighted, we sat down, with sharp appetite, to
a supper of fried capelin and cods' tongues, garnished
with cups of excellent tea. We ate and drank with the
relish of travellers, and talked of the continent from
Greenland to Cape Horn. After supper, we climbed out
of the valley, in advance of the wagons and our company,
to an eminence from which C—— sketched the surrounding scenery, more for the sake of comparison with some of
his Andean pencillings than for any thing really new. He
remarked that the wild and rocky prospect bore a strong
resemblance to the high regions of the Cordilleras.

While he was engaged with the pencil, I scrambled
to a high place, and looked at the Atlantic, touched
with long shafts of the light and shade of sunset. All
arrived at length, and we were fairly on our way back to
St. Johns. I buttoned my coat tightly, and wound my
cloak around me with a pleasing sense of comfort in the

clear and almost wintry air. All talked somewhat loudly, and in the best possible good humor, our three wagons keeping close company, and making a pleasant sound of wheels, as we ran down our serpentine way among the hills and lakes, now darkening in the dusk, and reflecting the colored skies. Although there was not a water-fowl in sight, the words came to memory spontaneously, and I recited them to myself:

> "Whither, midst falling dew,
> While glow the heavens with the last steps of day,
> Far through their rosy depths dost thou pursue
> Thy solitary way?"

As we approached the town, we were much amused with some boyish sports of a new kind. We saw what appeared through the darkness to be balls of fire, chasing each other down the craggy hill-side, but which turned out to be a company of frolicsome boys with lighted torches, bounding down the zigzag mountain road.

CHAPTER XV.

SATURDAY, *June* 25. This has been a quiet day, mostly spent in making calls and social visits. At an early hour, in company with Mr. Newman, the consul, we visited the Church Ship, a pretty vessel of not more than sixty tons, called the Hawk, a name suggested by that line in the Odyssey, where the poet says, " the auspicious bird flew under the guidance of God." By an ingenious arrangement, the cabin, which is a large part of the vessel, can be changed, in a few minutes, from state-rooms into a saloon, which, again, by a slight alteration, becomes a chapel. In this, at once home and church, the Bishop visits not only the harbors and islands of Newfoundland and Labrador, but the island of Bermuda. It was the gift of the Rev. Robert Eden, a clergyman of

England, some twelve years ago, and has been employed
in that benevolent and sacred service ever since, with the
promise of the same for years to come.   There are now
more than forty settled clergymen and missionaries along
those cold and rugged shores, who are visited from time
to time by their Bishop in this bold little ship, which I
shall dismiss for the present, for the reason that there
will be occasion to speak of it again.

From the Bishop's ship we went to his house, where
we had the honor of an introduction to General Williams,
the hero of Kars, and to Colonel Law, one of the few
now living who distinguished themselves at the battle of
Waterloo.   In the presence of one who had mingled in
the grand scenes of Napoleon and the Duke of Welling-
ton, emotions of admiration were spontaneous.   The hero
of Kars stands foremost among what are called fine-
looking military men,—a tall, commanding person, with
a most pleasing address.

We closed the day with the consul, who invited to
join us the Rev. George Hutchinson, a nephew of the
poet Wordsworth, and accustomed, in his youthful days,
to see at his uncle's such literary worthies as Lamb and
Southey.   He talked much of Hartley Coleridge, of whose
abilities he had a high opinion.   Southey, of all, seemed
to be his admiration.   He was, all in all, indeed a won-

derful man; a perfect Hercules in literary labors. A few years ago, Mr. Hutchinson, moved by a religious spirit, was induced to give up a pleasant living in Dorsetshire, under the Malvern Hills, and devote himself to the toils and privations of a missionary in Labrador. Upon the death of his mother he went home, over a year ago, and became possessed of a small property. He has returned recently, and is now waiting for an opportunity to get back to Labrador. This meeting and conversation with the Rev. George Hutchinson, has turned out to be of more than ordinary interest. C—— has determined to hire a vessel for a month, and set the missionary down in the midst of his people, without further trouble. We retired, pleasantly excited with visions of icebergs and northern coast scenery, and with thoughts of preparation for the voyage.

4

CHAPTER XVI.

MONDAY, *June* 27. We attended church, yesterday, at the cathedral, where we heard practical sermons and fine congregational singing. The evening was passed at the Bishop's, when the conversation was about Oxford, and Keble, English parsonages, and Christian art. A few poems were read from Keble's Christian Year, and commented upon by the Bishop, who is a personal friend and admirer of the poet. Before the company separated, all moved into a very beautiful private chapel, and closed the evening with devotions.

This has been a bright day, and favorable for our preparations. We took tea with the Consul, and had the pleasure of meeting the Rev. Mr. Wood, the Rector of St. Thomas', one of the city churches; who has true feeling, and a thorough appreciation of fine scenery, and whose descriptive abilities are rare.   He says that an iceberg is to him the most impressive of all objects.   Most beautiful in its life and changes, it is, next to an earthquake, most terrible and appalling, in the moment of its destruction, to those who may happen to be near it. Upon the falling of its peaks and precipices, waves and thunders carry the intelligence across the waters.   Lofty as it frequently is, the head only, helmeted and plumed with dazzling beauty, is above the sea.   In its solemn march along the blue main, how it steps upon the high places of the deep, is all unseen.   Around its mighty form, far down its alabaster cliffs and caverns, no eye plays but that of the imagination.   When it pauses in its last repose, and perishes, at times; as quickly as if it were smitten by the lightning, you may stand in the distance and gaze with awe, but never draw near to witness the motions and sounds of its dissolution.   After tea, we sat by the windows, which face the east and command the harbor, with its grand entrance from the Atlantic, and enjoyed the scene, one of unusual splendor, every cliff glowing with hues of reddish orange.

CHAPTER XVII.

WEDNESDAY, *June* 29. We are far advanced in our
preparations for the voyage. Yesterday and to-day, we
have been busily engaged, and now see the way clear for
leaving to-morrow morning. Bishop Field, who, with
many others, is pleased that C—— has volunteered to take
Mr. Hutchinson and Mr. Botwood, his associate, to Labrador, sailed on the visitation of his extended diocese to-
day. The Church Ship, which we visited in the morning,
looked, in her perfect order and neatness, with her signal
guns and her colors flying, quite like a little man-of-war.
We shall follow for awhile in her track, but with no expectation of seeing her again.

Allow me now to take you to the wharf, and show
you the craft which C—— has selected for his novel, and

somewhat perilous expedition. Here she lies, the Integrity, of Sydney, Cape Breton, a pink-sterned schooner, of only sixty-five tons, but reputed safe and a good sailer. Her forecastle contains the skipper and mate, a young man of twenty-two, the owner of the vessel, and three men, the youngest an overgrown Scotch lad, who has been serving, and will continue to serve us, in the capacity of cook. Her cabin is for Captain Knight, the commander, pro tem., with whom you will be made much better acquainted. Just forward of the cabin, in the hold, there has been a temporary cabin partitioned off, and furnished with beds, bedding, chairs and table ; in short, with every necessary article for the comfort and convenience of five individuals. In this snug little room, and in the hold, laden only with a light stone ballast, are stores and provisions, of the very best quality, for two full months, wood and water to be taken along shore as need shall require.

At C——'s sole expense, and under his control, this vessel is to cruise for a few weeks in the region of the icebergs, setting down the missionaries by the way. The sheet anchor and mainstay (I begin to speak the language of the mariner) of our hopes of a pleasant and successful trip, humanly speaking, is Captain Knight, a respected citizen of St. Johns, and an accomplished sailor, whom

C—— has had the good fortune to secure as master, pilot, and companion.

We have been startled by the intelligence, that the Argo, of the Galway line of steamers, from New York to Scotland, is ashore at St. Shotts, near Cape Race. As usual, a variety of reports have agitated the community, and made people look with eagerness for the return of the two small harbor steamers, which Mr. Shea, the agent for that line, dispatched yesterday to the scene of distress. One of the tugs, the Blue Jacket, has at length arrived with a part of the passengers in sad plight. It is the old story of shipwreck on these rocky coasts. Wrapped in fogs, and borne forward by a powerful current, the ill-fated ship struck the shore, a few moments after it was discovered. Providentially, it was calm weather, and the sea unusually quiet, or all had perished. As it was, all went safely to land, and encamped in the woods. Numbers of the passengers, saddened by the loss of trunks containing clothing and other valuables, excited and fatigued, tell bitter stories of carelessness and inefficiency.

While, with a crowd of people, we were at the pier, awaiting the arrival of the Blue Jacket, a funeral procession of boats with little white flags, half-pole, came slowly rowing in from sea, and across the harbor, and landed with the coffin near where we were standing. Not only the relatives were dressed in mourning, but the bearers. There were long flowing weeds of black crape upon all their hats, and wide white cambric cuffs upon the sleeves of their coats. They were of the fishing class, from some village up or down the coast, and conducted matters apparently with more dispatch than mournfulness. A hearse or black carriage, of very substantial make, with a high top, and white fringe or valance depending from its eaves instead of curtains, was waiting on the wharf, attended by a man with a flag of white linen attached to his hat.

Among our last calls to-day, was one of ceremony upon Sir Alexander and Lady Bannerman, from whom we had received an invitation to dine. Her ladyship, a fine-looking person, of graceful and dignified manners and pleasing conversation, talked with interest of C——'s excursion, and particularly of that part of it relating to his carrying Mr. Hutchinson to Labrador. After taking our leave, we went with Mr. Newman to look after some fireworks, which his Excellency has been pleased to order for our amusement at night among the icebergs.

CHAPTER XVIII.

THURSDAY EVENING, *June* 30. At sea. I am now writing, for the first time to-day, by the candles on our table in the main cabin of the Integrity. We are sailing northward with a fair wind, but with fog and rather rough water. But let me go back, and take the day from the beginning, passing lightly over its labors and vexations.

The morning opened upon us brilliantly, and all were employed about those many little things which only can be done at the last moment. Noon came and an early dinner, before that all were in readiness and aboard. And then, as if in retaliation for our delay during so many lovely hours, the wind was not ready, and so we were obliged to be towed by the Blue Jacket quite out into broad water, where she left us with our colors quivering in the sunshine, and all our canvas swelling in a mild southerly breeze. The coast scenery, and the iceberg of Torbay, and the last gleams of sunset upon land and ocean, were the lions of the afternoon.

We have taken our first tea, counting, with a lad in the charge of Mr. Hutchinson, six around the table, and making, with the crew, eleven souls, quite a little congregation, could all be spared to attend the short morning and evening services. We are just beginning to feel the effects of a small vessel with no lading beyond a light ballast. She rolls excessively, rises with every swell, and pitches into the succeeding hollow. This has already begun to disperse our company to their berths, as the more comfortable place for the random conversation which will close the day.

4*

CHAPTER XIX.

ICEBERGS OF THE OPEN SEA.—THE OCEAN CHASE.—THE RETREAT TO CAT HARBOR.

FRIDAY, *July* 1. The fog is so dense that the rigging drips as if it rained. In fact, if it be not the finest of all rain, then it is the thickest of all mists. C—— and I are sea-sick, almost as a matter of course, and look upon all preparations for breakfast with no peculiar satisfaction. Our consolation is, that we are sailing forward, although with only very moderate speed.

Delightful change! It is clearing up. The noon-day sun is showering the dark ocean, here and there, with the whitest light. And lo! an iceberg on our left. Lo! an iceberg on our right. An iceberg ahead! Yes, two of them!—four!—five—six!—and there, a white pinnacle just pricking above the horizon. Wonderful to behold, there are no less than thirteen icebergs in fair view. We run forward, and then we run aft, and then to this side, and that. We lean towards them over the railing, and spring up into the shrouds, as if these boyish efforts brought us nearer, and made them plainer to our delighted eyes. With a quiet energy, C—— betakes himself to painting, and I to my note-book. But can you tell me why I pause, almost put up the pencil, and pocket the book ? I am only a little sea-sick. The cold sweat starts upon the forehead, and I feel pale. We bear away now, such is the order, for the largest berg in sight. I freshen again with the growing excitement of this novel chase, and feel a pleasurable sense of freedom that I can never describe. I could bound like a deer, and shout like the wild Indian, for very joy. The vessel seems to sympathize, and spring forward with new spirit. The words leap out of the memory, and I give them a good strong voice :

"O'er the glad waters of the dark blue sea,
Our thoughts as boundless, and our souls as free."

Indeed, there is a hearty pleasure in this freedom of the ocean, when, as now with us, it is " all before you where to choose." Tied to no task, fettered to no line of voyage, to no scant time allowanced, the ship, the ocean and the day, are ours. Like the poet's river, that " windeth at its own sweet will," our wishes flow down the meandering channel of circumstances, and we go with the current.

And how lovely the prospect as we go ! That this is all God's own world, which he holdeth in the hollow of his hand, is manifest from the impartial bestowal of beauty. No apple, peach or rose is more within one network of sweet, living grace, than the round world. How wonderful and precious a thing must this beauty be, that it is thus all-pervading, and universal ! Here on these bleak and barren shores, so rocky, rough and savage, is a rich and delicate splendor that amazes. The pure azure of the skies, and the deeply blue waters, one would think were sufficient for rude and fruitless regions such as these. But look, how they shine and scintillate ! The iron cheeks of yonder headland blush with glory, and the west is all magnificent. Gaze below into the everlasting evening of the deep. Glassy, glittering things, like chandeliers dispersed, twinkle in the fluid darkness. The very fishes, clad in purple and satin, silvery tissues and cloth-of-gold, seem to move with colored lights. God hath apparelled all his creatures, and we call it beauty.

As we approach the bergs, they assume a great variety of forms. Indeed, their changes are quite wonderful. In passing around a single one, we see as good as ten, so protean is its character. I know of no object in all nature so marvelously sensitive to a steady gaze. Sit motionless, and look at one, and, fixture as it appears, it has its changes then. It marks with unerring faithfulness every condition of atmosphere, and every amount of light and shadow. Thus manifold complexions tremble over it, for which the careless observer may see no reason, and many shapes, heights and distances swell and shrink it, move it to and from, of which the mind may not readily assign a cause.

The large iceberg, for which we bore away this morning, resembled, at one moment, a cluster of Chinese buildings, then a Gothic cathedral, early style. It was curious to see how all that mimicry of a grand religious pile was soon transmuted into something like the Coliseum, its vast interior now a delicate blue, and then a greenish white. It was only necessary to run on half a mile to find this icy theatre split asunder. An age of ruin appeared to have passed over it, leaving only the two extremes, the inner cliffs of one a glistening white, of the other, a blue, soft and airy as the July heavens.

In the neighborhood, were numbers of block-like bergs, which, when thrown together by our perpetual change of position, resembled the ruins of a marble city. The play of the light and shadows among its inequalities was charming in the extreme. In the outskirts of this Palmyra of the waves, lay a berg closely resembling a huge ship of war, with the stern submerged, over which the surf was breaking finely, while the stem, sixty or seventy feet aloft, with what the fancy easily shaped into a majestic figure-head, looked with fixed serenity over the distant waters. As we ran athwart the bow, it changed instantly into the appearance of some gigantic sculpture, with broad surfaces as smooth as polished ivory, and with salient points cut with wonderful perfection. The dashing of the waves sounded like the dashing at the foot of rocky cliffs, indicative of the mass of ice below the surface.

As the afternoon advances the breeze strengthens, blowing sharply off to sea. We have the most brilliant sunshine, with a clear, cold, exhilarating air. It very nearly dispels all the nausea caused by this excessive rolling. We are now beating up from the east toward the land, and passing several of the bergs, in the chase of which we have spent so many joyous hours. Every few minutes we have new forms and new effects, new thoughts and fresh emotions. The grand ruins of the Oriental deserts, hunted on the fleetest coursers, would awaken, I fancy, kindred feelings. Full of shadowy sublimities are these great broken masses, as we sweep around them, fall away, tack and return again.

I never could have felt, and so must not think of
making others feel through the medium of language, the
possibility of being so deceived in respect of the bulk of
these islands-of-ice, as our sailors always call them.
What seems, in the distance, a mere piece of ice, of good
snow-bank size only, is really a mass of such dimensions
as to require you to look up to it, as you sail around it,
and feel, as you gaze, a sense of grandeur. What you
might suppose could be run down as easily as a pile of
light cotton, would wreck the proudest clipper as effectually as the immovable adamant.

Between the great northern current, and the breeze
which plumes the innumerable waves with sparkling
white, our course has become rather more tortuous and
rough than is agreeable to landsmen who have only come
abroad upon the deep for pleasure and instruction. The
painter has cleaned his pallet, wiped his brushes, shut his
painting-box, and gone below. I am sitting here, near
the helm, close upon the deck, screened from the spray
that occasionally flies over, heavily coated, and cold at
that, making some almost illegible notes. Life, it is
often said, is a stormy ocean. It is *on* the ocean, certainly, that one feels the whole force of the comparison.

The wind, which is blowing strongly, is getting into
the north, dead ahead, and sweeping us away upon our

back track. We are too lightly ballasted to tack with success, and hold our own. The bergs are retiring, and appear like ruins and broken columns. We are now fairly on the retreat, and flying under reefed sails to a little bay, called Cat Harbor. All aloft has the tightness and the ring of drums, and the whistling of a hundred fifes. The voice of the master is quick, and to the point, and the motions and the footsteps of the men, rapid. On our bows are the explosion and the shock of swells, the re-sounding knocks and calls of old Neptune, and upon the deck such showers of his most brilliant flowers and bouquets as I feel in no haste to gather. The sea-fowl whirl in the gale like loose plumes and papers, pouring out their wild complaints as they pass.

CHAPTER XX.

AT eight o'clock, our brave little pink-stern was lying
at anchor in her haven, as quietly as a babe in its cradle,
with the wind piping a pleasant lullaby in the rigging,
and the roar of the ocean nearly lost in the distance.
A few rude erections along the rocky shore, with a small
church, a store and warehouse, compose the town of Cat
Harbor, the life of which seems to be the water-craft
busy in the one common employment, some returning
with the catch of the day, others going for the catch of
the night. While C—— was painting a sketch of the
scene, the sun vanished behind the purple inland hills,
with unusual splendor, and left the distant icebergs in
such a white "as no fuller on earth can white them."

After dinner, notwithstanding the lateness of the

hour, Mr. Hutchinson, who knew that the clergyman in charge was absent, resolved to go ashore, and invite the people to attend divine service. As soon as we were landed, he left us to make our way to the church, at our leisure, while he ran from house to house to announce himself, and to give notice of the intended services. Our path, as usual in these coast hamlets, went in zigzag, serpentine ways, among evergreen fishing-bowers, and many-legged flakes and huts, and oddly-fenced potato-patches. In the marshy field around the church, we had some time to amuse ourselves with gathering slender bul-rushes tipped with plumes of whitest down. They were sprinkled all abroad like snow-flakes over the dusky green ground, and we ran about with the eagerness of boys, selecting the prettiest as specimens for home.

Twilight was already close upon the darkness. We turned from the chase of our thistle-down toys, and gazed upon the solemn magnificence around us—the dark and lonesome land—the bay, reflecting the colored heavens—the warm orange fading out into the cool pearl, and the pearl finally lost in the broad blue above.

It was fully candle-light when the congregation, about forty, assembled, and the service began. The mis-sionary preached extempore a practical sermon adapted to his hearers, and we sang, to the tune of Old Hundred, the One Hundredth Psalm, making the dimly-lighted sanctuary ring again. After church, our party were invited to warm at one of the houses, which we did most effectually before a broad and roaring fire, while mine host recounted the toil and the pleasure of getting winter wood over the deep snows with his team of dogs, and the more perilous and exciting labors of the fish-harvest, upon which life and all depend. At the mention of the puff-pig, the local name for the common porpoise, we indulged ourselves in a childish laugh. A more ludicrous, and at the same time a more descriptive name could not be hit upon.

During the half-hour around the exhilarating July fire, there dropped in, one by one, a room-full, curious to see and hear the strangers from St. Johns and America, as the United States are often called. We parted with a general shaking of hands, and plenty of good wishes, among which was one, "that we might have many igh hicebergs." Some half dozen attended us to the shore, and brought us off in handsome style over the calm and phosphorescent waters. At every dip of the oars it was like unraking the sparkling embers, so brilliant was that beautiful light of the sea. The boatmen called it the burning of the water. "When the water burnt," they said, "it was a sure sign of south wind and a plenty of fish."

It was one of those still and starry nights which require only an incident or so to make them too beautiful ever to be forgotten. Those incidents were now present, in a peculiarly plaintive murmur of the ocean, the kindling waves, and a delicate play of the Aurora Borealis. When we reached our vessel it was almost midnight, and still there was sweet daylight in the far north-west, moving along the circle of the northern horizon to brighten into morning before we were half through our light and dreamy slumbers. Weary and drowsy, all have crept to their berths ; and I will creep into mine when I have put the period to the notes of this long and delightful day. I hear the footfalls of the watch on deck. May God keep us through the short, but most solitary night, and speed us early on our northern voyage !

CHAPTER XXI.

SATURDAY, *July* 2.   It is five o'clock, and the morning has kindled in the clouds its brightest fires.   We are moving off to sea gracefully before a fair, light wind. The heart delights in this golden promise of a fine summer day, and the blue Atlantic all before us.   As the rising sun looks over it, the glittering waves seem to participate in these joyful emotions.   How marvelously beautiful is this vast scene !   Give me the sea, I say, now that I am on the sea.   Give me the mountains, I say, when I am on the mountains !   Henceforth, when I am weary with the task of life, I will cry, Give me the mountains *and* the sea.

The rugged islands, landward, have only an olive, not the living green, and seem never to have rejoiced in the blessing of a tree, or felt the delicious mercy of a leafy

shade. There blow the whales, and here is the edge of
an innumerable multitude of sea-birds feeding upon the
capelin, and flying to the right and left, thick as grass-
hoppers, as we advance among them. Poor things, they
are so glutted that they are obliged to disgorge before
they can gain the wing, and many of them merely scramble aside a few yards, and become the mark of the
roguish sailors, especially of Sandy, our young Scotch
cook, who is in a perfect frolic, pelting them with stones.
They sprinkle the sea by the million, and present, with
their white breasts and perpetually arching wings, a
lively and novel appearance. On the roll of the swells,
as the sunlight glances on them, they flash out white
like water-lilies.

How the pages of a book fail to carry these scenes
into the heart! I have been reading of them for years,
and, as I have thought, reading understandingly and
feelingly; but I can now say that I have never known,
certainly never felt them until now. The living presence
of them has an originality, a taste and odor for the
imagination, which can never be expressed even by the
vivid and sensuous language of the painter, much less by
the more subtle, intellectual medium of written records.
It is so new and fresh to me, that I feel as if none had
ever seen this prospect before. Old and familiar as these

waters are, I am thrilled with emotions, kindred to those of a discoverer, and remember and repeat the rhyme of the Ancient Mariner :

> We were the first that ever burst
> Into that silent sea.

Silent sea! This is any thing but that. The surf, which leaps up with the lightness and rapidity of flames, for many and many a white mile, roars among the sharp, bleak crags of the islands and the coast like mighty cataracts. Words of the Psalmist fall naturally upon the tongue, and I speak them in low tones to myself :

> Voices are heard among them.
> Their sound is gone out into all lands.

"And so sail we," this glorious morning, after the icebergs, several of which stand sentinel along our eastern horizon ; but we do not turn aside for them, for the reason that we confidently look for others more closely on our proper track.

CHAPTER XXII.

NOTRE DAME BAY.—FOGO ISLAND AND THE THREE HUNDRED ISLES.—THE FREEDOM OF THE SEAS.—THE ICEBERG OF THE SUNSET, AND THE FLIGHT INTO TWILLINGATE.

AFTER noon, with the faintest breeze, and the sea like a flowing mirror. We have sailed by the most eastern promontories, Cape Bonavista and Cape Freels, and have now arrived at a point where the coast falls off far to the west, and gives place to Notre Dame Bay, the great Archipelago of Newfoundland, of which there is comparatively little known. Our true course is nearly north, and along the eastern or Atlantic side of Fogo, which is now before us, the first and largest of some three hundred islands. For the sake of the romantic scenery, we conclude to take the inside route.

From the shores of Fogo, which are broken, and exceedingly picturesque further on, as Captain Knight informs us, the land rises into moderate hills, thinly wooded with evergreens, with here and there a little farm and dwelling. Perhaps there are twenty rural smokes in sight and a spire or two. Under the full-blown summer all looks pleasant and inviting. What will not the glorious sunshine bless and beautify? A dark and dusty garret wakes up to life and brightness, give it an open window and the morning sun.

The western headlands of Fogo are exceedingly attractive, lofty, finely broken, of a red and purplish brown, tinted here and there with pale green. The painter is busy with his colors. As we pass the bold prominences and deep, narrow bays or fiords, they are continually changing and surprising us with a new scenery. And now the great sea-wall, on our right, opens and discloses the harbor and village of Fogo, the chief place of the island, gleaming in the setting sun as if there were flames shining through the windows. Looking to the left, all the western region is one fine Ægean, a sea filled with a multitude of isles, of manifold forms and sizes, and of every height, from mountain pyramids and crested ridges down to rounded knolls and tables, rocky ruins split and shattered, giant slabs sliding edgewise into the deep, columns and grotesque masses ruffled with curling surf—the Cyclades of the west. ʹI climb the shrouds, and behold fields and lanes of water, an endless and beautiful network, a

5

little Switzerland with her vales and gorges filled with the purple sea.

After dinner, and nearly sunset. We are breaking away from the isles into the open Atlantic, bearing northerly for Cape St. John, where Captain Knight promises the very finest coast scenery. Far away on the blue, floats a solitary pyramid of ice, while a few miles to the east of us there stands the image of some grand Capitol, in shining marble. Looking back upon the isles, as they retire in the south and west, with the hues of sunset upon their green and cloud-like blue, we behold, the painter tells me, a likeness to some West-Indian views.

Once again the breeze swells every sail, and we are speeding forward after the icebergs. All goes merrily. It sings and cracks aloft, and roars around the prow. We speed onward. The little ship, like a very falcon, flies down the wind after the game, and promises to reach it by the last of daylight. A long line of gilding tracks the violet sea, and expands in a lake of dazzling brightness under the sun. Beneath all this press of sail, we ride on fast and steadily, as a car over the prairies. We seem to be all alive. This is fine, inexpressibly fine! This is freedom! I lean forward and look over the bow, and, like a rider in a race, feel a new delight and excitement. Wonderful and beautiful! Like the Arab on his sands,

I say, almost involuntarily, God is great ! How soft is the feeling of this breeze, and how balmy is the smell, " like the smell of Lebanon,". and yet how powerful to bear us onward ! We rise and bow gracefully to the passing swells, but keep right on. ⌊Fogo is sinking in the south, a line of roseate heights, and fresh ice sparkles like stars on the northern horizon.

We dart off a mile or more from our right path in order to bring a small berg between us and the sun, that we may look into his sunset beauties. A dull cloud, close down upon the waves, may defeat this manœuvre. We shall conquer yet. There, he rises from the sea, a sphinx of pure white against the glowing sky, and every man aboard is as full of fine excitement as if we were to grapple with, and chain him. We pass directly under the great face, the upper line of which overlooks our topmast. Every curve, swell and depression have the finish of the most exquisite sculpture, and all drips with silvery water as if newly risen from the deep. In the pure, white mass there is the suspicion of green. Every wave, by contrast, and by some optical effect, nearly black as it approaches, is instantly changed into the loveliest green as it rolls up to the silvery bright ice. And all the adjacent deep is a luminous pea-green. The eye follows the ice into its awful depths, and is at once startled and delighted to find that the mighty crystal hangs suspended in a vast transparency, or floats in an abyss of liquid emerald.

We pass on the shadow side, soft and delicate as satin, and changeable as costliest silk ; the white, the dove-color and the green playing into each other with the subtlety and fleetness of an Aurora-Borealis. As the light streams over and around from the illuminated side, the entire outline of the berg shines like newly-burnished silver in the blaze of noon. The painter is working with all possible rapidity ; but we pass too quick to harvest all this beauty : he can only glean some golden straws. A few sharp words from the captain bring the vessel to, and we pause long enough for some finishing touches. He has them, and we are off again. An iceberg is an object most difficult to study, for which many facilities, much time, and some danger are indispensable. The voyager, passing at a safe distance, really knows little or nothing of one.

Ten o'clock, and only twilight. We are now about to put up note-book and painting-box, and join our English companions in a walk up and down our little deck. Notwithstanding their familiarity with icebergs, they appear to enjoy them with as keen a zest as we, now that they are brought into this familiar contact with them.

After the walk, and by candle-light in the cabin. The wind is strengthening, and promises a gale. The black and jagged coast of Twillingate island, to the south, frowns upon us, and the great pyramid berg of sunset awaits us close at hand. For some time past, it has borne the appearance of the cathedral of Milan, shorn of all its pinnacles, but it now resumes its pyramidal form, and towers, in the dusk of evening, to a great height. After a brief consultation, we resolve to slip into the harbor of Twillingate, a safe retreat from the coming storm, and there pass our first Sunday out of St. Johns. To dare this precipitous coast, haunted with icebergs, and a gale blowing right on, in so light a craft as ours, would be rash. Much as I wish to make the most of our time, I am glad to find that we are making harbor, and intend to rest, according to the law.

I cannot take my mind's eye from the brilliant spectacle of the waves in conflict with the iceberg. I still hear the surf in the blue chasms. But with all the power of its charge, it is the merest toy to the great arctic mass, a playful kitten on the paws of the lion.

After ten, and after prayer. We are rolling most uncomfortably while we are beating towards our anchorage between the headlands of the harbor. It is midnight nearly, and yet I am not in the least sleepy. The day is so lengthy, and we are so continually stimulated with the grandeur and novelty of these scenes that it is quite troublesome to sleep at all. A few hours of slumber, so thin that the sounds on deck easily break through and wake the mind, is about all I have. We are coming about, and roll down almost upon the vessel's side. The sails are loose, and roar in the breeze. The anchor drops, home to its bed. The chain rattles and runs its length. We repose in safe waters, and I turn in thankfully to my berth.

CHAPTER XXIII.

THE SUNDAY IN TWILLINGATE.—THE MORNING OF THE FOURTH.

MONDAY MORNING, *July* 4, 1859. We were roused from our slumbers very suddenly, yesterday morning, by Mr. Hutchinson, in a loud and cheerful voice, telling us the pleasing news that the Church Ship was at anchor near by, and that he had exchanged salutations with the Bishop. His vessel had lost a spar in the same squall that drove us into Cat Harbor. To that accident we owed the pleasure of meeting him in Twillingate, and of passing a profitable and happy Lord's day. The wind was blowing a perfect gale, and roared among the evergreen woods on the surrounding hills. At half-past ten, the Bishop's boat glided alongside, and bore us ashore, from which we walked past the church, through the assembling congregation, to the house of the Rector, the Rev. Thomas Boone, where we joined the Bishop and two or three of the leading persons of the island. There were the regular morning and evening services, and a third service at night, completed though by good strong daylight. The house was filled, and the sermons plain and practical, their burden being repentance, faith in Christ, and obedience to his law. After supper, and a social hour with the Rector and his family, we returned to our vessels respectively, the north-western sky still white with daylight, and the thunder of the ocean breaking with impressive grandeur upon the solemn repose, into which all nature seemed gladly to have fallen after the tempest.

I was up this morning at an early hour, and away upon the hills with Mr. Hutchinson and Master William Boone, a fine youth of fifteen, for our guide and companion. The main object was to get a view of the iceberg of Saturday evening. To my surprise and disappointment, the ocean was one spotless blue. The berg had foundered, or gone off to sea. It was barely possible that it lay behind a lofty headland, beneath which we passed in making the harbor. To settle a question, which in some measure involved the pleasure of the day, we climbed a rocky peak beset with brushwood, and descried the berg close in upon the headland apparently, and, as I supposed, rapidly diminishing, a lengthy procession of fragments moving up the coast. Looking south, there was unrolled to view, spread out from east to west, the splendid island scenery of Notre Dame Bay, already described. A single reach of water, with islets and mountainous shores, had a striking resemblance to Lake George.

At eight o'clock, we were again on board and ready for the boat, which, by appointment, was to take our party to the Hawk for a farewell breakfast with the Bishop. It is needless to say that we were most kindly and pleasantly entertained. The Bishop was pleased to accompany us back to our vessel, and to give us his parting blessing, on our own more humble deck. Just before sailing, Master Boone came off to us in a boat with a gift of milk and eggs, and a nice, fat lamb. By ten o'clock, both the Union Jack and the Stars and Stripes were waving on high in a south-west breeze, and we glided through the narrows toward the open sea, the chasms of the precipices heavily charged with the last winter's snow.

5*

CHAPTER XXIV.

THE ICEBERG OF TWILLINGATE.

TWELVE o'clock. The day we celebrate. Three cheers! Now we are after the iceberg. Upon getting near, we find it grounded in fifty fathoms of water, apparently storm-worn, and much the worse for the terrible buffeting of the recent gale. Masses of the huge, glassy precipices seem to have been blasted off within the last hour, and gone away in a lengthy line of white fragments upon the mighty stream. We are now bearing down upon it, under full sail, intending to pass close under it. Our good angels bear us company as we pass.

What an exquisite specimen of nature's handiwork it looks to be, in the blaze of noon! It shines like polished silver dripping with dews. The painter is all ready with his colors, having sketched the outlines with lead. The water streams down in all directions in little rills and falls, glistening in the light like molten glass. Veins of gem-like transparency, blue as sapphire, obliquely cross the opaque white of the prodigious mass, the precious beauty of which no language can picture. Fragments lie upon the slopes, like bowlders, ready to be dislodged at any moment, and launched into the waves. Now we dash across his cool shadow, and take his breath. There looks to be the permanency of adamant, while in reality all is perishable as a cloud, and charged with awful peril. Imagine the impressive grandeur and terrific character of cliffs, broad and lofty cliffs, at once so solid, and yet so liable at any moment to burst asunder into countless pieces. We all know the danger, and I confess that I feel it painfully, and wish ourselves at a safe distance.

The wind increases, and all is alive on deck. To my relief, we have fallen off to leeward beyond all harm. But we are on the back track, and mean to take him again, and take the risques also of his terrible, but very beautiful presence. Now we run. If he were a hostile castle, he would open upon us his big guns, at this instant. Bravely and busily the waves beat under the hollow of the long, straight water-line, rushing through the low archways with a variety of noises,—roaring, hissing, slapping, cracking, lashing the icy vaults, and polishing

and mining away with a wild, joyous energy.   Poor
Ishmael of the sea ! every hand and every force is against
him.   If he move, he dashes a foot against the deep
down stones.   While he reposes, the sun pierces his
gleaming helmet, and strikes through the joints of his
glassy armor.

In the seams and fissures the shadows are the softest
blue of the skies, and as plain and palpable as smoke.
It melts at every pore, and streams as if a perpetually
overflowing fountain were upon the summit, and flashes
and scintillates like one vast brilliant.   Prongs and reefs
of ice jutting from the body of the berg below, and over
which we pass, give the water that emerald clearness so
lovely to the eye, and open to the view something like
the fanciful sea-green caves.   We now lie to, under the
lee side, fearfully close, it seems to me, when I recollect
the warning of the Bishop, never, on any account, to venture near an iceberg.   Its water-line, under which the
waves disappear in a lengthy, piazza-like cavern, with explosive sounds, is certainly a remarkable feature.   Occasional glimpses unfold the polish, the colors, and the
graceful winding of sea-shells.   A strong current in connection with the wind forces us, I am glad to say, to a
more safe and comfortable distance.   The last ten minutes has given us a startling illustration of the dangers

of which we have been forewarned : a crack like a field-
piece was followed by the falling of ice, on the opposite
side of the berg, attended with a sullen roar.

We round to, and take the breeze in our faces.   The
ice is up the wind, square before us, and we must after it
by a tack or two.   The stars and stripes yet float aloft,
and seem to tremble with delight as we sport through
these splendid hours of Freedom's holiday.   The berg
with its dazzling white, and dove-colored shadows,—the
electric breeze,—the dark sea with its draperies of sparkling foam, north, east, south, out to the pure azure of the
encircling sky,—the sunshine, that bright spirit and ceaseless miracle of the firmament,—the white-winged vessel
boxing the billow, now rolling on black and cloud-like,
now falling off with the spotless purity of a snow-drift,—
the battle of the surges and the solid cliffs, all conspire
to enliven and excite.

While the painter is busy, overlooked by Mr. Hutchinson, and I lean over the bow and scribble in my
note-book, a sailor comes forward and gazes upon the iceberg as if he, too, was looking at something new.   He has
passed them by, time out of mind, either idly or with dis-
like, as things to be shunned, and not to be looked back
at when safely weathered.   Now that his attention is
called, he finds that this useless mass, tumbling about in

the path of mariners, is truly a most wonderful creation. Like all the larger structures of nature, these crystalline vessels are freighted with God's power and glory, and must be reverently and thoughtfully studied, to " see into the life of them." The common clouds, which unnoticed drop their shadows upon our dwellings, and spot the landscape, are found to be wonderful by those alone who watch them patiently and thoughtfully. " The witchery of the soft blue sky did never melt into the poet's heart ; he never felt the witchery of the soft blue sky" but from silent, loving study.

Captain Knight backs the sails, and we hold on near enough to the ice to see the zone of emerald water, a fearfully close proximity. Look up to those massy folds and wreaths of icy drapery, all flashing in the sun ! See that gigantic wing, not unlike the pictured wings of angels, unfolded from one of the vast shoulders, and spread upon the high air. As the wind sweeps over and falls upon us, we feel an icy chilliness. Beyond a very short distance, however, we are unable to perceive the smallest influence.

We are now to the leeward, half a mile or so, and are watching the Captain, who has gone with the boat and a couple of men to gather ice out of the drift, which stretches from the berg in a broken line for two miles or more. Portions of this have fallen within the last hour, keeping up a kind of artillery discharge, very agreeable to hear at this distance, and quite in harmony with the day at home. They have struck the ice, a mile off, and the chips sparkle in the sunshine as they ply the axe. As they return, we drop down the wind to meet them. Here they come with a cart-load of the real arctic alabaster, the very same, I have no question, that hung an hour ago as one of the shining crags of the lofty ice-cliff. And now, with all sail spread, and a spirited breeze, away to the north-west for Cape St. John.

CHAPTER XXV.

THE waves are crisp with a snowy mane, and the rocky shores of Twillingate are draped with splendid lights and shadows. While the seams and surfaces of the cliffs are strikingly plain in the sunlight, they are dark as caverns in the shade. This gives the coast a wonderfully broken, wild, and picturesque look.

Once more the sea "is all before us where to choose." The joy of this freedom is utterly inexpressible, although, in consideration of the day, we—we Yankees—occasionally hurra right heartily. But no words can do justice to the delightful emotions of moments such as these. "Messmates, hear a brother sailor sing the *dangers* of the sea," runs the old song. None that I have ever heard or read express at all the real pleasure of its *freedom*. The freedom of the seas ! If any great city council would do a man of feeling a noble pleasure, let them vote him that.

A lonely isle of crystalline brightness, all the way from Melville Bay, most likely, gleams in the north-east. Pale and solitary, like some marble mausoleum, the iceberg of Twillingate stands off in the southern waters. After all, how feeble is man in the presence of these arctic wonders ! With all his skill, intelligence and power, he passes, either on the sunny or the shady side, closely at his peril, only in safety at a distance too great to satisfy his curiosity, and gazes at their greatness and their splendor, and thinks and feels, records his thoughts and feelings, draws their figure and paints their complexion, but may no more lay his hand upon them than the Jew of old might lay his hand upon the ark of the covenant. He may do it and live, do it twice or thrice, and then he may perish for his temerity. There now reposes, amid the currents and billows of the ocean, the huge, polar structure, which has been to us an object of the liveliest interest and wonder ; its bright foundations fifty fathoms in the deep ; an erection suggestive of the skill and strength of the Creator ; with a mystery enveloping its story, its conception, birth and growth, its native land, the hour of its departure, its strange and labyrinthine voyage. While the body of this building-of-the-elements sleeps below, and only its gables and towers glow and melt in the brightness of these summer days, yet is it as dissolvable as the clouds from which it originally fell. It is but the clouds condensed and crystallized. A column of vapor, mainly invisible, perpetually ascends into its native heavens, while the atmosphere, and the warm, briny currents melt and wear, at every imaginable point of the vast surface. Pass a few sunny weeks, and all will be melted, and, like a snow-flake, lost in the immensity of waters.

Still the flags wave above. We fill our glasses with iceberg-water, and drink with cheers to the Queen and President. As the breeze dies away in the long, long afternoon, and we roll lazily on the glassy swells, the painter and I, the poorest of sailors, lapse into sea-sickness, and go below.

CHAPTER XXVI.

TUESDAY, *July 5.* Off Cape St. John, with fog and head winds. We are weary of this fruitless beating about, and resolve to put into smooth water for the sake of relief from sea-sickness. While our English guests seem to enjoy the breakfast, we have gone no further than to sip a little tea, take a few turns on deck in the chilly morning air, and return to the cabin, where I pencil these notes.

There is a dome-shaped berg before us in the mist, but not of sufficient beauty in the dull gray atmosphere to attract attention. Exclamations of our friends on deck have brought me up to look at the ice as we pass it, distant, it may be, five hundred yards. It bears a strange resemblance to a balloon lying on its side in a collapsed condition. It has recently undergone some heavy disruptions, and rolled so far over as to bring its late waterline, a deep and polished fissure, nearly across the top of it.

There is a promise of clear weather. The clouds, to our delight, are breaking, and giving us peeps of the sunny azure far above. The Cape is in full view, a promontory of shaggy precipices, suggestive of all the fiends of Pandemonium, rather than the lovely Apostle, whose name has been gibbeted on the black and dismal crags. The salt of that saintly name cannot save it. Nay, it is better fitted to spoil the saint. Cape St. John! Better, Cape "Moloch, Horrid King," or some other demon of those that figure in the dark Miltonic scenes. It is terribly awful and impressive. Our lamb, poor innocent, seems to feel lonely under the frown of a coast so inhospitable and savage, and comes bleating around us as if for sympathy. The wind is cold and bracing, sweeping alike the sea and the sky of all fog and clouds, and driving us to heavy winter clothing.

As we bear down toward the Cape, we pass Gull Isle, a mere pile of naked rocks delicately wreathed with lace-like mists. Imagine the last hundred feet of Corway Peak, the very finest of the New Hampshire mountain tops, pricking above the waves, and you will see this

little, outpost and breakwater of Cape St. John. All
things have their uses. Even this bone of the earth,
picked of all vegetable growth and beauty, and flung into
the deep, has the marrow of goodness in it to a degree
that invites a multitude of God's fair creatures to make
it their estate and dwelling-place. Gulls with cimetar-
like pinions, cut and slash the air in all directions.
Pretty little sea-pigeons fly to and fro, flying off with
whistling wings in straight lines, and flying back, full of
news, and full of alarm.

A grand iceberg is before us, remarkable, in this particular light, for its pure, white surface. A snow-drift,
with its icy enamel, after a silver thaw, might be taken
as a model of its complexion. This is a berg evidently
of more varied fortunes than any we have yet seen. It is
crossed and recrossed with old water-lines, every one of
which is cut at right angles with its own system of lines,
formed by the perpendicular dripping. It is ploughed
and fluted and scratched deeply in all possible directions.
At this very moment a new system of lines is rapidly
forming by the copiously descending drip, over-streaming
all those made when the berg had other perpendiculars.
Any large fall of ice, for example, from the opposite side,
would bow the berg toward us, sinking the present sea-
line on this side, and lifting it on the other. In nearly

every case the berg, when it rolls, loses its old horizontal position, and settles in a new one. Immediately a new horizon-line, if it may so be called, with its countless vertical ones, of course, instantly commences forming, to be followed by a similar process, at each successive roll of the berg, unto the end. There are draperies of white sea-shell-like ice, with streaks of shadow in their great folds, which rival the softest azure. Indicative of the projections of the submarine ice, the light-green water extends out in long, radiating points, a kind of emerald spangle, with its bright central diamond on the purple sea.

It is a wonderfully magnificent sight to see an almost black wave roll against an iceberg, and instantly change in its entire length, hundreds of feet, into that delicate green. Where the swell strikes obliquely, it reaches high, and runs along the face, sweeping like a satellite of loveliness in merry revolutions round its glittering orb. Like cumulous clouds, icebergs are perpetually mimicking the human face. This fine crystal creature, by a change in our position, becomes a gigantic bust of poet or philosopher, leaning back and gazing with a fixed placidity into the skies. In the brilliant noon, portions of it glisten like a glassy waterfall. The cold, dead white, the subtle greens, the blues, shadows of the softest slate, all contrast

... lasting brightness in a way most exquisite to
... True to all the forms of nature that swell to the
..., an iceberg grows upon the mind astonishingly.
... the boundless plains of water, of course, it is the
... molehill: in itself, it has the lonely grandeur of a
... precipice in the mountains.

... of several bergs, now hovering about the
..., is one of greater magnitude than any we have pre-
... met. It is, on this front, a broad and lofty pre-
..., very nearly resembling the finest statue-marble,
... broken. It is losing its upper crags, every now
... then, and vibrating very grandly. At short intervals,
... hear sharp reports, like those of brass ordnance, fol-
... by the rough, rumbling crash of the descending
... and the dull roar of its final plunge into the ocean.
... this awful burial of its dead, with such grand
..., a splendid regiment of waves retreats from the
... scene, in a series of concentric circles, rivalling
... finest surf that rolls in upon the sand. It is the very
... of the ocean cavalry. Under its fierce and bril-
... charge, an ordinary ship's boat would go down,
... to a certainty. It is what we have been most
... warned to avoid. This fine iceberg presents, I
... much the same appearance it had in the Greenland
... water-line, which is the only one visible, is

with the flashing brightness in a way most exquisite to behold. True to all the forms of nature that swell to the sublime, an iceberg grows upon the mind astonishingly. On the boundless plains of water, of course, it is the merest molehill : in itself, it has the lonely grandeur of a broad precipice in the mountains.

Foremost of several bergs, now hovering about the Cape, is one of greater magnitude than any we have previously met. It is, on this front, a broad and lofty precipice, very nearly resembling the finest statue-marble, newly broken. It is losing its upper crags, every now and then, and vibrating very grandly. At short intervals, we hear sharp reports, like those of brass ordnance, followed by the rough, rumbling crash of the descending ice, and the dull roar of its final plunge into the ocean. After this awful burial of its dead, with such grand honors, a splendid regiment of waves retreats from the mournful scene, in a series of concentric circles, rivalling the finest surf that rolls in upon the sand. It is the very flower of the ocean cavalry. Under its fierce and brilliant charge, an ordinary ship's boat would go down, almost to a certainty. It is what we have been most carefully warned to avoid. This fine iceberg presents, I fancy, much the same appearance it had in the Greenland waters. Its water-line, which is the only one visible, is not less than fifteen feet deep, and rises and falls, in its ponderous rockings back and forth, not more than twenty feet, so vast the bulk below. I have little doubt that the Alpine slopes and summits are its primitive surface. \

THE SPLENDID ICEBERGS OF CAPE ST. JOHN.

WE are making a round of calls on all the icebergs of Cape St. John, painting, sketching, and pencilling as we go. Our calls are cut short for the want of wind, and we lie becalmed on the low, broad swells, majestically rolling in upon the Cape, only a mile to the south-west. Captain Knight is evidently unquiet at this proximity. A powerful current is setting rapidly in, carrying us over depths too great for our cables, up to the very cliffs. If the adventurous mariner, who first sighted this bold and forward headland, was bent upon christening it by an apostolic name, why did he not call it Cape St. Peter ? All in all, it is certainly the finest coast scenery I have ever seen ; and Captain Knight assures us it is the very finest on the eastern shore of Newfoundland. It is a black, jagged wall, often four, and even five hundred feet

6

in height, with a five-mile front, and the deep sea close
in to the rock, without a beach, and almost without a
foothold.   This stupendous, natural wharf stretches back
into the south-west toward the main.land, widening very
little for twenty miles or more, dividing the large expanse
of White Bay on the west from the larger expanse of
Notre Dame Bay on the east and south, the fine Ægean,
before mentioned, with its multitudinous islands, of which
we get not the least notion from any of our popular maps.

Such is a kind of charcoal sketch of Cape St. John,
toward which, in spite of all we can yet do, we are slowly
drifting.   Unless there be power in our boat, manned by
all the crew pulling across the current, with the Captain
on the bow cracking them up with his fine, firm voice,
I do not see why we are not in the greatest danger of
drifting ashore.   It is possible that there is a breath of
wind under the cliffs, by which we might escape round
into still water.   With all the quiet of the ocean, I see
the white surf spring up against the precipices.   In the
strongest gales of the Atlantic, the surges here must be
perfectly terrific, and equal to any thing of the kind on
the globe.   The great Baffin current, sweeping past with
force and velocity, makes this a point of singular danger.
To be wrecked here, with all gentleness, would be pretty
sure destruction.   In a storm, the chance of escape would

be about the same, as in the rapids of Niagara.   After
all, there is a fine excitement in this rather perilous play
with the sublime and desolate. Would any believe it ?
I am actually sea-sick, and that in the full enjoyment of
this grandeur of adamant and ice.   I find I am not alone.
The painter with his live colors falls to the same level of
suffering with the man of the dull lead-pencil and the
note-book.   A slight breeze has relieved us of all anxiety,
and all necessity of further effort to row out of danger.
We are moving perceptibly up the wide current, and
propose to escape to the north as soon as the wind shall
favor.

We have just passed a fragment of some one of the
surrounding icebergs that has amused us.   It bore the
resemblance of a huge polar bear, reposing upon the base
of an inverted cone with a twist of a sea-shell, and whirling slowly round and round.   The ever-attending green
water, with its aerial clearness, enabled us to see its
spiral folds and horns as they hung suspended in the deep.
The bear, a ten-foot mass in tolerable proportion, seemed
to be regularly beset by a pack of hungry little swells.
First, one would take him on the haunch, then whip back
into the sea over his tail and between his legs.   Presently
a bolder swell would rise and pitch into his back with a
ferocity that threatened instant destruction.   It only

washed his satin fleece the whiter. While Bruin was turning to look the daring assailant in the face, the rogue had pitched himself back into his cave. No sooner that, than a very bull-dog of a billow would attack him in the face. The serenity with which the impertinent assault was borne was complete. It was but a puff of silvery dust, powdering his mane with fresher brightness. Nothing would be left of bull but a little froth of all the foam displayed in the fierce onset. He too would turn and scud into his hiding-place. Persistent little waves! After a dash singly, all around, upon the common enemy, as if by some silent agreement under water, they would all rush on, at once, with their loudest roar and shaggiest foam, and overwhelm poor bear so completely, that nothing less might be expected than to behold him broken into his four quarters, and floating helplessly asunder. Mistaken spectators! Although, by his momentary rolling and plunging, he was evidently aroused, yet neither Bruin nor his burrow were at all the worse for all the wear and washing. The deep fluting, the wrinkled folds and cavities, over and through which the green and silvery water rushed back into the sea, rivalled the most exquisite sculpture. And nature not only gives her marbles, with the finest lines, the most perfect lights and shades, she colors them also. She is no monochromist, but polychroic, imparting such touches of dove-tints, emerald and azure, as she bestows upon her gems and her skies.

We are bearing up under the big berg as closely as we dare. To our delight, what we have been wishing, and watching for, is actually taking place : loud explosions with heavy falls of ice, followed by the cataract-like roar, and the high, thin seas, wheeling away beautifully crested with sparkling foam. If it is possible, imagine the effect upon the beholder : This precipice of ice, with tremendous cracking, is falling toward us with a majestic and awful motion. Down sinks the long water-line into the black deep ; down go the porcelain crags, and galleries of glassy sculptures, a speechless and awful baptism. Now it pauses and returns : up rise sculptures and crags streaming with the shining, white brine ; up comes the great, encircling line, followed by things new and strange, crags, niches, balconies and caves ; up, up it rises, higher and higher still, crossing the very breast of the grand ice, and all bathed with rivulets of gleaming foam. Over goes the summit, ridge, pinnacles and all, standing off obliquely in the opposite air. Now it pauses in its upward roll : back it comes again, cracking, cracking, cracking, "groaning out harsh thunder" as it comes, and threatening to burst, like a mighty bomb, into millions of glittering fragments. The spectacle is terrific

and magnificent.   Emotion is irrepressible, and peals of
wild hurra burst forth from all.

The effect of the sky-line of this berg is marvellously
beautiful.   An overhanging precipice on this side, and
steep slopes on the other, give a thin and notched ridge,
with an almost knife-like sharpness, and the transparency
and tint of sapphire, a miracle of beauty along the heights
of the dead white ice, over which the sight darts into the
spotless ultramarine of the heavens.   On the right and
left shoulders of the berg, the slopes fall off steeply this
way, having the folds and the strange purity peculiar
to snow-drifts.   One who has dwelt pleasantly upon
draperies in marble,—upon those lovely swellings and
depressions,—those sweet surfaces and lines of grace and
beauty of the human form, perfected in the works of
sculptors, will appreciate the sentiment of the ices to
which I point.

At the risque of being thought over-sentimental and
extravagant, I will say something more of the great iceberg
of Cape St. John, now that we are retiring from it, and
giving it our last look.   Of all objects an iceberg is in the
highest degree multiform in its effects.   Changeable in its
colors as the streamers of the northern sky, it will also
pass from one shape to another with singular rapidity.
As we recede, the upper portions of the solid ice have a

light and aerial effect, a description of which is simply impossible. Peaks and spires rise out of the strong and apparently unchanging base with the light activity of flame. A mighty structure on fire, all in ice !

Cape St. John !—As we slowly glide away toward the north, and gaze back upon its everlasting cliffs, confronted by these wonderful icebergs, the glorious architecture of the polar night, I think of the apostle's vision of permanent and shining walls, "the heavenly Jerusalem," "the city which hath foundations, whose builder and maker is God."

"The good south wind" blows at last with strength, and we speed on our way over the great ocean, darkly shining in all its violet beauty. Pricking above the horizon, the peak of a berg sparkles in the glowing daylight of the west like a silvery star. C—— has painted with great effect, notwithstanding the difficulty of lines and touches from the motion of the vessel. If one is curious about the troubles of painting on a little coaster, lightly ballasted, dashing forward frequently under a press of sail, with a short sea, I would recommend him to a good, stout swing. While in the enjoyment of his smooth and sickening vibrations, let him spread his pallet, arrange his canvas, and paint a pair of colts at their gambols in some adjacent field.

The novelty and grandeur of these Newfoundland seas and shores have busied the pencil so completely as to exclude much interesting matter, especially such as Captain Knight is continually contributing in his conversation. As we have been, for some time past, crossing the fields of the sealer, and as the Captain himself has a large experience in that adventurous business, seals and sealing have legitimately a small place, at least, in this recital.

CHAPTER XXVIII.

THE sealers from St. Johns, for example, start upon their northern voyage, early in March, falling in with both ice and seals very frequently off the Capes of Conception and Trinity Bays. The ice, a snowy white, lies in vast fields upon the ocean, cracked in all ways, and broken into cakes or " pans " of all shapes and sizes. At one time, it resembles a boundless pavement dappled with dark water, into which vessels work their way, and upon which the seals travel : at another time, without the displacement of a block, this grand pavement of the sea rolls with its billows, rising and falling with such perfect order, that the men run along the ridges and down the hollows of the swells in safety. But this order goes into confusion in a storm, presenting in the succeed-

6*

ing calm a waste of ruins, masses of ice thrown into a thousand forms. In the long, starry nights, or the moonlight, or in the magic brilliancy of the aurora-borealis, the splendor of the scene,—dark avenues and parks of sleeping water, the silent glittering of mimic palaces and temples, sparkling minarets and towers, is almost supernatural. As will be seen at once, both the beauties and the perils incident to the ice, in calm and tempest, enter largely into the experience of the sealers. To-night, their vessel may repose in a fairy land or fairy sea, of which poets and painters may dream without the least suspicion that any mortal ever beholds the reality, and to-morrow night, it may encounter the double dangers of ice and storm.

Upon the fields just mentioned, the seals come from the ocean, in the depth of winter, and bring forth their young by thousands. There, while their parents come and go, the young things lie on the ice, fattening on their mothers' milk with marvellous rapidity, helpless and white as lambs, with expressive eyes almost human, and with the piteous cries of little children. In March, about as soon as the voyagers can reach them, they are of suitable age and size for capture, which is effected by a blow on the head with a club, a much more compassionate way of killing these poor lambs of the sea than by the gun, which is much used in taking the old ones.   Occasionally they are drawn bodily to the vessel, but usually skinned on the spot, the fat, two or three inches deep, coming off from the tough, red carcass with the hide, which, with several others is made into a bundle, dragged in by a rope, and thrown upon deck to cool.   After a little, they are packed away as solidly as possible, to remain until discharged in port.   Five, six, and seven thousand skins are frequently thus laid down, loading the vessel to the water's edge.   An accident to which the lucky sealer was formerly liable, was the melting of the fat into oil from the sliding of the skins, caused by the rolling of the ship in stormy weather.   To such an extent was this dissolving process sometimes carried, as to reduce the cargo to skins and oil, half filling cabin and forecastle, driving the crew on deck, rendering the vessel unmanageable in rough weather, and requiring it to be abandoned.   This is now securely guarded against by numbers of upright posts, which crib, and hold the cargo from shifting.

Several years ago, Captain Knight, while beset with the kind of ice, described as so beautiful in the bright nights, encountered, with many others, a terrific gale, to this day, a mournful remembrance to many people.   If I am not mistaken, some eighty sail were wrecked, at the time, along these iron shores. In fact, very few that were out escaped. Several crews left their vessels and fled to land over the rolling ice-fields, the more prudent way. A forlorn hope was to put to sea, the course adopted by Captain Knight. By skill and coolness he slipped from the teeth of destruction, and in the face of the tempest escaped into the broad ocean. It was but an escape, just the next thing to a wreck. One single sea, the largest he ever experienced in numerous voyages along this dreadful coast, swept his deck, and nearly made a wreck of him in a moment, carrying overboard one man, nine boats, every sealing-boat on board, and every thing else that could be wrenched away. Another gigantic roller of the kind would have destroyed him. But he ·triumphed, and returned to St. Johns in time to refit, and start again.

Captain Knight was less fortunate, no later than last April, when he lost a fine brig with a costly outfit for a sealing voyage, under the following circumstances: Immersed in the densest fog, and driven by the gale, he was running down a narrow lane or opening in the ice, when the shout of breakers ahead, and the crash of the bows upon a reef, came in the same moment. Instantly, overboard they sprang, forty men of them, and saw their strong and beautiful vessel almost immediately buried in the ocean. There they stood, on the heaving field of ice, gazing in mournful silence upon the great, black billows as they rolled on, one after another, bursting in thunder on the sunken cliffs, a tremendous display of surf where the trembling spars of the brig had disappeared forever. To the west of them were the precipitous shores of Cape Bonavista, lashed by the surge, and the dizzy roost of wild sea-birds. For this, the nearest land, in single file, with Captain Knight at their head, they commenced at sunset their dreadful, and almost hopeless march. All night, without refreshment or rest, they went stumbling and plunging on their perilous way, now and then sinking into the slush between the pans or ice-cakes, and having to be drawn out by their companions. But for their leader and a few bold spirits, the party would have sunk down with fatigue and despair, and perished. At daybreak, they were still on the rolling ice-fields, be-clouded with fog, and with nothing in prospect but the terrible Cape and its solitary chance of escape. Thirsty, famished, and worn down, they toiled on, all the morning, all the forenoon, all the afternoon, more and more slowly, and with increasing silence, bewildered and lost in the dreadful cloud travelling along parallel with the coast, and passing the Cape, but without knowing it at the time. But for some remarkable interposition of

Divine Providence, the approaching sunset would be their last. Only the most determined would continue the march into the next night. The worn-out and hopeless ones would drop down singly, or gather into little groups on the cold ice, and die. As the Captain looked back on them, a drawn-out line of suffering men, now in the hollow of the waves, and then crossing the ridge, the last of them scarcely seen in the mist, he prayed that God would interpose, and save them. A man who prays in fair weather, may trust God in the storm. So thought Captain Knight, when he thought of home, and wife and children, and the wives and the children of his men, and made his supplication. They had shouted until they were hoarse, and looked into the endless, gray cloud until they had no heart for looking any longer. Wonderful to tell! Just before sundown they came to a vessel. A few rods to the right or to the left, and they must have missed it, and been lost. It was owing to this disaster that Captain Knight was at leisure in St. Johns upon our arrival, and found it agreeable to undertake, for a few weeks, our guidance after the icebergs.

CHAPTER XXIX.

BELLE ISLE AND THE COAST.—AFTER-DINNER DISCUSSION.—FIRST
VIEW OF LABRADOR.—ICEBERGS.—THE OCEAN AND THE SUNSET.

WEDNESDAY, *July* 6. After a quiet night, with a
mild and favorable breeze, the morning opens with the
promise of a bright day. Our little cloud of sail is all up
in the early sunshine, and moving before the cool south
wind steadily forward down the northern sea. Brilliantly
as the summer sun looks abroad upon the mighty waters,
I walk the clean, wet deck, in the heaviest winter clothing, and have that pleasant tingling in the veins which
one feels in a brisk walk on a frosty autumnal morning.
We are abreast of South Belle Isle, high lands fronting
the ocean, with huge precipices, the fashion of most of the
eastern coast of Newfoundland. With all their sameness, their rugged grandeur and the ceaseless battle of
the waves below make them ever interesting. Imagine

the Palisades of the Hudson, and the steeper parts of the Highlands exposed to the open Atlantic, and you will have no imperfect picture of these shores. They have no great bank of earth and loose rocks heaped up along their base, but step at once into the great deep ; so deep that the icebergs, several of which are in sight, float close in, and seem to dare their very crags.

Afternoon. We have a pleasant custom of coming up, after dinner, and eating nuts and fruits on deck. It is one of the merry seasons of the day, when John Bull and Jonathan are apt to meet in those pleasant encounters which bring up the past, and draw rather largely upon the future, of their history. John is always the greatest, of course, and ever will be, *secula seculorum.* Jonathan, "considering," is greater than John. To be sure he is thinner, and eats his dinner in a minute ; but then he has every thing to do, and the longest roads on earth to travel, in the shortest time. In fact, he has many of the roads to make, and the least help and the shortest purse of any fellow in the world that undertakes and completes grand things. John's first thousand years is behind him ; Jonathan's, before him. One's work is done ; the other's begun. John's fine roads were made by his forefathers ; Jonathan is the forefather himself, and is making roads for his posterity. In fact, Jonathan is a

the Palisades of the Hudson, and the steeper parts of the Highlands .... and you will have no .... They have no great .... and .... rocks .... along their .... but stop at once .... the great .... so that the icebergs, several of which are in sight, float close in, and seem to dare their very crags.

Afternoon. We have a pleasant custom of coming up, after dinner, and .... on deck. It is one of the .... of the day, ... John Bull and Jonathan are apt to .... pleasant encounters which bring up the past, and .... rather largely upon the future, of their history. John .... always the greatest, of course, and ever will be, ... Jonathan, "considering," is greater than .... To be sure he is thinner, and eats his dinner in a minute; but then he has every thing to do, and the longest roads on earth to travel, in the shortest time. In fact, he has many of the roads to .... and the least help and the shortest purse of any fellow .... and completes good things. John's first thousand years is behind him; Jonathan .... done; the other's .... John's .... made by his forefathers; Jonathan is the forefather himself, and is making roads for his posterity. In fact, Jonathan is a

Lith of Saxony Major &

AN ARCHED ICEBERG IN THE AFTERNOON LIGHT

youth only, and John an old man. When the lad gets his growth, he will be everywhere, and the old fogy, by that time, comparatively nowhere. Jonathan insists that he is up earlier in the morning than John, and smarter, faster, and more ingenious. He contends that he has seen his worst days, and John his very best. The longer the diverging lines of the dispute continue, the further they get from any end ; and wind up finally with one general outburst of rhetoric, distinguished for its noise, in which each springs up entirely conscious of a perfect victory. In the complicated enjoyment of almonds, figs, and victory, we betake ourselves to reading, the pencil and the brush.

We are coasting along the extreme northern limb of Newfoundland, bound with its endless girdle of adamant, upon which the white lions of old Neptune are perpetually leaping, but which they will never wrench away. The snow lies in drifts along the heights, a novel, but rather dreary decoration for a summer landscape. Between us and the descending sun stands a berg, church-like in form. The blue shadows in contrast with the pure white, have a deep, cloud-like, and grand appearance. It is certainly a most superb thing, rising out of the blue-black waves, now gleaming in the slant sunlight like molten silver. So vast and varied is the scene, at this moment, that many pencils and many pens would fail to keep pace with the rapid description of the mind.

Directly west, is the Land's End of Newfoundland, Cape Quirpon—in the seaman's tongue, Carpoon, which we now shoot past. A few miles to the north, as if it might have been split off from the Cape, lies Belle Isle. The broad avenue of dark sea, extending westward between the cape and the island, opens out into the Strait of Belle Isle, and carries the eye to the shore of Labrador, our first view of that bony and starved hermit of a country. In this skeleton sketch, as it shows on paper, there is nothing very remarkable ; but with the flesh and the apparel of nature upon it, it is more beautiful than language can paint to the reader's eye. The entire east is curtained by one smooth cloud, of the hue called the ashes-of-roses. Full against it, an iceberg rises from the ocean, after the figure of a thunderhead, and of the color of a newly-blown rose of Damascus—a gorgeous spectacle. The waters have that dark violet, with a silvery surface, lucent like the face of a mirror, and a complexion in the deeps reminding one of the soft, dusky hues of a Claude Lorraine glass. The painter is busy with his colors, and all are silently opening mind and heart to the universal beauty. We move on over the lovely sea with a quiet gracefulness, in harmony with the visible scene and with our emotions. We are looking for unusual splendors, at the approaching sunset. I close the note-book, and give myself entirely to the enjoyment of the lonely and still magnificence.

The book is open to record. The sun on the rugged hills of Labrador, a golden dome ; Belle Isle, a rocky, blue mass, with a wavy outline, rising from the purple main pricked with icebergs, some a pure white, others flaming in the resplendent sunset like red-hot metal. We are sailing quietly as an eagle on the still air. Our English friends are heard singing while they walk the deck, and look off upon the lonesome land where their home is waiting for them.

All that we anticipated of the sunset, or the after-sunset, is now present. The ocean with its waves of Tyrian dye laced with silver, the tinted bergs, the dark-blue inland hills and brown headlands underlie a sky of unutterable beauty. The west is all one paradise of colors. Surely, nature, if she follows as a mourner on the footsteps of the fall, also returns jubilant and glorious to the scenes of Eden. Here, between the white light of day and the dark of the true evening, shade and brightness, like Jacob and the angel, now meet and wrestle for the mastery. Close down along the gloomy purple of the rugged earth, beam the brightest lemon hues, soon deepening into the richest orange, with scattered tints of new straw, freshly blown lilacs, young peas, pearl and blue intermingled. Above are the royal draperies of the twilight skies. Clouds in silken threads and skeins ; broad velvet belts and ample folds black as night, but pierced and steeped and edged with flaming gold, scarlet and crimson, crimson deep as blood ; crimson fleeces, crimson deep as blood ; plumes tinged with pink, and tipped with fire, white fire. And all this glory lies sleeping on the shore, only on the near shore of the great ethereal ocean, in the depths of which are melted and poured out ruby, sapphire and emerald, pearl and gold, with the living moist blue of human eyes. The painter gazes with speechless, loving wonder, and I whisper to myself: This is the pathway home to an immortality of bliss and beauty. Of all the days in the year, this may be the birth-day of the King-of-day, and this effulgence an imperial progress through the grand gate of the west. How the soul follows on in quiet joy, dreaming of lovely ones, waiting at home, and lovely ones departed, waiting with Christ ! Here come those wondrous lines of Goethe, marching into the memory with glowing pomp :

. . . . "The setting Sun ! He bends and sinks—the day is overlived. Yonder he hurries off, and quickens other life. Oh ! that I

have no wing to lift me from the ground, to struggle after, forever
after him! I should see, in everlasting evening beams, the stilly world
at my feet,—every height on fire,—every vale in repose,—the silver
brook flowing into golden streams. The rugged mountain, with all
its dark defiles, would not then break my god-like course. Already
the sea, with its heated bays, opens on my enraptured sight. Yet the
god seems at last to sink away. But the new impulse wakes. I hurry
on to drink his everlasting light,—the day before me and the night
behind,—the heavens above, and under me the waves. A glorious
dream! as it is passing, he is gone." . . . . .

Here come the last touches of the living coloring,
tinging the purple waves around the vessel. Under the
icebergs hang their pale and spectral images, piercing the
depths with their mimic spires, and giving them a lustrous, aërial appearance. The wind is lulling, and we rise
and fall gracefully on the rolling plain. "The day is
fading into the later twilight, and the twilight into the
solemn darkness." No, not into darkness; for in these
months, the faint flame flickering all night above the
white ashes of day from the west circling around to the
north and east, the moonlight and the starlight and the
northern-light, all conspire to make the night, if not
"more beloved than day," at least very lovely. A gloomy
duskiness drapes the cape, beneath the solitary cliffs of
which lies half entombed a shattered iceberg, a ghostly
wreck, around whose dead, white ruins the mad surf
springs up and flings abroad its ghastly arms. Softly

comes its sad moaning and blends with the plaintive melodies of the ocean.   Hark! a sullen roar booms across the dusky sea—nature's burial service and the funeral guns.   A tower of the old iceberg of the cape has tumbled into the billows.   We gather presently into the cabin for prayer, and so the first scene closes on the coast of Labrador.

CHAPTER XXX.

PAST Midnight. I have been up and watching forward for more than an hour, roused from my berth by the cry of ice. A large ship, with a cloud of sail, passed just across our head, bound for Old England. "That's a happy fellow," says the man at the helm; "past the dangers of the St. Lawrence and the Straits, and fairly out to sea." The wind is rising, and promises a rough time. "There is something," I said to myself, as I leaned, and looked over the bow, "there is something in all this, familiar as it is to many, very grand and awful, as we rise upon the black seas, and plunge into the darkness, rushing on our gloomy, strange way. We seem to be above the very 'blackness of darkness,' and riding upon the bosom of the night. The sounding foam, sweeping forward from beneath our bows, looks like a cloud of supernatural brightness, its whiteness filled, as it is, with the fire and electric scintillations of the sea.   One could easily imagine himself sailing on the breeze through the night, with sparks of lightning and a cloud at his vessel's bow." The wind freshens to a gale nearly, and all hands are called on deck.   We are rolling in a most uncomfortable manner, and I have retreated to my cabin, and will creep back to my berth.

THURSDAY NOON, *July* 7.   A few scrawls of the pencil will serve to give an outline of our experience for the last twelve hours.   A dense fog, high wind and a heavy swell.   As a matter of course, our little ship has been in great commotion, and we, miserably sea-sick, regardless of breakfast, absent from the cold, wet deck, and rolled up below, dull and speechless in bed.   We have been gradually creeping up into the world, of late, sipping a little coffee and nibbling at crackers.   We are off Cape St. Louis, the most eastern land of the continent.   The few turns on deck have sufficiently electrified the brain to enable me to get on thus far with my notes, and to venture upon a short description of a cabin-scene, at a very late hour last night.

Three sides of our cabin, a room some ten feet by twelve, and barely six feet under the beams, are taken up by four roughly-made berths; one on each side, and two extending crosswise, with a space between them, fitted up with shelves, and used for the flour-barrel, and as a cupboard. Beneath the berths are trunks, tubs, bags, boxes and bundles, most of our choicest stores. From the centre, and close upon the steep, obtrusive stairs, covered with a glossy oil-cloth, of a cloudy brown and yellow, our table looks round placidly upon this domestic scene, so indicative of refreshment and repose. With this little sketch of our sea-apartment, the stage upon which was enacted our last night's brief play, I will undertake its description, promising a brevity that rather suggests, than paints it.

After the midnight look-out forward for ice, and the retreat to the cabin, I soon joined in the general doze, rather suffered than enjoyed. In the uproar above, sharp voices and the rush of footsteps over the deck, occasionally stamping almost in our very faces, we were too frequently called back to full consciousness, to escape away into any thing better than the merest snatch of a dream. In my own case, the stomach, as usual, indulged itself in taking the measure of those motions, so disastrous to its peace and equipose; those rollings, risings, sinkings, divings, flings and swings, in which there is the sense of falling, and of vibrations smooth and oily. Where one's mind's eye is perpetually looking down in upon the poor remains of his late departed dinner, there is no possibility for the outter eye to sink into any true and honest slumber. The shut lid is a falsehood. It is not sleep. The live, wakeful eye is under it, looking up against the skinny veil. Occasionally the veil is lifted just to let the dark out ; occasionally the dumb blackness falls in upon the retina like a stifling dust, and dims it, for a moment, to a doze. But the fire of wakefulness soon flashes up from the cells of the brain, and throws out the sleepy darkness, as the volcanic crater throws out its smoke and ashes.

Through some marine manœuvre, thought necessary by the master spirit on deck, and which could be explained by a single nautical word, if I only knew what the word is, we began to roll and plunge in a manner sufficiently violent and frightful to startle from its staid quiet almost every movable in the cabin. Out shot trunks and boxes—off slid cups and plates with a smash —back and forth, in one rough scramble with the luggage, trundled the table, followed by the nimble chairs. At this rate of going on, our valuables would soon mix in one common wreck. Determining to interfere, I sprang into the unruly confusion, and succeeded in lighting a candle just in time to join in the rough-and-tumble, at the risk of ribs and limbs, and the object of mingled merriment and alarm to the more prudent spectators. Botswood, an experienced voyager, shouted me back to my berth instantly, if I would not have my bones broken at the next heavy lurch of the vessel. I was beginning to feel the force of the counsel, when another roll, almost down upon the beam-ends, overturned the butter-tub and a box of loaf-sugar, and brought their contents loose upon the field of action. They divided themselves between the legs of the table and the individual, and so, candle in hand and adorned in modest white, he sat flat down upon the floor among them, at once their companion in trouble and their protector. The marble-white sugar and the yellow butter, our luxuries and indispensable necessaries, there they were, on the common floor, and disposed for once to join in a low frolic with plebeian boots and shoes and scullion trumpery. With an earnest resolve to prevent all improprieties of the kind, one hand grasped, knuckle deep, the golden mellow mass, of the size of a good Yankee pumpkin, and held on, while the other was busy in restoring, by the rapid handful, the sugar to the safety of its box. The candle, in the mean time, encouraged by the peals of laughter in the galleries, slid back and forth in the most trifling manner possible. When we tipped one way, then I sat on a steep hill-side, looking down to-

ward the painter, roaring in his happy valley : away slid
the candle in her tin slippers, and away the barefooted
butter wanted to roll after, encouraged to indulge in the
foolish caper by a saucy trunk jumping down from behind. When we tipped the other way, then I sat on the
same hill-side, legs up, looking up, an unsatisfactory
position : back slid the candle, followed by a charge of
sharp-pointed baggage, and off started the butter with
the best intentions toward the tub, waiting prostrate and
with open arms. Notwithstanding the repetition and
sameness of this performance, the beholders applauded
with the same heartiness, as if each change back and forth
was a novel and original exhibition. What heightened
the effect of the scene, and gave it a suspicion of the
tragic, was a keg of gunpowder, which evinced, by several
demonstrations of discontent in the dark corner where it
tumbled about, a disposition to come out and join the
candle. By a happy lull, not unusual in the very midst
of these cabin confusions during a brush at sea, the powder did not enter, and I was enabled to pitch the butter
into the tub, and finally myself, after some few prelimi-
naries with a towel, into my berth, where, in the course
of the small remnant of the night, I fell into some broken
slumbers.

CHAPTER XXXI.

THE CAPE AND BAY OF ST. LOUIS.—THE ICEBERG.—CARIBOO ISLAND. —BATTLE HARBOR AND ISLAND.—THE ANCHORAGE.—THE MISSIONARIES.

FIVE o'clock, P. M. What a pleasing contrast! We have been tossing nearly all day upon a rough, inclement ocean, and are now on the sunny, smooth waters of the bay, gliding westward, with Cape St. Louis close upon our right. We have sailed from winter into summer, almost as suddenly as we come out of the fog, at times—bursting out of it into the clear air, as an eagle breaks out of a cloud. It is fairly a luxury to bask in this delicious sunshine, and smell the mingled perfume of flowers and the musky spruce. Mr. Hutchinson is filled with delight to find himself once more on this beautiful bay. The rocky hill-country along the western shores, nine or ten miles distant, is not the mainland, he tells us, but islands, separated from the mainland, and from each other, by narrow waters, occasionally expanding into lakes of great depth, and extending more than forty miles from the sea. Were these savage hills and cliffs beautified with verdure, and sprinkled with villages and dwellings, this would class among the finest bays of the world. Across it to the south, some seven miles, and partly out to sea, lies a cluster of picturesque islands, where is Battle Harbor, the home of the missionaries, and the principal port on the lengthy coast of Labrador.

A fine iceberg, of the fashion of a sea-shell, broken open to the afternoon sun, and unfolding great beauty, lies in the middle of the bay. We are sailing past it, on our passage to the harbor, just near enough for a good view. It gleams in the warm sun like highly-burnished steel, changing, as we pass it, into many complexions— changeable silks and the rarest china. The superlatives are the words that one involuntarily calls to his aid in the presence of an iceberg. From this bright creation floating in the purple water, I look up to the bright clouds floating in the blue air, and easily discover likenesses in their features, ways and colors.

The coast of Labrador is the edge of a vast solitude of rocky hills, split and blasted by the frosts, and beaten by the waves of the Atlantic, for unknown ages. Every form into which rocks can be washed and broken, is visible along its almost interminable shores. A grand headland, yellow, brown and black, in its horrid nakedness, is ever in sight, one to the north of you, one to the south. Here and there upon them are stripes and patches of pale green—mosses, lean grasses, and dwarf shrubbery. Occasionally, miles of precipice front the sea, in which the fancy may roughly shape all the structures of human art, castles, palaces and temples. Imagine an entire side of Broadway piled up solidly, one, two, three hundred feet in height, often more, and exposed to the charge of the great Atlantic rollers, rushing into the churches, halls, and spacious buildings, thundering through the doorways, dashing in at the windows, sweeping up the lofty fronts, twisting the very cornices with snowy spray, falling back in bright green scrolls and cascades of silvery foam. And yet, all this imagined, can never reach the sentiment of these precipices.

More frequent, though, than headlands and perpendicular sea-fronts are the sea-slopes, often bald, tame, and wearisome to the eye, now and then the perfection of all that is picturesque and rough, a precipice gone to pieces, its softer portions dissolved down to its roots, its flinty bones left standing, a savage scene that scares away all thoughts of order and design in nature. If I am not mistaken, there are times when a slope of the kind, a mile or more in length, and in places some hundreds of feet in breadth from the tide up to the highest line of washing, is one of the most terribly beautiful of ocean sights. In an easterly gale, the billows roll up out of the level of the ocean, and wreck themselves upon these crags, rushing back through gulfs and chasms in a way at once awfully brilliant and terrific.

This is the rosy time of Labrador. The blue interior hills, and the stony vales that wind up among them from the sea, have a summer-like and pleasant air. I find myself peopling these regions, and dotting their hills, valleys, and wild shores with human habitations. A second thought, and a mournful one it is, tells me that no men toil in the fields away there ; no women keep the house off there ; there no children play by the brooks, or shout around the country school-house ; no bees come home to the hive ; no smoke curls from the farm-house chimney ; no orchard blooms ; no bleating sheep fleck the mountain-sides with whiteness ; and no heifer lows in the twilight. There is nobody there ; there never was but a miserable and scattered few, and there never will be. It is a great and terrible wilderness of a thousand miles, and lonesome to the very wild animals and birds. Left to the still visitations of the light from the sun, moon, and stars, and the auroral fires, it is only fit to look upon, and then be given over to its primeval solitariness. But for the living things of its waters, the cod, the salmon and the seal, which bring thousands of adventurous fishermen and traders to its bleak shores, Labrador would be as desolate as Greenland.

We are now entering Battle Harbor, a most romantic nook of water, or Strait rather, between the islands forming the south side of the bay St. Louis. Cariboo Island fronts to the north on the bay, five or six miles, I should guess, and is a rugged mountain-pile of dark gray rock, rounded in its upper masses, and slashed along its shores with abrupt chasms. It drops short off, at its eastern extremity, several hundred feet, into a narrow gulf of deep water. This is Battle Harbor. The billowy pile of igneous rock, perhaps two hundred and fifty feet high, lying between this quiet water and the broad Atlantic, is Battle Island, and the site of the town. We pass a couple of wild islets, lying seaward, as we glide gently along toward our anchorage. There is little to be seen but hard, iron-bound bay, and yet we are all out, gazing abroad with silent curiosity, as if we were entering the Golden Horn. Up runs the Union Jack, and flings its ancient crosses to the sun and breeze, and the fishermen look down upon us from their rude dwellings perched

7*

among the crags, and wonder who, and from whence we are. For the moment, nothing seems to be going on but standing still and looking, men, women, and children. And now they will look and wonder still more : up run the Stars and Stripes, higher up than all, and overfloat the flag of England, and salute the sun and cliffs of Labrador. The missionary waves his handkerchief—waves his hat—calls pleasantly to a group upon the nearest shore. They look, and hearken, in the stillness of uncertainty. Instantly there is a movement of recognition. The people know it is their pastor. The intelligence has caught, and runs from house to house. Down drop the sails, rattling down the masts ; the anchor plunges, and the cable runs, runs rattling and ringing from its coil. Round the vessel swings in line with the breeze, and comes to its repose. We congratulate the missionary on his safe return, while he points us feelingly to the little church and parsonage, just above us on the mossy hillside, and bids us welcome as long as we shall find it agreeable to remain. With light and thankful hearts, and pleasant anticipations, we prepare to go ashore, and take our first run upon the hills.

CHAPTER XXXII.

WE sit down upon the summit of Battle Island, after a zigzag scramble up its craggy side, and talk and sketch and scribble, as we rest and look upon the blue, barren sea, and the brown and more barren continent, with its mountains of desert rock. With all this desolateness, the approaching sunset and the warm skies, the stern headlands, the white icebergs and bleak islands, and the bay with its rays and points of water, like a vast spangle on the savage landscape, all compose a picture of singular novelty and grandeur ; at the present moment, wonderfully heightened in beauty and spirit by a distant shower, itself a spectacle of brilliancy and darkness sweeping up from the north. Mr. Hutchinson here joins us, looking all the pleasure that he feels, and points out what is visible of the lengthy, but narrow field of his religious labors. The harbor, with its vessels and various buildings, lies quite below. One could very nearly throw a stone over the little church spire, and shoot a rifle ball into the cliffs opposite. The air is spiced with the most delicate odors, which invites us to a short ramble in search of flowers, after which we descend to the parsonage for tea.

I have stolen out upon the small front piazza with a chair, to enjoy the warm sunshine and the sights of a Labrador village. The parsonage, which has been closed for more than a year past, has been cleaned and put in order by some kind Esquimaux parishioners, and looks neat and comfortable. H—— has taken us all through, from room to room—to the kitchen, pantry, bed-rooms, parlor, which serves also for dining-room, library and study, to the school-room up stairs, which is used at times as a chapel. As we passed the house clock, the pointer still upon the hour where it stopped more than eighteen months ago, the painter wound it up, and gave it a fresh start and the true time, which it began to measure by loud and cheerful ticks, as if conscious that life and spirit had returned again to the vacant dwelling. On the shelf, over the fireplace, lay a prayer-book, the gift of Wordsworth to his nephew, with an affectionate inscription on a fly-leaf, in his own handwriting, while near by stood a couple of small pictures of the poet and his wife.

As some fishermen are now drawing in their capelin seine, we are going to run down and see the sight. And quite a pretty sight it was. Not less than a barrel or two were inclosed, which they dipped with a small scoop-net into their boat, where they lay for a moment, fluttering like so many little birds of gaudy plumage under the fowler's net. The males and females of these delicate fishes, are called here, very comically, cocks and hens. As our boat, just then, came across from the vessel, the fishers gave us a mess for breakfast, all of half a bushel, which we carried over at once. At the sight of several fine salmon, on the fishing-flake close by, fresh from the net, the poor little capelin sank into immediate contempt. We must have a salmon or two. It was a question whether we could not eat several. It resulted in the purchase of one of sixteen pounds, at the cost of a dollar. We were pulled back immediately in order to sup with Mr. Hutchinson, and spend the remainder of the long, light evening in running over Battle Island. I shall not yield to the temptation to dwell upon the brilliant sunset which we saw from the summit rocks. Its glories were reflected in the bay, and shed upon the grim wilderness, dissolving all its gloomy ruggedness into softest beauty. No language can depict the still and. solemn splendor of the icebergs, reposing upon the burnished waters. Temples and mausoleums of dazzling white, warming into tints of pink, or deepening on their shaded side into the sweetest azure, seemed to be standing upon a mighty mirror with their images below. I thought of that standing on the sea of glass, in the glorious visions of St. John, and was filled with emotions of wonder and admiration. The words of the psalmist could hardly fail to be remembered : "These men see the works of the Lord, and his wonders in the deep."

One would think that all is couleur de rose in these lands beyond the reach of fashionable summer tourists. Let him remember that nature here blooms, beautifies, and bears for the entire year, in a few short weeks. We are in the very flush of that transient and charming time. Believe me, when I speak of the plants and flowers, shrubbery and mosses. At this moment, the rocky isle, bombarded by the ocean, and flayed by the sword of the blast for months in the year, is a little paradise of beauty. There are fields of mossy carpet that sinks beneath the foot, with beds of such delicate flowers as one seldom sees.

There is a refined delicacy in the odor, which the

ordinary flora of warmer climes seldom has. Some rare exotic, reared with cost, and pampered by all the appliances of art, may suggest the subtle spirit of these tiny blossoms. It steals upon the sense of smell with the indescribable tenderness of the music of the æolian harp upon the ear. As I enjoy it, I know that I cannot paint it to the reader, and that I shall probably never " look upon its like again." It is very likely that the cool and very pure air, a refinement of our common atmosphere, has much to do with it.

In our stroll, we found banks of snow still sleeping in the fissures above the showering of the surf, and peeping out from beneath their edges were clusters of pretty flowers. As we returned in the twilight, upon the mournful stillness of which broke the voice of the surge, I lingered upon the cliffs to listen to the wood-thrush, the same most plaintive and sweet bird that sings in the Catskill mountain woods, at dusk and in the early morning. The pathos of its wild melody stole in upon the heart, waking " thoughts too deep for tears," and calling up a throng of tender memories of Cole and others, with whom the songster, the hour, and mountain scenery are forever associated. Startled by the voices of my companions, one a nephew of the famous poet, and the other a pupil of the painter scarcely less renowned, I hastened

to join them at the humble parsonage below the cliffs,
when we went across to the vessel, and united, for the
last time in the cabin, in those pleasant devotions which
we had enjoyed, morning and evening, since our departure from St. Johns.

CHAPTER XXXIII.

FRIDAY, *July* 8, 1859. A bright, cool morning. After breakfast at the parsonage, we went rambling again up and down the moss-covered fields of Battle Island, smelling the fine perfume, gathering flowers, and counting the icebergs. There are more than forty in the neighborhood, and some of them grand and imposing at a distance. Have you thought, as I did, that there are no flowers, or next to none, in Labrador? You might as well have thought that all, or nearly all the flowers were in Florida. Along the brook-banks under the Catskills—to me about the loveliest banks on earth, in the late spring and early summer days—I have never seen such fairy loveliness as I find here upon this bleak islet, where nature seems to have been playing at Switzerland. Green and yellow mosses, ankle-deep and spotted with blood-red stains, car_ pet the crags and little vales and cradle-like hollows. Wonderful to behold! flowers pink and white, yellow, red and blue, are countless as dew-drops, and breathe out upon the pure air that odor, so spirit-like. Such surely was the perfume of Eden around the footsteps of the Lord, walking among the trees of the garden in the cool of the day. What grounds these, for such souls as write, " The moss supplicateth for the poet," and the closing lines of the " Ode, Intimations of Immortality from recollections of early Childhood." The Painter, passionately in love with the flowers of the tropics, lay down and rolled upon these soft, sweet beds of beauty with delight. Little gorges and chasms, overhung with miniature precipices, wind gracefully from the summits down to meet the waves, and are filled, where the sun can warm them, with all bloom and sweetness, a kind of wild greenhouse. We run up them, and we run down them, fall upon the cushioned stones, tumble upon their banks of softness as children tumble upon deep feather-beds, and dive into the yielding cradles embroidered with silken blossoms. Willows with a silvery down upon the leaves, willow-trees no larger than fresh lettuce, and the mountain laurel of the size of knitting-needles, with pink flowers to correspond, cluster here and there in patches of a breadth to suit a sleeping child.

After our ramble, we returned on board, arranged the cabin, now become quite roomy from the departure of our friends, and prepared for dinner, to which a small company is invited. Our cook, a young Sandy, excelling in good nature, but failing in all the essentials of his art, was suspended, for the time, from the exercise of all duties about the caboose, except those of the mere lackey, and two more important personages self-inducted into his place. Some pounds of fresh salmon bagged in linen, a measure of peeled potatoes, a pudding of rice well shotted with raisins, one after another, found their way to the oven and the boilers; from which, in due time and order, they emerged in a satisfactory condition, and, with appropriate sauce and gravy, descended in savory procession to the cabin, to which they were unexpectedly welcomed by a whole dress circle of fashionable dishes seated in the surrounding berths, jelly-cake, sponge-cake, raspberry-jam, nuts, figs, almonds and raisins, and a corpulent pitcher, sweating in his naked white, filled with iceberg water. It is not necessary to dwell upon the fact, that the cooks subsided into the more quiet character of hosts, and made themselves, and endeavored to make their guests, merry at their own expense. Whether the Queen of England, or the President of the United States will be pleased, it never occurred to us at the time, when, without thinking of either, we drank to their health in the transparent vintage of Greenland.

CHAPTER XXXIV.

AFTER dinner. Mr. Hutchinson has placed at our service his parish vessel, at once a schooner and a row-boat, of which Captain Knight, of course, is master, and our men the sailors. We are all ready, waiting its arrival alongside, in order for our first excursion after icebergs, equipped entirely to our mind.

An hour's sail has brought us off into the broad waters, south of Battle Harbor, close to a berg selected from the heights this morning. We drop sails, and row rapidly around it, for the best point of observation in the present light. The intention is to study the ices of these waters, at all points, and in all lights, with great care. From this, the western side, now glittering in the face of the sun, at six o'clock, it is alpine in its form, with one crowning peak, supported by pinnacles and buttresses, with intervening gulfs and hollows, each with its torrent hissing along down in white haste over glassy cliffs and in alabaster channels, until it comes spouting into the sea from an overhanging precipice, varying from six, to twenty feet in height. Between the upper edge of this ice-coast and the great steeps of the berg, lies a broad slope, smooth as ivory, a paradise for the boys of a village school. We are actually tempted to land at a low place, and have a run. Without skates, or some arming of the boots, how-ever, we guess it would be rather perilous sport; in short, simply impossible. We content ourselves with catching a panfull of water, fresh from the great Humboldt gla-cier, quite likely, and cold and pure it is. While we are busy at the fountain, we amuse ourselves with looking down through the clear, green water—right under us, clear almost as air—at the roots and prongs of the moun-tain mass. They shoot out into the dark sea below far beyond our boat, not a pleasing vision to dwell upon, when we reflect, that these very prongs and spurs only wait to take their turn in the sunshine, under the aspect of up-right towers. A heavy fall of ice, which may happen in a minute, on the opposite side of the berg, instantly gives the preponderance to this, when over this way slowly rolls the alpine peak, down sinks all this precipice, and after it, all the slanting field above; then on rushes the sea in curling waves, and we are swept on with them. Before we can get back, and get away to a safe distance, by the force of mere sailor power, back rolls the berg, up rises the broad slope, followed quickly by the precipices rising up, up, and up into lofty cliffs, with a foreground, a new revelation of ice ; in a word, the prongs and spurs now below us in the transparent deep. In all this play of the iceberg and the sea, what will be our part ? And who knows whether the moment is not now close upon us for this sparkling planet of the main to burst asunder, a common process by which the mother berg throws off her little ones, rather, resolves herself entirely into a shoal of small icebergs ? Should that moment really come while we are in this fearful proximity, you need not ask any questions about us, except those which you yourself can answer. There are the dead in these very waters, I believe, whose last earthly experience was among the final thunders of these ices.

I am struck with the rapid rate at which the bergs are perishing. They are dissolving at every point and pore, both in the air and in the sea. One sheet of water, although no thicker than a linen sheet, covers the entire alp. It trickles from every height, yonder glimmering like a distant window in the sunset, here cutting into the glassy surface and working out a kind of jewelry, which sparkles with points of emerald and ruby. It rains from eves and gables, cornices and balconies, and spouts from gutters. All around, there is the pattering of a shower on the sea, and the sharp, metallic ringing of great drops, similar to what is heard around a pond in the still woods, when the dew-drops fall from the overhanging boughs. Below, the currents, now penetrated with the summer warmth, are washing it away. Around the surface-line, the ever-busy waves are polishing the newly-broken corners, and cutting under, and mining their way in, with deceitful rapidity. Unceasingly they bore and drill, without holiday or sabbath, or rest at night, as the perpetual thunders of their blasting testify. Thus their ruin is hourly hastening to a consummation, and the danger of approaching them made more and more imminent. The iceberg in winter, in the Arctic regions, and even here, is a different affair. In the cold, they are tolerably safe and sound. But now, in these comparatively tepid seas, and in this warm atmosphere, lone wanderer, it finds no mercy. Motionless as this and several bergs appear, they are all slowly moving in toward the Strait of Belle Isle, borne forward by the great Baffin current, a stream of which bends around Cape St. Louis and these adjacent isles, and sets along the shore of Labrador into the Gulf of St. Lawrence.

CHAPTER XXXV.

THE ALPINE BERG.—STUDIES OF ITS SOUTHERN FRONT.—FRIGHTFUL
EXPLOSION AND FALL OF ICE.—STUDIES OF THE WESTERN SIDE.
—OUR PLAY WITH THE MOOSE HORNS.—THE SPLENDOR OF THE
BERG IN THE SUNSET.

WE are now lying under oars, riding quietly on the
swells, distant, say, a hundred yards south of the berg,
which has a visible, perpendicular front of five hundred,
by one hundred and fifty feet or more elevation. It resembles a precipice of newly-broken porcelain, wet and
dripping, its vast face of dead white tinged with green,
here and there, from the reflection of the green water at
its base. We are in its shadow, which reaches off on the
sunny sea, a long, dark track. The outline of the berg is
one edge of dazzling brightness, a kind of irregular, flowing frame, gilt with sunlight, which comes pouring over
in full tide from behind. Where the ice shoots up into
thin spear-points, or runs along a semi-transparent blade,

8

the light shines through, and gives the tint of flame, with a greenish band below, and lower still, a soft blue, presently lost in the broad white. In these ices, never think of any such as you see at home, from Rockland and Catskill. Frozen under enormous pressure, and frozen to dry and flinty hardness, it has all the sparkle of minutest crystallization, and resembles, as I have said already, freshly broken statue-marble or porcelain, as you see it on the edge newly snapped. The surface of this ice is in itself a study singularly complex and subtle. How the mere passer-by, at a distance, is going to know any thing of value to a painter, I cannot tell. The fact is, he knows just nothing at all. A portrait-painter might as well pretend to have a knowledge of flesh, from seeing people at a distance. I think if I could study just here, for hours, I should be able to speak more correctly. Of course, the Painter, whose eye is trained to look into the texture of surfaces, sees all more readily. I am looking up to rough crags, and enormous bulges, where the recent fracture would seem to have an almost painful sharpness to the touch. Where the surfaces have been for a time exposed to the weather, they have the flesh-finish of a statue. Along the lower portion, where you see the glassing effects of the waves, there it resembles the rarest Sèvres vase, or even pearl itself, so exquisitely fine is the polish. It is almost mirror-like. You perceive the dim images of passing objects, shadowy ships and shores. Where the light pours over it in its strength, it shines like burnished steel in the sunshine.

Under the manifold effects of atmosphere, light and shade, none can imagine, through the medium of mere description, the grandeur and glory of these moving Alps of ice. Here now, is one simple feature, which our dangerous proximity alone enables us to view, the wondrous beauty of which—beauty to the feelings as well as to the eye—I cannot find any language to paint. I may talk of it through a hundred periods, and yet you will never feel and see a tithe of what you would in a moment, were you here upon the spot. The berg, in the deep shadow of which we now sit painting and writing, as I have intimated, is in form a mountain pinnacle, split down from the summit square, and the split side toward our boat. What has became of the lost half, the Great Builder of icebergs only knows. We are under the cliffs, from which that unknown part burst off and fell away. It is an awful precipice, with all the features of precipices, such as are seen about capes, headlands and ocean shores. Here it swells out, there it sinks in, masses have slidden out, and left square-headed doorways opening into the solid porcelain, ridges run off, and hollows run in and around. In these very hollows and depressions is the one feature of which I am speaking. And, after all, what is it? It is simply shadow. Is that all? That is all: only shadow. All the grand façade is one shadow, with a rim of splendor like liquid gold leaf or yellow flame, but in those depressions is a *deeper* shadow. Shadow under shadow, dove-colored and blue. Thus there seems to be drifting about, in the hollow lurking-places of the dead white, a colored atmosphere, the warmth, softness, and delicate beauty of which no mind can think of words to express. So subtle is it and evanescent, that recollection cannot recall it when once gone, but by the help of the heart and the feelings, where the spirit of beauty last dies away. You can feel it, after you have forgotten what its complexion precisely is, and from that emotion you may come to remember it. You would remember nothing more beautiful.

Any doubt that I may have entertained about the danger of lying under the shadow of this great ice-rock is now wholly dispelled. We have just witnessed what was, for the moment, a perfect cataract of ice, with all its motion, and many times its noise. Quick as lightning and loud as thunder, when bolt and thunder come at the same instant, there was one terrific crack, a sharp and silvery ringing blow upon the atmosphere, which I shall

PLATE Nº 4

forget, nor ever be able to describe. It shook me enough, and struck the very heart. The only response on my part, and I was not alone in the fright, was a convulsive spring to the feet, and a shout to the oarsmen, of fierce command, "Row back! row back!" The spectators were watching the explosion. At once, the ■■■■ burst out upon the air, as if it had ■■■■ swept down across the great cliff, a huge ■■■■ of green and snowy fragments, with a wild, roar, followed by the heavy, sullen thunder of the plunge into the ocean, and the rolling away of the high-crested seas, and the rocking of the mighty mass back and forth, in the effort to regain its equilibrium. I dreaded the encounter; but our whale-boat was quite and breasted the lofty swells most gracefully.

■■■■ impressive is all this! I recall the ■■■■ ■■■■ and recollect the ■■■■ ■■■■ the ■■■■ of St.

We now pass round to the other side of the berg, and take a position between it and the sun. Upon our first circumnavigation, we found this edge of the ice, in its lowest part, about six feet above the sea, with a cavernous hollow running all round, into which the waves were ■■■■ with their strange and many sounds. Now, from

never forget, nor ever be able to describe. It shook me
through, and struck the very heart. The only response on
my part, and I was not alone in the fright, was a convulsive spring to the feet, and a shout to the oarsmen, of
fierce command, " Row back ! row back ! " The spectacle was nearly as startling as the explosion. At once, the
upper face of the berg burst out upon the air, as if it had
been blasted, and swept down across the great cliff, a huge
cataract of green and snowy fragments, with a wild,
crashing roar, followed by the heavy, sullen thunder of
the plunge into the ocean, and the rolling away of the
high-crested seas, and the rocking of the mighty mass
back and forth, in the effort to regain its equilibrium.
I dreaded the encounter ; but our whale-boat was quite
at home, and breasted the lofty swells most gracefully.
But how fearfully impressive is all this ! I recall the
warning of the Bishop of Newfoundland, and recollect the
conversation of the Rev. Mr. Wood, the rector of St.
Thomas'.

We now pass round to the other side of the berg, and
take a position between it and the sun. Upon our first
circumnavigation, we found this edge of the ice, in its
lowest part, about six feet above the sea, with a cavernous hollow running all round, into which the waves were
playing with their strange and many sounds. Now, from

the recent loss of ice on the opposite heights, all this edge
has sunk below the waves, leaving only an inclined plane
sweeping up from the water's edge to the steeper parts of
the berg, at an angle of about 20 degrees.   Fancy a slab
of Italian marble, four and five hundred feet in width,
extending from the eaves of the City Hall, New York,
half-way or more down the park.   I think you will have
a tolerable notion of the slope now before us.   Up this
slippery field of ivory hardness roll the waves, dark as
night until they strike the ice, when, in a flash, they
turn into that lovely green of the sea, and afterward
break in long lines of tumultuous foam.   The spectacle
is perfectly magnificent.   A seam of ice, apparently six
inches in diameter, of the hue of a sapphire, cuts the berg
from its very top down, and doubtless cuts through the
entire submarine body.   This jewel of the iceberg is a
wonderful beauty.   Sparkles of light seem to come from
its blue, transparent depths.   What, at first, appears singular is, that these blue veins are much softer than the
surrounding ice, melting faster, and so becoming channels
in which little torrents glitter as they run.   At first, we
were at a loss to know how they originated, but presently
felt satisfied, that they were cracks filled with water, and
frozen when the berg was a glacier.   This indelible mark
of primitive breakage and repair indicates with some cor-

rectness the original perpendicular of the ice. According to the blue band in the berg now before us, it is occupying very nearly the position it was in when it was a fissure or crevasse of the glacier. Long processional lines of broken ice are continually floating off from the parent berg, which, in the process of melting, assume many curious shapes, huge antlers of the moose and elk, and sea-fowl, geese and ducks, of gigantic figure. We have just succeeded in securing one of these antlers, and a merry time we had. Before reaching it, we supposed one could bend over and lift it out of the water as easily as he stoops and picks up a buck's horn out of the prairie grass. It was a match for three of us, and escaped out of our hands and arms repeatedly, slipping back into the waves, and requiring us to round to again and again before we fairly had it. As it is the hardest and the heaviest, so it is the most slippery of all ices, and certainly it seems to me the coldest thing upon which human hands were ever laid. Our summer cakes, handed in by the ice-man, are warm, I fancy, in comparison. I do not wonder that the face of icebergs burst off, under the expansion of the heat they receive in these July days. The surface of this horn is not the least curious feature of it : it is melted into circular depressions about the depth and size of a large watch-crystal, all cutting into each other with such regularity that their angles fall into lines parallel and diagonal in the most artistic manner. Now that we have it in the boat, it resembles a pair of mammoth moose-horns sculptured from water-soaked alabaster. We see several of them now, five or six feet tall, rocking and nodding on the swells as if they were the living append-ages of some old moose of the briny deep, come up to sport a little in the world of warmth and sunshine.

C—— finds great difficulty in painting, from the motion of the boat; but it is the best thing in the ser-vice, after all, for the men can take a position, and keep it by the help of oars, in spite of the waves and currents which beset an iceberg. The moments for which we have been waiting are now passing, and the berg is immersed in almost supernatural splendors. The white alpine peak rises out of a field of delicate purple, fading out on one edge into pale sky-blue. Every instant changes the quality of the colors. They flit from tint to tint, and dissolve into other hues perpetually, and with a rapidity impossible to describe or paint. I am tempted to look over my shoulder into the north, and see if the "merry dancers" are not coming, so marvellously do the colors come and go. The blue and the purple pass up into peach-blow and pink. Now it blushes in the last look of the sun-red blushes of beauty—tints of the

roseate birds of the south—the complexion of the roses
of Damascus.   In this delicious dye it stands embalmed
—only for a minute, though ; for now the softest dove-
colors steal into the changing glory, and turn it all into
light and shade on the whitest satin.   The bright green
waves are toiling to wash it whiter, as they roll up from
the violet sea, and explode in foam along the broad
alabaster.   Power and Beauty, hand in hand, bathing the
bosom of Purity.   I need not pause to explain how all
this is ; but so it is, and many times more, in the passing away of the sunshine and the daylight.   It is wonderful !   I had never dreamed of it, even while I have been
reading of icebergs well described.   As I sit and look at
this broken work of the Divine fingers,—only a shred
broken from the edge of a glacier, vast as it is—I whisper
these words of Revelation : "and hath washed their
robes, and made them white in the blood of the Lamb."
It hangs before us, with the sea and the sky behind it,
like some great robe made in heaven.   Where the flowing folds break into marble-like cliffs, on the extreme
wings of the berg, an inward green seems to be pricking
through a fine straw tint, spangled with gold.   Weary,
chilly, and a little sea-sick, I am glad to find the Painter
giving the last touches to a sketch, and to hear him give
the word for return.   The men, who in common with

8*

all these people of this northern sea have a terror of ice-bergs, gladly lift the sails, and so, with Captain Knight at the helm, we are speeding over the waves for Battle Harbor.

CHAPTER XXXVI.

RAMBLE AMONG THE FLOWERS OF BATTLE ISLAND.—A VISIT TO
THE FISHERMEN.—WALK AMONG THE HILLS OF CARIBOO.

SATURDAY, *July* 9. We are abroad again on the
rocky hills, fanned with the soft, summer wind, and
blessed with the loveliest sunshine. The mosses sparkle
with their sweet-scented blossoms of purple, white, and
red, and the wood-thrush is pouring out its plaintive
melody over the bleak crags, and the homes of fishermen,
around whose doors I see the children playing as merrily
as the children of fortune in more favored lands. How
many a tender parent, now watching over a sick child in
the wealthy city, would be glad to have the sufferer here,
to be the playfellow of these simple boys and girls, if he
could have their health and promise of life. Captain
Knight comes with his hands full of flowers, not unlike the
daisy ; and here come Hutchinson and the Painter. We

meet around this moss-covered crag, where I am sitting with my book and pencil, and resolve at once to go down, and visit an islet of the harbor, where a few families have a summer residence during the fishing season.

Here we are among the huts and dogs, and English people, with the ways of Labrador. A kind woman, with whom I have been talking about the deprivations of her lot in life, has offered to bake bread for us when we can send the flour. The Painter is out sketching this summer nest upon the bleak, surf-washed rocks, about as wild-looking as the nesting-place of sea-birds. Generous-hearted people ! I am pleased with their simple ways, and their affectionate, but most respectful manner toward their pastor. Well, indeed, they may be both respectful and affectionate. His life is a sacrifice for them and their children. What but the love of Christ and of men could lead one here, and keep him here, who can ornament and bless the most cultivated society ? I thank God, that He gives us witness, in such men, of the power and excellency of His grace upon the human heart. We sail across the harbor to a cove, or chasm in the lofty sea-wall, with the intention of a walk over the hills of Cariboo, while Hutchinson visits a few of his pa- rishioners thereabouts.

After a pleasant ramble, during which we were often

tempted to run and jump with very delight along the spongy, springy moss, blushing here and there with its sweet bloom, we sit down on the top of a high hill, and look off upon the ocean and the bay of St. Louis, extending far into the desolate interior like a series of blue lakes. All the beauteous apparel of summer has been stripped off, and the brown and broken bones of the sad earth are bleaching in the wind and sun. You would be delighted, though, with the little vales, notched and shelved with craggy terraces that catch and hold the sunshine. They have the sultry warmth and scent of a conservatory, and are frequently rich with herbage, now in flower. It seems a pity that these nooks of verdure and floral beauty should thus " waste their sweetness on the desert air." For a few days, the woolly flocks of New England would thrive in Labrador. During those few days, there are thousands of her fair daughters who would love to tend them. I prophesy the time is coming when the invalid and tourist from the States will be often found spending the brief, but lovely summer here, notwithstanding its ruggedness and desolation. Upon reflection, a broad and ancient solitude like this has a sadness in it which no bloom, no sun can dispel. Never, never, in all my life, have I beheld a land like this, the expression and sentiment of which are essentially mournful and melancholy. The sunshine, skies, "the pomp and circumstance of" ocean, sweet smells, and sounds, and one's own joyous, healthy feelings, flowing out and washing out as they flow the natural sadness of the soul, cannot take away nor cover up that which really and everlastingly is, and ever will be, namely, the sentiment of mournfulness. Nature here is at a funeral forever, and these beauties, so delicately fashioned, are but flowers in the coffin.

It is a coincidence a little curious that I should have written these periods above, and then have plunged into just the most lonesome little valley in all the world to hit upon a graveyard. But there it was, a gloomy, silent field, enclosed with the merest dry skeleton of a fence, for no purpose to keep a creature out where no creature is, but just to make a scratch around the few narrow beds where the dead repose, unpraised and unnamed, under the lightest possible covering of dust, as undisturbed as in the deeps of the Atlantic. From the tombless cemetery, our way back to the vessel over the hills resembled the crossing of mountains just below the line of perpetual snow. Upon the summit we encountered a small lake and marshes with water-plants and flowers. At the eastern extremity of the island, where the rocks break off steeply some hundreds of feet, we saw every object of the port nearly beneath, and apparently within stone's throw.

A novel sight to us was the bottom of the harbor, seen through the clear, greenish water with considerable distinctness almost from end to end.   Patches of sea-weed, dark rocks, and white gravel, seemed to be lying in the bottom of. a shallow mirror, across which small fishes, large ones in reality, were wandering at their leisure. This was a picturesque revelation.   Upon the surface of the harbor, the depth of water very nearly shuts out all view of the bottom.   I am beginning to think that a few thousand feet above the ocean, in a bright day, would enable the eye to pierce it to an extraordinary depth.

CHAPTER XXXVII.

AFTER THE BAY ST. LOUIS ICEBERG.—WINDSOR CASTLE ICEBERG.—
FOUNDERS SUDDENLY.—A BRILLIANT SPECTACLE.

AFTER dinner, upon the heights of Battle Island,
gathering roots, plants, and mosses to carry home. We
notice with pleasure the largest iceberg by far that we
have ever yet seen. It is the last arrival from Greenland, and is abreast Cape St. Louis, in the northeast.
It is a stupendous thing, and reminds me of Windsor
Castle, as I know it from pictures and engravings. It
appears to be wheeling in toward the bay, with a front of
great elevation and extent, finely adorned with projections and massive towers not unlike those of the regal
structure of which it reminds me. I see by the
watch it is nearly 4 P. M., the time set for our departure to a Bay St. Louis berg. Pencil and note-book

must be pocketed, and haste be made with my vegetable gatherings.

Pencil and note-book reappear, and the sketch recommences. Half-way to the chosen iceberg, in the mouth of the bay, rowing slowly over the glassy, low swells, as they move in from sea. These are the swells for me: broad, imperial swells, full of majesty, dignity, and grace; placid and serene of countenance; solemn, slow, and silent in their roll. They are the swells of olden time, royal and aristocratic, legitimately descended from those that bore the ark upon their bosom, and used to bear the unbroken images of the orbs of heaven. Replete with gentleness and love and power, they lift us lightly, and pass us over tenderly from hand to hand, and toss us pleasantly and softly from breast to breast, and roll us carefully from lap to lap, and smile upon us with their shining smiles. Grand and gracious seas! With you I love the ocean. With you I am not afraid. And with you, how kind and compassionate of you, ye old patrician billows! with you I am not sea-sick. Save us from those plebeian waves, that rabble-rout of surges, that democratic "lop," lately born, and puffed into noisy importance! They scare me, and, worst of all, make me sick and miserable.

Every few minutes we hear the artillery of the icebergs, and are on the watch for fine displays, this warm afternoon. C—— is sketching hastily, with the pencil, Windsor Castle berg, now in complete view, and distant, I should guess, five miles. It is a mighty and imposing structure.

Between making my last dot and now—an interval of ten minutes—Windsor Castle has experienced the convulsions of an earthquake, and gone to ruin. To use the term common here, it has " foundered." A magazine of powder fired in its centre, could not more effectually, and not much more quickly, have blown it up. While in the act of sketching, C—— suddenly exclaimed : when, lo ! walls and towers were falling asunder, and tumbling at various angles with apparent silence into the ocean, attended with the most prodigious dashing and commotion of water. Enormous sheaves of foam sprung aloft and burst in air ; high, green waves, crested with white-caps, rolled away in circles, mingling with leaping shafts and fragments of ice reappearing from the deep in all directions. . Nearly the whole of this brilliant spectacle was the performance of a minute, and to us as noiseless as the motions of a cloud, for a length of time I had not expected. When the uproar reached us, it was thunder doubled and redoubled, rolling upon the ear like the quick successive strokes of a drum, or volleys of the largest ordnance. It was awfully grand, and altogether the most startling exhibition I ever witnessed. At this moment, there is a large field of ruins, some of them huge masses like towers prone along the waters, with a lofty steeple left alone standing in the midst, and rocking slowly to and fro.

CHAPTER XXXVIII.

SUNDAY EVENING, *July* 10. We have had a beautiful and interesting day. Early in the morning, flags were flying from the shipping, and from the tall staff in front of the church, the only bell-tower of the town. Boats, with people in their Sunday best, soon came rowing in from different quarters, for the services of the day, in which I had the pleasure of assisting. The house, seating about two hundred people, was crowded, morning and afternoon, with a devout and attentive congregation, responding loudly, and singing very spiritedly.

Before sunset, we left the parsonage for a quiet walk. Falling into a crooked path, we followed it to the burying-ground in the bottom of a narrow, deep hollow, where time has gathered from the surrounding rocks a depth of earth sufficient for shallow graves. While yet the sunshine was bright upon the high, over-hanging cliffs, dotted with lichens and tufted with their summer greenery, the little vale below, with its brown gravestones nearly lost in the rank verdure, was immersed in cool and lonesome shadows. An unavoidable incumbrance of the sacred field was several large bowlders, among which the long grass, and weeds and tablets were irregularly dispersed.

It is the custom of the English church to consecrate burying-grounds. Eleven years ago, Bishop Field consecrated this. It was a pleasant Sunday morning, and the procession, with the bishop at its head clothed in his official robes, descended by the winding path, and performed the appointed service. Nearly the whole population of the region was present, either in the procession, or looking down with silent admiration from the rocky galleries around. A better resting-place, when one lies down weary from the tasks and troubles of the present life, could not well be imagined. Its perpetual solitude, never profaned by the noisy feet of the busy world, draped alternately with snowy fleeces and blooming verdure, is always made musical by the solemn murmurs of the ocean. I found by the inscriptions, that England was the native country of most of those whose bones repose below, and whose names are gathering moss and lichens, while the sea, close by, sings their mournful requiem.

From this lone hamlet of .the dead, we picked our way among broken rocks out to the sea shore, all white with the sounding surf, and gazed with silent pleasure on the blue Atlantic, the dark headlands, and the icebergs glittering in the sunset. Glittering in the sunset! They glowed with golden fire—pointed, motionless, and solid flames.

Battle Island, had there never been any bloody contest of angry men, would be an appropriate name. The whole northeastern shore, once a lofty precipice, no doubt, but now a descent of indescribable ruggedness, is an extended field, whereon for ages flinty rocks and mighty waves have contended in battle. A favorite walk of Hutchinson's, during the wintry tempests, is along the height overlooking this mighty slope or glacis. His quiet description of the terrible grandeur of the scene, was truly thrilling. In the course of our walk, we came upon the verge of a fissure, which looked like an original intention to split the island through its centre. Banks of snow still lay in the nooks and closets of its gloomy chambers, through which, every now and then, boomed the low thunder of the plunging surf.

Upon our return, late in the evening, although quite light, we wandered over tracts of the elastic, flowering moss. The step is rendered exceedingly bouyant, and invites you to skip and bound through the richly carpeted hollows. After prayer at the parsonage, we returned to the vessel, and talked in our berths until slumber made us silent, past midnight.

CHAPTER XXXIX.

MONDAY, *July* 11. After icebergs in St. Michael's
Bay, was to have been the order of the morning. It lies
northward forty miles, and usually abounds in icebergs
of the largest size, Mr. Hutchinson informs us. There
is not, however, the least necessity for passing Cape St.
Louis, south of which there is ice enough in sight for all
the painters in the world. But the charm of novelty is
almost irresistible. Had we the time, we would see the
glaciers themselves, of which these bergs are merely the
chippings. What has suddenly caused this change in
our plans is an approaching storm. It will never do for
us to be out at sea in a cold northeaster, if it possibly can
be avoided. The painter and I are so given over to sea-
sickness, in rough weather, that nothing can be enjoyed,

and nothing done with pen or pencil. The work and play of the day are finally determined. · C—— with the Captain will cruise southerly among the bergs of Belle Isle, and I will go with Mr. Hutchinson and Botwood north, across St. Louis water to Fox Harbor, one of the points of this extended parish.

We leave, past noon a little, sailing very pleasantly by the ices, which appear to be in considerable motion. Several are going to sea, and may reach the track of New Yorkers voyaging to Europe, and be thought very wonderful and fine ; and so indeed they will be, should they lose half of their present bulk. There appears to be no end to the combinations of these icy edifices. They mimic all the styles of architecture upon earth ; rather, all styles of architecture may be said to imitate them, inasmuch as they were floating here in what we please to call Greek and Gothic forms long before Greek or Goth were in existence. Yonder, now, is a cluster of Gothic cottages. I trace out a multitude of peaked gables and low porches, and think of Sunny Side upon the Hudson.

Two hours have slipped away, and we approach the northern shore, attended by no less a travelling companion than a small whale. Now he blows just behind us, disappears, and blows again upon our right. There he blows ahead of us. Here he is close upon our left.

9

The fellow is diving under us. All this may be very pretty sport for the whale, but with all the merry remarks of Hutchinson, respecting the good nature of our twenty-foot out-rider, I confess I am relieved to find that he is gradually enlarging the field of his amusements.

The mouth of Fox Harbor all at once discovers itself, and lets us in upon a small sheet of water, not unlike a mountain lake with its back-ground of black, wild hills. A few huts, a wharf, and fish-house appear upon the margin of the narrow peninsula that lies between the harbor and the bay. The people are pure Esquimaux and English, with a mixture from intermarriage. The patriarch of the place, perhaps sixty years of age, with his wife, and, I believe, the elder members of the family, are natives of a high latitude, and a good specimen of the arctic race. They are now members of the English Church, and for piety and virtue compare well with Christians anywhere.

In the course of the afternoon, their pastor held divine service, and administered the sacrament of baptism. There were between twenty and thirty present, old and young, some of whom had prayer-books and responded. The sermon, which I was invited to preach, I made as simple and practical as possible, and found earnest and honest listeners. After an examination of

furs and snow-shoes, reindeer horns, and seal-skin, fresh
from the seal, and still loaded with its fat or blubber, we
had an exhibition of the kayak. It was light and tight,
and ringy as a drum, and floated on the water like a
bubble. Under the strokes of the kayaker, it darted forward over the low swells with a grace and fleetness unknown to the birch bark canoe. After tea, and a very
good tea, too ; in fact, after two teas, we bade the
Esquimaux farewell and sailed away, taking one of their
number along with us, who had formerly been a servant,
and was now to resume her old place as such, in the
parsonage. About half way across the bay, a squall from
sea struck us with startling suddenness. But our bold
young sailing-master, Mc Donald, the mate and owner
of our vessel, managed the boat admirably, and we fairly
flew through the white-caps to the smooth water of our
harbor. In the evening we gathered in at the parsonage,
taking tea, made and served by the Esquimaux woman,
telling the adventures of the day, both north and south,
and returning at midnight to our cabin.

CHAPTER XL.

TUESDAY, *July* 12. Cold as November, and a gale outside. After a late breakfast, we roam the hills of Cariboo, under the cliffs of which the Integrity now lies tied to the rocks. We gather roots and flowers, gaze upon the vast and desolate prospect, count the icebergs, and watch the motions of the fog driving, in large, cloud-like masses, across the angry ocean. It is surprising how much we do in these, to us, almost interminable days. But for the necessity of it, I believe that we should not sleep at all, but work and play right on from midnight into morning, and from morning down to midnight. We have a large afternoon excursion before us. Previous to that, however, the Captain and myself are going upon an exploring expedition.

Coasting the southern shores of St. Louis water, having a little private amusement by ourselves. The breeze, in from sea, gives us about as much as we can manage. Gives *us* about as much as *we* can manage ! "Us" and "We" have not a great deal to do with it. This half of the "us" and the "we," the Me and the subjective I, as your Kantian philosopher calls his essential self, sits here about midship, bear-skinned in with a fleecy brown coat, holding on, and dodging the spray that cuffs him on the right and left ; while the other, and vastly larger half, in the shape of the captain, holds all the reins of this marine chariot in his own single hand—ropes, rudder and all, and holds them, too, well and wisely. But we enjoy the freedom of these spirited, though harmless seas, and dash along through most charmingly.

What coasts these are ! " Precipitous, black, jagged rocks," savage as lions and tigers showing their claws and teeth, and foaming at the lips. Here a chasm called a cove, up which the green water runs in the shape of a scimetar or horn—the piercing and the goring of the sea for unknown centuries. Away in the extreme hollow of this horn is a fishing-flake, and half-way up, where the sea-birds would naturally nest, a Scotch fisherman has his summer-home. We are going in to see him.

He met us at the water's edge, and welcomed us with a fisherman's welcome—none heartier in the world—and sent us forward by a zigzag path to the house hidden away among the upper rocks. In the very tightest place of the ascent, there swept down upon us an avalanche of dogs furiously barking—a kind of onset for which I have had a peculiar disrelish ever since I was overthrown by a ferocious mastiff in my childhood. I sprang to the tip of a crag, and stood out of their reach, while they bristled and barked at the Captain, who coolly maintained his ground. The shout of the fisherman's wife, who now appeared on the edge of the scene above, instantly stilled the uproar, and invited us up with the cheering assurance that they seldom bit anybody, and were rather glad than angry that we had come. The language of dogs being very much the same in all countries, I took occasion to doubt any pleasure that Bull, Brindle, and Bowse were thought to have felt at our presence. The rascals smelt closely at my heels and hands, with an accompaniment of bristling backs and tails, and deep-throated growls. We were no sooner in the house and seated than the goodman himself arrived, and ordered the kettle to the fire for a " bit of tea." " It would do us good," he said. " When strangers came, he commonly had a bit of tea." His

life had been a struggle for food and raiment : such was
the tenor of his brief history. Four children were with
him ; four were in a better world. Forty years he had
been a fisherman. Thirty, on these shores. They came
up yearly from Carbonear in the early days of June,
cleared the house of ice and snow, and got ready for the
fish. Their dogs, which are their only team in Newfoundland, would be lost if left behind, and so they
brought them along to save them. After tea, a fine
game-cock took possession of the floor, walking close in
front, looking up sideways in an inquisitive and comical
manner, and crowing very spiritedly. Hard by, in a box
beneath a bed, I caught a glimpse of the red comb of a
hen, his only mate. A little, flaxen-haired, blue-eyed
girl ran and brought her out as something to surprise
and delight us. And so with cock and hen, and children, the fisherman and his wife, mariner and minister,
we were a social party. Thus the human heart spins
out its threads of love, and fastens them even to the
far-distant rocks of cold and barren Labrador. They took
us through their fish-house, which hung like a birdcage
among the crags, and afterwards followed us down to
the water, and gave our bark a kindly push," and thus
we parted."

CHAPTER XLI.

Two o'clock P. M. The wind has moderated, and blows from the land. We sail out upon the eastern or ocean side of Great Island. This is not precisely the excursion proposed in the morning, which was to an iceberg in the bay. It is the best, though, that we can do, and may turn out very well. I could wish a less exciting passage in than we had out, when, for the first, I learned the power of wind to knock a vessel over at a single blow. It pounced upon us, as it swept over the lofty ridge of the island, in puffs and gusts quite frightful. At one moment, the sails would be without a breath ; at another, the wonder is that they were not burst from their fastenings. As the Captain turned into the wind, the boat would jump as if going out of the water. Some training is necessary for your landsman to bear this with perfect coolness. After landing us, the Captain, with a couple of men, plays off and on between a fishing-fleet and shore, while C—— paints the particular part of the coast for which we have come.

It consists of what once might have been a grand cavern, but now fallen in, and all its cragged gulf opened to the day. Into the yawning portal of this savage chasm plunge the big waves of the Atlantic. In an easterly gale, there is performed in this gloomy theatre no farce of the surges, but the grandest tragedy. In fact, this whole coast, a thousand miles or more, is built up, rather torn down, on the most stupendous scale—vast and shattered—terrifically rough—tumult and storm all in horrid stone. It would well pay the painter of coast scenery to spend a fall and winter upon these shores. The breaking of the waves upon such rocks as these must be an astonishing spectacle of power and fury. The charge and the retreat of billows upon slopes of rock so torn and shattered, for miles and miles at the same moment, Mr. Hutchinson repeatedly declares, is one of the most brilliant and imposing sights on earth. While C—— is painting, I have been writing these periods, and clambering the mossy cliffs for plants and flowers. Half-past 7, and Captain Knight below, waiting for us near the mouth

9*

of the chasm.   The fishing-fleet is dispersing, homeward-bound, and we are now ready to put up paint and pencil, and join in the general run.

There is nothing like a dash of peril to wake one up. Now that I am quietly sitting by the cabin candles, I will sketch you our passage in.   These notes are usually taken on the spot ; upon the occasion of which I am at present speaking, my note-book was buttoned in pretty tightly in its pocket.

It was blowing a gale, but, fortunately for us, from the land.   In from sea, the same wind would have driven all into the surf.   Close-reefed as we were, and under the island, with a capital craft, and Captain Knight, the very best of sailors, it was quite enough for us.   We were almost over at times.   The sharp, short seas thumped our bows like sledge-hammers.   The spray flashed across like water from an engine.   There were the hum and trembling of a swiftly revolving wheel.   When she came into the wind for a tack, all shook and cracked again, and then sang on shrill and wildly as shuttle-like we shot to the next point of turning.   A few small islands make a net-work of channels.   Through this entanglement we and the fishing-fleet were now making our way home, crossing and recrossing, shooting here and there, singly and in pairs, with sails black, white, and red—a lively and picturesque sight, and just the prettiest play in all the world. In a narrow strait leading into the harbor, we were nearly baffled. The tempest, for to such it had increased, at some moments, seemed to fall upon us from above, flattening the swells, and sweeping the spray about as a whirlwind sweeps the dust. Back and forth we darted between the iron shores, wheeling in the nick of time, and losing nearly as often as we gained. C—— and I lay close below the booms, and watched the strife as one might watch a battle round the corner of a wall. Wrapped in heavy overcoats, and wet and chilly, we came, notwithstanding, to enjoy it vastly. C—— fairly overflowed with fun and humor. But what admirable sailors are these northern seamen, in their schooner whaleboats ! the very Tartars and Camanches of the ocean ! They go off to the fishing-grounds in stormy weather, and stay with unconquerable patience at their hard and dangerous labor. Under the cliffs of Cariboo we glided into calm water, and looked back at the dark and troubled deep, in broad contrast with the clouds and icebergs resplendent with rosy sunlight.

CHAPTER XLII.

AFTER THE ICEBERG OF BELLE ISLE.—THE RETREAT TO CART-
WRIGHT'S TICKLE.—BRIDGET KENNEDY'S COTTAGE, AND THE
LONELY STROLL OVER CARIBOO.

WEDNESDAY, *July* 13. We rise with the intention of spending the day in Belle Isle water to the
south, around what we call the Great Castle Berg—an
object, from the first, of our particular regard. The
breeze freshens from the north, but the Captain thinks
we may lie safely to the leeward of the ice, and so sketch
and write. Battle Harbor has a narrow and shallow passage into the south water. We have slipped through
that, and are now scudding before a pleasant northeaster, directly toward the castle, and the northern cape
of Bell Isle. We are having a long ground-swell, rough-
ened with a "lop" or short sea, and the promise of
high wind. The fishing boats, more out to sea, are putting in—a signal for our retreat. We confess ourselves
beaten for the day, and run for Cartwright's Tickle, a

small inlet, a mile or so distant.   And a merry run of it we are having ; a kind of experience to which we were put yesterday afternoon.   Wet with spray, and chilly, we are glad to jump ashore at Mrs. Bridget Kennedy's fishing-flake.

Kind woman, she was on the spot to ask us up "to warm, and take a drop of tea," although no later than 10 o'clock.   Mrs. Kennedy, a smart Irish widow of Newfoundland, is " the fisherman ; " and has men and maidens in her employ.   While the tea was really refreshing, and the fire acceptable, the smoke was terrible—a circumstance over which I wept bitterly, wiping away the tears with one hand, while I plied the hot drink with the other.   From this painfully affecting scene I was presently fain to retire to a sunny slope near by, where I was soon joined by my companion in suffering, who indulged himself, perhaps too freely, in remarks that reflected no great credit on the architect and builder of Mrs. Kennedy's summer-house and chimney.   I cannot say that we wasted, but we whiled away, not overwillingly, the best part of two hours, looking around—looking across a bight of water, at a nest of flakes and huts on the hill-side, to which Swiss cottages are tame—looking over upon the good woman's garden, the merest spot of black, in which there is nothing but soil slightly freckled with vegetation, fenced in with old fish-net to keep out the fowls, and a couple of goats— looking at the astonishment of our sailors over a syphon, made from the pliant, hollow stalk of a sea-weed, through which water flowed from the surface of the sea into a basin placed upon the beach ; quite a magical performance they fancied it, until explained.

Tired of waiting for the wind to lull sufficiently for an escape back by sea, I resolved to foot it over the hills to Battle Harbor, and have come off alone. I am sitting on the moss, out of the breeze, on the warm side of a crag, " basking in the noontide sun ; disporting here like any other fly." A part of the aforesaid amusement consists in scribbling these notes, and especially the ones relating our enjoyments and trials at hospitable Bridget Kennedy's.

From the hill-top above me I had a wide prospect of the dark, rough ocean ; and of darker and rougher land. Looking westerly, what should I discover but the painter, silent and motionless, looking out from another hill-top ? Beyond him, far inland, is a chain of purple mountains, lording it over the surrounding tumult of brown and sterile hills, in the mossy valleys of which, they say, are dwarf woods of birch and spruce, pretty brooks, and reaches of blue sea-water.

I have turned my walk back to the vessel, into a regular holiday stroll, jotting down from time to time whatever happens to please me. These deep amphitheatres opening out of the hills to the sea, are quite charming, and novelties in landscape. And how almost painfully still they are! But for the dull roar of the surf, they would be silent as paintings. The cloudless sun, pouring its July brightness into them, gives them a hot-house sultriness; and, in their moist places, almost a hot-house growth. The universal moss, the turf of the country, carpets their depths and graceful slopes, and lies upon their shelves like the richest rugs; bright red, green, and yellow, and sprinkled with small, sweet-smelling flowers. Along the margin of the sea all is cracked and slashed, and has no pretty beach. Here now is a fast little brook, eagerly driving its spirited steed down one of these rocky cuts. Pleased with its speed, it hurras and cracks its whip, and swings its white-plumed cap, all in its way, as if rivers were looking on, and cataracts were listening with delight. Silly rivulet! it sounds like water in a mill-wheel, and will in a moment more be lost in the great deep. Here again, a few steps higher up the vale, the rill expands into a pool, daintily cushioned round its edges. I lie down and drink; kneel down and wash my hands; wash my handkerchief and spread it in the sun to dry. Poor little fishes! They dart and dodge about, as if they had never felt before the look of a human face. Over there is a bed of grass, luxuriant as grain, with a sprinkling of those cotton-tufted rushes. And I sing, as I sang in my boyhood :

"Green grow the rushes, O!
'Tis neither you nor I do know,
How oats, peas, beans, and barley grow."

After this lyrical feat, I straighten up, and look all around, to see if any one hears me, but only catch a glimpse of a tiny waterfall ; a little virgin all in white, spinning her silvery thread, as she looks out of her chamber window among the rocks above. For all the world! Here comes a fly—one of our own house flies—the same careless, familiar fellow, whose motto is : "The dwelling owes me a living." Now what do you expect, you self-complacent little vagabond, standing here on my hand, and rubbing your head at this rate, looking me in the face, with all the thousand eyes you have, and none of the modesty of bugs finely dressed, and vastly your superior? I do suppose myself the first Yankee here, and here you are. Away with you! I have a mind to run up yonder soft and sunny hill-side, and roll over and over to the bottom. I did run up the hill-side, but not to roll back to the foot of it, on this most springy of all turfs. I sat down and panted, wiping the moisture from my forehead, and breathing the cool ocean breeze. A half hour's walk brought me over to the brow of the mountain, with the harbor and its vessels at my feet.

CHAPTER XLIII.

LATE in the afternoon, and the breeze gone down. We are off on the gentle rollers of the Bay of St. Louis, after a low, broad iceberg, covering, say, an acre of surface, and grounded in forty fathoms of water. It has upon one extremity a bulky tower of sixty feet, on the other, forty, and in the middle a huge pile of ice blocks of all shapes and sizes, the ruins of some spire. While the outside of this heap of fragments is white, with tints of green, touched here and there with what seems to be the most delicate bronze and gilding; every crevice, where there is a shadow lurking, is a blue, the purity and softness of which cannot be described nor easily imagined. To one who has any feeling for color, it has a sentiment as sweet as any thing in all visible nature. A pure, white surface, like this fine opaque ice, seen through deep shade produces blue, and such a blue as one sees in the stainless sky when it is full of warmth and light. It is quite beyond the rarest ultramarine of the painter. The lovely azure appears to pervade and fill the hollows like so much visible atmosphere or smoke. One almost looks to see it float out of the crystal cells where it reposes, and thin away into colorless air.

We have just been honored by a royal salute from the walls of the alabaster fortress. Our kind angels will keep us at a safer distance than we are disposed to keep ourselves. A projecting table has fallen with that peculiarly startling crack, quick as lightning and loud as thunder. It seems impossible for my nerves to become accustomed to the shock. I tremble, in spite of myself, as one does after a fright. The explosion unquestionably has the voice of the earthquake and volcano. To my surprise, I find myself with cold feet and headache—those unfailing symptoms of sea-sickness. By the painful expression of his face, I suspect the painter is even worse off than myself. It is impossible to avoid feeling both vexed and amused at this companionship in misery. In his case, the climax has been attained. Laying down box and brushes with uncommon emphasis, he made a rapid movement to the edge of the boat, and looked over at his own image reflected in the glassy, oily-rolling

swell, with loud and violent demonstrations of disagree-
ment with himself. After this unhappy outbreak, he
wiped away the tears, and returned subdued and com-
posed to the gentler employment of the paint-box.

It is nearly nine o'clock in the evening, with the
downiest clouds dropped around the retiring sun. What
light must be behind them to fill them with such wealth
of color, and dye their front with such rich and varied
red! The very waves below bloom with a crimson
splendor. C—— has finished his pictures, and we row
around the berg, a singularly irregular one, both above
and below the surface. The surrounding water, to the
eye nearly black, is irradiated, star-like, with tracts of
the clear, tender green. The effect upon us is inde-
scribably fine. I think of deep down caverns of light
shining up through the dark sea. The blocks and bowlders, wrecks of former towers, which lie scattered and in
heaps upon the main berg, are like the purest alabaster
on their outer and upper sides, but of that heavenly
azure in their fissures and spaces, although wrapped in
the one great shade of evening. We now pause at the
corner of the ice, and look down both its northern and
western fronts ; the upper stories, to all appearance, in
rough marble—the lower, polished as a mirror. Almost
over us, a Greek-like figure-head, sculptured from shin-

ing crystal, gazes with serene majesty upon the white daylight in the northwest. Possessed with the mournful and nearly supernatural beauty, we forget the dangers of this intimacy. There is a strange fascination, and particularly at this hour, that draws like the fabulous music of the Sirens. We are headed homeward, riding silently over the glassy waves. The surf rings in the hollows of the iceberg, and sounds upon the shores like the last blows of the weary day.

CHAPTER XLIV.

CAPE ST. CHARLES.—THE RIP VAN WINKLE BERG.—THE GREAT
CASTLE BERG.—STUDIES OF ITS DIFFERENT FRONTS.

THURSDAY, *July* 14. Off again for the Great Castle
Berg. The passage from Battle Harbor into the south
waters is a shallow, rocky lane, and furnishes very rare
studies of color in stone. A large agate cut across would
serve the painter very well as a sample of much that is
seen here along the rough margin of this little strait.
Wave-washed, and sparkling with mica and crystalliza-
tions, and tinged with green and yellow mosses soft as
plush, the rocks are frequently very beautiful. Foremost
along the coast, reaching southwest into the straits of
Belle Isle, is Cape St. Charles, a brown promontory, rising,
as it recedes from the sea, into rocky hills tinged with a
pale green, the moss-pastures of the reindeer. Beyond the
cape is a bay with mountain shores, not unlike those of
Lake George. The fine smoke-like shadow along their

ICEBERG IN THE MORNING MIST.—WHALEBOAT

Lith of Sarony Major & Knapp. 449 Broadway NY

sides is dappled with olive-green and yellowish tracts of moss and shrubbery. The annual expenditure of nature, on those poor mountains, for clothing and decoration is very small. She furnishes holiday suits of cheap and flimsy cloud, and the showy jewelry of the passing showers, but refuses any bounteous outlay for the rich and sumptuous apparel of green fields and forests. Beneath those sunny but desolate heights, there slumbers, in the purple, calm waters, an iceberg with a form and expression that harmonize with the landscape. I would call it the Rip Van Winkle iceberg. It seems to have been lying down, but now to be half up, reposing upon its elbow. Its head, recently pillowed on the drowsy swells, wears a shapeless, peaked hat, from the tip of which is dropping silvery rain through the warm, dreamy air. Between the calm and the currents, our oarsmen are having a warm time of it. I lay hold and labor until my hands smart, and I feel that hot weather has come at last to Labrador.

We rest in front of the Great Castle Berg, the grand capitol of the city of icebergs now in the waters of Belle Isle, and, if I except the Windsor Castle Berg which we saw founder, the largest we have seen, and, what is most likely, the largest we ever shall see. We merely guess at the dimensions. Sailing up the Niagara in the little steamer, how wide should you judge the falls to be from

Table Rock across to the horse-shoe tower? I judge this ice-front to be two-thirds that width, and quite as high, if not higher, than the cataract. If this were float-ed up into that grand bend of Niagara, I think it would fill a large part of it very handsomely, with a tower rising sufficiently above the brink of the fall to be seen from the edge of the river for some distance above. Imagine the main sheet, reaching from Table Rock toward the Horse-shoe, to be silent ice, and you will have no very wrong no-tion of the ice before us at this moment. I do not mean to say that it hàs the bend of the great cataract, for it is on this side quite devoid of flowing lines, and abounds with the perpendicular and horizontal for about fifty feet from the water, when the long and very level lines begin to be crossed by a fluted surface, resembling the folds of carefully arranged drapery hanging gracefully from the serrated line at the top. No other side will present this view at all. Change of position gives an iceberg almost as many appearances as a cumulous cloud assumes at sun-set in the summer sky.

We have rounded an angle to the southern front, and look upon a precipice of newly broken alabaster crowned with a lofty peak and pinnacles. A slight sketch seems to satisfy the painter, and so we pass round to the eastern or ocean side, at which Captain Knight, an experienced iceberger, expresses both delight and surprise. It is a cluster of Alpine mountains in miniature : peaks, precipices, slopes and gorges, a wondrous multitude of shining things, the general effect of which is imposing and sublime. We have been looking out from Battle Island upon this for days, and never dreamed of all this world of forms so grand and beautiful. Besides the main, there are two smaller bergs, but all nothing more than the crowning towers and spires of the great mass under the sea. Here is quite a little bay with two entrances, in which the pale emerald waves dash and thunder, washing the pearly shores, and wearing out glassy caverns. The marvellous beauty of these ices prompts one to speak in language that sounds extravagant. Had our forefathers lived along these seas, and among these wonders, we should have had a language better fitted to describe them. I can easily suppose that there must be a strong descriptive element in the Icelandic, and even in the Greenlandic tongues. I am quite tired of the words : emerald, pea-green, pearl, sea-shells, crystal, porcelain and sapphire, ivory, marble and alabaster, snowy and rosy, Alps, cathedrals, towers, pinnacles, domes and spires. I could fling them all, at this moment, upon a large descriptive fire, and the blaze would not be sufficiently brilliant to light the mere reader to the scene. I will give it up,

10

at least for the present, and remark merely that we have received what the French newspapers occasionally receive —a warning. It came in the shape of a smart cracking of rifles in some large reverberating hall. There is undoubtedly at hand the finest opportunity one could wish of witnessing an ice-fall. As it is now nearly 8 o'clock P. M., and the painting done, we shall take a hasty leave, and content ourselves with a distant view of ice-exhibitions, tame as they are, when contrasted with those more dangerously close by. Our men have had some trouble in keeping the boat up to the berg in the right place for painting, (so powerful is the current on this side setting away,) and are glad of a change.

CHAPTER XLV.

THE SAIL FOR ST. CHARLES MOUNTAIN.—THE SALMON FISHERS.—
THE CAVERN OF THE ST. CHARLES MOUNTAIN.—BURTON'S COT-
TAGE.—MAGNIFICENT SCENE FROM ST. CHARLES MOUNTAIN.—
THE PAINTING OF THE RIP VAN WINKLE BERG.—THE ICE-VASE,
AND THE RETURN BY MOONLIGHT.

OUR sails are up, and we glide landward, stopping to warm at a hut on a rocky islet. Two young fellows, engaged here in the salmon fishery, welcomed us to their cabin, and soon made their rusty old cooking-stove hot enough. The salmon are taken very much like our river shad, in nets set in sheltered waters. We have frequently sailed past them, and seen the salmon entangled in the meshes at quite a depth in the clear sea water, where they have the singular appearance of yellow serpents writhing and bounding in the folds of the seine—an optical illusion caused by the distorting and magnifying effects of the rolling surface. These young fishermen have several hogsheads filled, and are about closing up for the season. They were not a little amused with the idea of our coming so far to visit icebergs, but expressed surprise that we would run the risk of being close about them in such warm weather. After a walk over their island, the merest crest of rough rocks, in a storm washed very nearly from end to end, we set off for St. Charles Mountain, quite lofty and rising perpendicularly from the sea. It is gashed and pierced with black chasms, some of which are whitened with a kind of snowy glacier. We are now approaching a cavern to all appearance spacious enough for the dusk of a very pretty little twilight, with a doorway fifty feet in width and a clear three hundred feet high. The summit of the hill is six hundred and twenty feet above the tide, and the square-headed portal reaches all but half-way up. The ocean goes deep home to the precipice, and so we sail right in. With the wet, black walls and the chilly shade behind, we look back upon the bright, sparkling sea and the shining icebergs. The sound of the waves rings and rolls through the huge space like the deep bass of a mighty organ. We retreat slowly, rising and sinking on the dark, inky swells coming in, and steer for Mr. Burton's, the sole inhabitant of the small bay close by, where we hope for supper.

Between our landing and the supper, two hours

passed, during which C—— painted the Rip Van Winkle berg; and I ascended the mountain. Crossing a little dell to the west of the house, through which flow a couple of tinkling rills bordered with rank grass, and sheeted with flowers white and fragrant, I struck the foot of a small glacier, or chasm filled with perpetual snow, and commenced the ascent. At first I was pleased with the notion of climbing this mer-de-neige, and went up right merrily, crossing and recrossing, stepping sharply into the thawing surface in order to secure a good foothold. But as I wound my way up the cold track, beginning to be walled in by savage crags, it seemed so lonesome, and sounded so hollow below, and looked so far down and steep behind me, that I became suspicious, and afraid, and timidly crept out upon its icy edge, and leaped to the solid cliff. By this time I was too warm with a heavy overcoat, and left it hanging upon a rock against my return. Cold and windy as it was, I was glowing with heat when I reached the top.

The prospect was a new one to me, although long accustomed to mountain views, and more impressive than any thing of the kind I can remember. Rather more than half of the great circle was filled with the ocean ; the remainder was Labrador, a most desolate

extent of small rocky mountains, faintly tinted here and
there with a greenish gray, and frequently slanting down
to lakes and inlets of the sea. It may be said that
Neptune, setting his net of blue waters along this
solitary land, sprung it at last and caught it full of
these bony hills, so hopelessly hard and barren, that
he, poor old fellow, appears to have thought it never
worth his trouble to look after either net or game.
Quite in the interior were a few summits higher than
the St. Charles, the one upon which I was standing.
The sun was looking red and fiery through long lines
and bars of dun clouds, and shed his rays in streams
that bathed the stern and gloomy waste with wonderful brightness. Seaward, the prospect exceeds any power
of mine at description. I have no expectation of witnessing again any such magnificence in that field of
nature. Poets and painters will hereafter behold it,
and feel how suggestive it is of facts and truths, past,
present, and to come. The coast—that irregular and
extended line far north, and far away south and west,
upon which the ocean and the continent embrace and
wrestle—with its reefs and islets, inlets, bays, and capes,
waves breaking into snowy foam, twilight shadows
streaming out upon the sea from behind the headlands,
and the lights of sunset glancing through the gorges and

valleys of the shore, all combined to weave a fringe of glory both for land and ocean. The sky over the ocean was of great extent, and gave a wonderful breadth and vastness to the water. There was truly " the face of the deep." And a most awful, yet a glorious countenance it was, and most exquisitely complexioned, reflecting faintly both the imagery and the hues of heaven, the bright, the purple and the blue, the saffron and the rosy. Belle Isle, with its steep shores reddening with light, lay in the south, lovely to look upon but desolate in reality, and often fatal to the mariner. Looking farther south and southwest, a dark line lay along the sky—the coast of Newfoundland. I was looking up the straits of Belle Isle. All the sea in that quarter, under the last sunlight, shone like a pavement of amethyst, over which all the chariots of the earth might have rolled, and all its cavalry wheeled with ample room. Wonderful to behold ! it was only a fair field for the steepled icebergs, a vast metropolis in ice, pearly white and red as roses, glittering in the sunset. Solemn, still, and half-celestial scene ! In its presence, cities, tented fields, and fleets dwindled into toys. I said aloud, but low : " The City of God ! The sea of glass ! the plains of heaven " ! The sweet notes of a wood-thrush, now lost in the voices of the wind, and then returning with soft murmurs of the surf, recalled me from the reverie into which I had lapsed unconsciously, and I descended carefully the front of the mountain until I stood just above the portal of the lofty cavern into which we had sailed.   The fishing-boats in a neighboring cove, moored for the night, appeared like corks upon the dark water, and Burton's house like the merest box.   He was just ashore from his salmon-nets, and was tossing the shining fishes from his boat to the rocks.   I counted seven.

Coming round upon the northern slope, I was tempted by the mossy footing to try the reindeer method, and went bounding to the right and left until I was brought up waist-deep in a thicket of crisp and fragrant evergreens.   When I say thicket, do not fancy any ordinary cluster of shrubs, such as is common, for example, among the Catskills.   This, of which I am speaking, and which is found spotting these cold hillsides, is a perfect forest in miniature, covering a space twenty or thirty feet across, compact as a phalanx of soldiery, and from three feet to six inches high.   In fact, it reminds me of a train-band standing straight and trim, and bristling with bayonets.   The little troop looked as if it was marching up the mountain, the taller ones in front, and the little inch-fellows following in the rear, all keeping step and time. There are gentlemen on the Hudson and around our cities, that would give a thousand dollars for such a tiny little wood. It is an exquisite curiosity, and must excel the dwarf shrubbery of the Japanese. The little trees—no mere yearlings playing forest—are venerable with moss and lichens, and bear the symbols of suffering and experience. All are well-developed, complete trees, mimicking the forms and the ways of majestic firs. The lower boughs droop with a sad, mournful air, and their pointed tops look up into the sunshine and down upon the minute shrubbery below, with the gloomy repose of dark, old pines. It made me laugh. As I waded through the pigmy woods, running my fingers through the loftier tops, as I would run them through the hair of a curly-headed child, and stepping over hills and dales of green forest, I was highly amused, both at the little woodlands and the moral of the thing. Cutting an armful of the sweet-scented branches, and thinking of the children at home as I dinted the mossy pincushions bright as worsted-work all over the ground, I hastened to regain my coat, and get down to the fisherman's. The painter soon came in, when we sat down to an excellent supper of tea and fried salmon, and presently set sail by moonlight.

10*

Among the incidents of painting the berg, C——
related one of some novelty. It was in deep water,
but close to the shore, and so nicely poised that it
was evidently standing tiptoe-like on some point, and
vibrating largely at every discharge of ice. Near by as
it was, he could paint from the shore with security—a
rare chance in summer. A heavier fall than usual
from the part fronting the land was followed by correspondingly large vibrations, leaving the berg, after it
had settled to rest, leaning toward the sea with new
exposures of ice. Among these was an isolated mass
resembling a superbly fashioned vase. Quite apart from
the parent berg, and close to the rocks, it first appeared
slowly rising out of the sea like some work of enchant-
ment, ascending higher and higher until it stood, in the
dark waters before him, some twenty feet in height—a
finely proportioned vase, pure as pearl or alabaster, and
shining with the tints of emerald and sapphire throughout its manifold flutings and decorations. It was actually startling. As it was ascending from the sea, the
water in the Titanic vase, an exquisite pale green,
spouted in all directions from the corrugated brim, and
the waves leaped up and covered its pedestal and stem
with a drift of sparkling foam. While in the process of
painting this almost magical and beautiful apparition,

nearly one half of the bowl burst off with the crack of a rifle, and fell with a heavy plunge into the sea. How much in olden times would have been made of this! In the twilight of truth it is easy to see that there is but a step, an easy and a willing step, from plain facts into wild and fanciful forms of superstition. On our way back to harbor, we passed the Rip Van Winkle iceberg, and saw his broken goblet pale and spectral in the moonlight. How lengthy will be the slumbers of the venerable wanderer beneath the shadows of the mountain, there is none but the hospitable Burtons to report. For their sakes, whose salmon-nets his ponderous movements along shore have greatly disturbed, it is to be hoped he will speedily perish and be buried where he is, or wake up and be off to sea with the dignity befitting an iceberg of so much character.

CHAPTER XLVI.

AFTER OUR LAST ICEBERG.—THE ISLES.—TWILIGHT BEAUTIES OF
ICEBERGS.—MIDNIGHT ILLUMINATION.

FRIDAY, *July* 15. This is another of the summer days of Labrador, with a soft, southerly wind, tempting one to ramble in spite of musquitoes and black flies, which, though few, are uncommonly pestilent. The painter is sleeping from very weariness, and I am loitering about these cliffs, note-book in hand, in a drowsy state, for a similar reason. These long days and late hours about headlands and icebergs are attended with their pains as well as pleasures. From the tenor of my pages one would think that all was joyous and interesting. Let him reflect, that for his sake I record the joyous and the interesting, and pass by the dull and the vexatious. I flit from frowning cliff to cliff where the surf thunders and Leviathan spends his holiday among the capelin, and linger in the sunshine and shadow of an iceberg, the choicest among fifty, but give you but a suspicion of the common things between. The sparkling points of the life of this novel voyage are for the reader's eye; the chill and the weariness, and the sea-sickness, and the mass of things, lumpish and brown in "the light of common day," are for that tomb of the Capulets away back in the fields of one's own memory. But to return: this kind of life begins to wear upon us, to wear upon the nerves, and suggests the importance of keeping dull and still awhile.

I find myself looking towards home, looking that way over the sea from the hill-tops, and rather dreading the rough and tumble and chances of the journey. I regret that time will not permit a continuation of the voyage, at least as far as Sandwich Bay, where the mountains are now covered with snow. We shall visit, this afternoon and evening, our last iceberg, and mainly for some experiments with lights. The rocks here, among which I saunter, are a kind of gallery tufted with wild grass and herbage, up to which a few goats climb from the dwellings near our vessel, and upon a patch of which I lounge and scribble. If there were any spirit in me, the fine prospect, although somewhat familiar, would awaken some fresh thoughts and feelings. One thought comes swelling up from the sluggish depths—it is this: There is a fascination in these northern seas, with their ices and their horrid shores. The arctic voyagers feel and act under its impulse. I can understand their readiness to return to polar scenes.

Late in the afternoon, sailing up the bay, after an ugly iceberg of no particular shape or remarkable attraction. In New York Bay, it would be thought a most splendid thing, and so indeed it would be ; but here, in contrast with the great berg of Belle Isle water, and many others, it is a small matter, a harmless and dull specimen of its kind. Its merit is its convenience. And yet, let me tell you, we pause in our approach at a distance of seventy yards. I am not willing to go any nearer upon this, the cliff side. The agent, Mr. Bendle, told us this morning, that when he first came from England to these shores, he was fond of playing about icebergs, and once rowed a boat under a lofty arch, passing quite through the berg, a thing that he could not now be persuaded to attempt. The wind blows rather strongly, and we lie to the leeward of the ice, rolling quite too much for painting. There is no accounting for these currents which flow in upon, and flow away from these bergs. The submarine ice so interferes with the upper and lower streams that the surface water rolls and whirls in a manner upon which you cannot calculate.

Under the leeward here, one would naturally suppose that the current would set toward the ice, and require an effort on our part to keep away. The contrary is the case. Two good oars are busy in order to hold us up to our present position. The wind and the swell increase, and so we make sail and scud to some small islands distant half a mile. We moor our boat under the shelter of the rocks and clamber up, look around upon the ruins washed and rusty, and take a run.

At seven o'clock I sit down on the warm side of a crag, and look about with the intention of seeing what there is worth looking at in a spot to which one might flee who was tired of seeing too much. Upon the word of a quiet man, I find myself in the very middle of the beautiful, and ought to be thankful that we are here, and wish that we might be suffered to come again. And what is there here? Wise men have written volumes over less. I do not know but here are groups of the South Sea Isles in miniature. For example, separated from us by a narrow gulf of water, and such clear, bright water, is an islet with a ridge, a kind of half-moon crest, carpeted with olive-tinted moss, over which the lone sun pours a stream of almost blinding light. What glory the God of nature sheds upon these rugged outworks of the earth! The painter that could faithfully repeat

upon canvas this one effect of light would leave Claude
and Cole, and the like, far enough behind to be forgotten.
The wind is lulling ; the sun touches and seems to burn
the crest of the island opposite, after eight o'clock.
C—— is finishing a sketch ; the Captain and I have
been hunting the sea-pigeons' nests, a pair of which keep
flying off and on ; and now the men are making the boat
ready for our twilight and evening play around "the
ugly iceberg." How glad the poor little family of ducks
must be, from whose home we have driven them, that we
are going away. They have been pretending to swim off,
and yet have managed to keep back near enough to watch
us over the shoulder, ever since we arrived. Timid,
cunning fellows, how much they appear to know ! A
stone disperses them, some to the wing and some to the
bottom ; and now here they are again, all riding the
same swell, and seeming to swim away while they watch
our motions, continually turning their slick, black heads
quickly over the shoulder.

If you would look upon the perfectly white and pure,
see an iceberg between you and the day's last red
heavens. If you would behold perfect brilliancy, gaze
at the crest of an iceberg cutting sharply into those
same red heavens. To all appearance it will burn and
scintillate like a crown of costly gems. In all its

notched, zigzag and flowing outline, it palpitates and glitters as if it were bordered with the very lightning. He that watches the Andean clouds of a July sunset, and beholds them rimmed, now with pink and rose-hues, and now with golden fire, will see the edges of an iceberg when it stands against the sky glowing with the yellow and orange blaze of sunset. We go to the skies for pure azure ; you will find it at twilight in these wonderful Greenland ices. I am looking now upon what mimics the ruins of a tower, every block of which, in one light, gleams like crystal ; in another, as if they had been quarried from the divinest sky. Cloud-like and smoke-like, they look light as the cerulean air. This, as I have said already, is the effect of perfect white seen through deep, transparent shadow. True azure is the necessary result. More than enough, it would seem, has been said of these forms and colors. But really the eye never wearies of these arctic palaces so grandly corniced and pillared ; these sculptures so marvellously draped. As we gaze at them, even in this meagre and common berg, under this delicate light veiled with the dusk of evening, they are astonishing in their beauty. I look at them with joyful emotions, with wonder and with love. Why do they not rustle with a silken, satin rustle ?

After dark, we sailed round to the northern extremity, where from the lowness of the ice it was more safe to approach it, and dropped sail in order to experiment with the blue lights furnished us by the governor. Rowing up quite closely, within eight yards perhaps, C——, who stood ready upon the bow, fired a couple. In the smoke and glare "we were a ghastly crew," while the berg was rather obscured than beautified. We then rowed round to the side where the current was setting rapidly towards the ice, and launched a flaming tar-barrel. With a stone for ballast, it kept upright, and floated in fine style directly into the face of the berg—an irregular cliff of sixty feet, pierced with caverns. It was kept for some time under a succession of the brightest flashes of pink light. Upon one slope of the swells the sheaf of red flames gushing from the barrel would be turned from, on the other, toward the ice. Thus the whole eastern front was kept changing from light to darkness, from darkness to light. As the brightness was flung back and forth from the sea to the berg, and from the berg to the sea, the effect was exceedingly novel and beautiful. When the swells bore the full-blown torch into a cave, and its ruddy tongues were licking the green, glassy arches, we hoisted sail and went gaily bounding back to harbor. For a while, the fire shot its fitful rays over the lonely waters, and gleamed "like a star in the midst·of the ocean." At last it was quenched in the distant gloom. A ghostly figure with dim outline was all that was visible, and our work and play with icebergs were over—over forever. It was midnight and past, when we dropped sails alongside the vessel, after a quick run, enlivened, as we entered the harbor, by a sudden display of the northern-light.

CHAPTER XLVII.

FAREWELL TO BATTLE HARBOR.—THE STRAITS OF BELLE ISLE.—
LABRADOR LANDSCAPES.—THE WRECK OF THE FISHERMEN.

SATURDAY, *July* 16. " Once more upon the waters, yet
once more." We were awakened from sound slumbers by
the footsteps and voices of the men above, making ready
for sea. It was a pleasant sound, and the sunshine
streaming down into the cabin was welcome intelligence
of the brightness of the morning. We dressed in time to
get on deck, and wave a final adieu to our friends, from
whom we had formally parted yesterday, as well as from
Mr. and Mrs. Bendle, of whose hospitality we bear away
agreeable recollections.

And now the broad Atlantic is before, and Cape
St. Louis, its waters and its ices, behind the intervening
islands. The signal staffs of Battle and Cariboo Islands
are yet visible from the high rocks that overlook that
busy nest of fishermen, with its steepled church and par-

sonage. God's love abide with the man that lives there, and ministers to the religious wants of men, women, and children, who have little else than respect and affection to make his home comfortable and happy. While kind hearts, and none kinder than those of the Esquimaux, throb beneath rough manners and uncomely raiment, there are wicked spirits there, no doubt, as everywhere, that hurt and hinder, and never help, and render the solitary path among the rocks insufferably lonesome and painful. The remembrances of famous and beloved kindred, of old and honored Cambridge, and of the quiet rectory under the Malvern Hills, are much to a cultivated and sensitive nature ; the bliss that flows from daily duties cheerfully done with an habitual resignation to the will of God, and with hopes of glory in the future, is more than recollections, to a heart whose motive powers are Christian faith and love. But amid all the sweetest memories, and the brightest hopes, and the comforting satisfaction of believing well and doing well, it is a fearful thing for cultivated man to toil in solitude and deprivation. Although heaven is above him, and his pathway certainly upward, yet a double portion of all those good and perfect gifts coming from above, be awarded to the man whose parish is in Labrador ; who, when he leaves the still companionship of books for the toils of the

gospel from door to door, must take down either his oars
or his snow-shoes, and sweep over the snow-drift or the
billow.

We now beat slowly up the straits of Belle Isle for the
Gulf of St. Lawrence, hoping to pass these dangerous
waters by daylight. They are very fair to look upon at
this time of day, studded in all directions with those shining palaces of ice seen from the top of St. Charles Mountain. The coast hills have a graceful outline, and slant
quite smoothly down, abutting on the sea in low broken
cliffs. They resemble the hills of Maine and Canada
after April thaws, while the heavier snow-drifts yet remain, and the yellow brown sod is patched with faint
green. Forsaken country ! if that can be called forsaken
which appears never to have been possessed. Doleful and
neglected land ! Chilly solitude keeps watch over your
unvisited fields, and frightens away the glory of the fruit-
ful seasons. The loving sunshine and the healing warmth
wander hand in hand tenderly abroad, calling upon the
lowly moss to wake up and blossom, and to the tiny,
half-smothered, flattened willows to rise and walk along
the brook banks. But the white-coated police of winter,
the grim snow-drifts, watch on the craggy battlements
of desolation, and luxuriance and life peep from their
dark cells only to sink back pale and spiritless. To a

traveller there is real beauty on the tawny desert and the wild prairie ; but there is to me an awful lonesomeness and gloom in these houseless wastes where the eye with an insane perverseness will keep looking for cottage smokes and pasture fences. I think of landscapes drying off after the flood.

The bergs are in part behind us, and we are rocking on the easy swells of Henly Harbor, where we can glean no more signs of human " toil and trouble " than are just enough to tie a name to, and quite a pretty name too. The lazy sails flap idly in the sunshine, and the cold air cuts with the sharpness of a frosty October morning. I sit in the July heat with overcoat, and cloak over the overcoat, woollen mittens and woollen stockings, and with cold feet at that. And yet this miserable shore has, in its cod and salmon, attractions for thousands of people during the transient summer. Even the long and almost arctic winter with its seals and foxes detains hundreds. But, as a fisherman told me one day, while tossing upon the dock with his pitchfork a boat-load of cod, " It is a poor trade." It is a little trying to patience to be rolling in this idle way, with the creak of spars and the rattling of blocks and rigging, especially as a breeze has been winging the blue water for an hour not more than a mile ahead of us. We do move a little, just a little, enough to keep the hope breathing that we shall soon move off with reasonable speed.

The current is almost a river stream, and we are drifting rapidly, which is not a pleasant thing to be thinking about, with these waters scouring the very banks, and a short cable. I am gazing back upon the southern point of Belle Isle with a mournful interest. It was only the night of the second, the same night we ran into Twillingate to escape a gale, that a vessel was lost there, and all, or nearly all, on board perished. At this moment there is a faint line of white, but not a murmur. All looks quiet there and peaceful, as if the lion was going up to lie down with the lamb.

ICEBERG IN THE STRAIT OF BELLE ISLE.

of Sarony Major & Knapp.

painter is a model of industry, sketching and
the bergs as we pass them. They are now clus-
the northern horizon, with a few exceptions.
e been for some time near one, out of which
cut an entire block of Broadway buildings, evi-
resenting the same upper surface that it had
as a glacier from the polar shore. If such is
infer that in its long glacial experience it
long near any mass of earth
an for there is not a stone or particle of
arthy stain upon it. It is as spotless as a cloud
he tempest." How beautiful is the sentiment of
carries the imagination away to those heavenly
icted in Revelation, and sends it back upon the

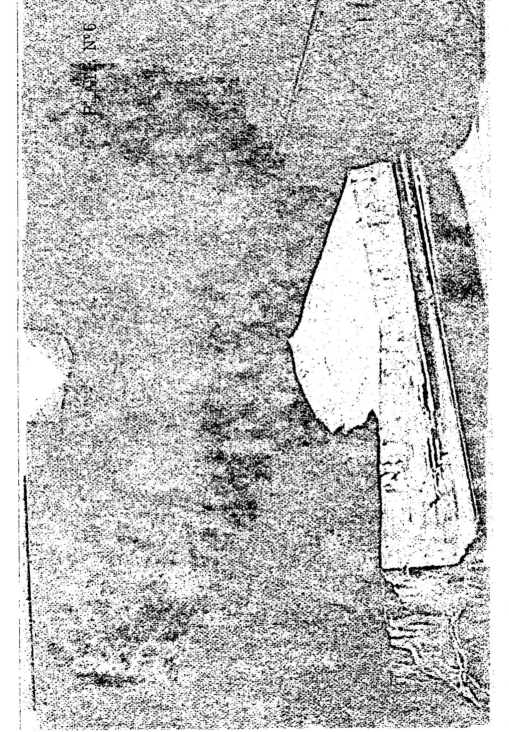

Pleuraflug Nr. 6

CHAPTER XLVIII.

THE painter is a model of industry, sketching and painting the bergs as we pass them. They are now clustered on the northern horizon, with a few exceptions. We have been for some time near one, out of which might be cut an entire block of Broadway buildings, evidently presenting the same upper surface that it had when it slid as a glacier from the polar shore. If such is the fact, we infer that in its long glacial experience it could not have remained - long near any mass of earth higher than itself, for there is not a stone or particle of dust or earthy stain upon it. It is as spotless as a cloud " after the tempest." How beautiful is the sentiment of it ! It carries the imagination away to those heavenly walls depicted in Revelation, and sends it back upon the track of its own story.

11

The story of an iceberg! yes, indeed; and a most wonderful tale would it be, could it be truthfully written. It would run up into, and become lost in the story of the great glaciers of Greenland; the half of which science itself has not learned, profoundly as it has penetrated the mysteries of the Alpine glaciers.

There are valleys reaching from the interior to the coast, filled with glaciers of great depth and breadth, which move forward with an imperceptible but regular motion. The continent, as one might call Greenland, does not shed the bulk of its central waters in fluid rivers, but discharges them to the ocean in solid, crystalline, slowly progressing streams. They flow, or rather march, with irresistible, mighty force, and far-resounding footsteps, crossing the shore line, a perpetual procession of block-like masses, flat or diversified with hill and hollow on the top, advancing upon the sea until too deeply immersed longer to resist the buoyant power and pressure of the surrounding waters, when they break upwards, and float suspended in the vast oceanic abyss. The van of the glacial host, previously marked off by fissures into ranks, rushes from the too close embrace of its new element, and wheels away, an iceberg—the glistening planet of the sea, whose mazy, tortuous orbit none can calculate but Him who maps the unseen currents of the main.

When and where, on the lengthy Greenland coast, did this huge block make the grand exchange of elements ? Which, if any of these great buildings " not made with hands," now whitening the blue fields of Neptune, followed or preceded it ? What have been its solemn rounds ? Through what winters has it slept, and caught the snows upon the folds of its sculptured draperies ? How many summers has it bared its spotless bosom to the sun and rains ? What nights of auroral splendors have glassed their celestial countenance in its shining mirrors ? What baths and vases of blue water have opened their pure depths to moon and stars ? What torrents and cascades have murmured in its glassy chasms, crystal grottoes, Alpine dells ? And who shall count its battles with the waves and tempests, when with the surf about its shoulders and among its locks, and the clouds around its brow, it stood far up from the unsounded valleys of ocean " tiptoe on the mountain top " ?

In the defiles and gorges of the Arctic coast are prodigious accumulations of ice—the congelation of small streams flowing from the adjacent mountains—the glaciers of the coast range, in short. These gradually encroach upon, and overhang the sea ; and are continually breaking off, from the undermining of the waves which beat at their base. Such is the depth of water, that the hugest avalanche of ice can fall with safety to itself, and float away.

When, and in what bay or inlet, may this Great Northern have been launched ? Out of what gloomy fiord may have rolled the billows, after its icy fastenings were loosed, and it slid, with the thunder of an earthquake, down its slippery ways, and plunged into the black deep ?

Until science have her beaten pathway over polar waves and hills, and measure the rain-falls and the snow-falls, and the freezings of the one and the compactings of the other, the story of the glacier and the iceberg, in their native land and seas, will be left, in part, to the imagination—a faculty, after all, that will ever deal with those wonderful ices about as satisfactorily as the faculty that judges according to the sense, as Bishop Leighton calls the mere scientific faculty. The truth of this is illustrated by the very icebergs about us. Emphatically as they speak to the naturalist with his various instrumentalities, they speak, at the same moment, with marvellous eloquence to the poet and the painter. There are forces, motions, and forms, voices, beauties, and a sentiment, which escape the touch of science, and are scarcely caught by the subtle, poetic mind. Icebergs, to the imaginative soul, have a kind of individuality and life.

They startle, frighten, awe ; they astonish, excite, amuse, delight and fascinate ; clouds, mountains and structures, angels, demons, animals and men spring to the view of the beholder. They are a favorite playground of the lines, surfaces and shapes of the whole world, the heavens above, the earth and the waters under : of their sounds, motions and colors also. These are the poet's and the painter's fields, more than they are the fields of the mere naturalist, much as they are his. Do not these fifty bergs, in sight from any crag frowning in its iron strength above the surf, speak more a living language to the creative, than to the mensural faculty ? Let us see.

They have a daily experience, and a current history more remarkable now than ever. Whatever may have been the wonders of their conception, birth and growth ; however lengthy and devious their voyage, they are present in these strange seas, in these tepid waters and soft airs, to undergo their last, fatal changes, and dissolve forever into their final tomb. There are fifty icebergs, more or less. Apparently similar in appearance, yet each differs widely from all others. Exhibiting similar phenomena, yet each has complexions, movements, sounds and wonders of its own. If we choose, though, to add to the performances of to-day, those of yesterday and to-morrow, we shall find that the experience of any one berg closely resembles that of all. The entire circle of its looks and doings corresponds with the circle of nearly every other berg, and so of all together, differing merely in the matter of time—as to *when* the changes take place. The description upon which I will venture, and which might be gleaned from the foregoing pages, is, therefore, strictly true, except that the phases and accidents are supposed to occur in rapid succession. In a word, what you would behold in all of these fifty, within twenty-four hours, you are to fancy of one, in the course of an afternoon.

I have before me, in my mind's eye, the Windsor Castle berg, fresh from the north, and the Great Castle berg, of Belle Isle water, which it entered early last May, and as large, at the time of its arrival, as both of them at present combined. And so I am looking at a veritable berg of Cape St. Louis, small, though, in comparison with the berg of Cape St. Francis, "a vast cathedral of dazzling white ice, with a front of 250 feet perpendicular from the sea," visited by the Bishop of Newfoundland in the summer of 1853.

I will describe, first, the figure of the berg. It is a combination of Alp, castle, mosque, Parthenon and cathedral. It has peaks and slopes ; cliffs, crags, chasms and caverns ; lakes, streams and waterfalls. It has towers, battlements and portals. It has minarets, domes and steeples ; roofs and gables ; balustrades and balconies ; fronts, sides and interiors ; doors, windows and porches ; steps and entrances ; columns, pilasters, capitals and entablatures ; frieze, architrave and cornice ; arches, cloisters, niches, statuary and countless decorations ; flutings, corrugations, carvings, panels of glassy polish and in the rough ; Greek, Roman, Gothic, Saracenic, Pagan, Savage. It is crested with blades and needles ; heaped here and there with ruins, blocks and bowlders, splintered and crumbled masses. This precipice has a fresh, sharp fracture ; yonder front, with its expanse of surface beautifully diversified with sculptured imagery and other ornament, has.the polish of ivory—the glassy polish of mirrors—the enamel of sea-shells—the fierce brightness of burnished steel—the face of rubbed marble—of smoothest alabaster —of pearl—porcelain—lily-white flesh—lily-white wax— the flesh-finish of beauty done in the spotless stone of Italy. This, though, is but the iceberg of the air ; the head and crown only of the iceberg of the deep sea.

From the figure of the berg, I will come to describe an important feature of its life and history : its motion ; not its movement from place to place, but upon its centre—its rotation and vibration. Where the berg is not grounded—in which case it only beats and sways to and fro, vibrating through the arc of a circle like an inverted pendulum—when it is not grounded, it must be supposed to hang suspended at the surface—all but the topmost part—just *under* the surface of the ocean, very much as a cloud, a great white thunder-head, hangs suspended in the upper air. Balanced around its heart, far down in the deep, and in its cold solidity " dry as summer dust " —poised upon its centre with perfect exactness, it is evident that the loss of a single ton of ice shifts that centre, shifts it an ounce-notch on the bar of the mighty scale, destroys the equilibrium, and subjects the whole to the necessity of some small movement in order to regain its rest. When, instead of one ton, thousands fall off, it sets a rolling the whole clifted and pinnacled circumference.

And here begins that exhibition of novel forms and shapes, and of awful force, and the sublimity of stupendous masses in motion, that so impresses, awes, startles, and fascinates the beholder. A berg in repose, wondrous as it is to him that dares to linger in its presence, differs from itself in action, as a hero in his sleep differs from himself upon the field of battle.

With regard to the motions of the berg, it must be borne in mind, that, from the fact of its centre being not on a level with the surface of the sea, but at depths below, they are quite different from what might at first be imagined. A rough globe, revolving upon its axis, with but a small portion of its bulk, say a twelfth, above the water ; or, better still, the hub and spokes merely of a common wagon wheel, slowly rolling back and forth, will serve for illustration. The uppermost spoke, in its vibrations to the right and left, describes a line of some extent along the surface, not unlike an upright stick moving to and fro, and gradually rising and sinking as it moves. In this movement back and forth, the two adjacent spokes will be observed to emerge and disappear correspondingly. In this way, a berg of large diameter, instead of falling over upon the sea like a wall or precipice, appears to advance bodily, slowly sinking as it comes, with a slightly increasing inclination toward you. In its backward roll, this is reversed. It seems to be retreating, slowly rising as it floats away, with a slightly increasing inclination from you. In these grand vibrations, projecting points and masses of opposite sides correspondingly emerge and disappear, rising apparently straight up out of the sea on this side, going down as straight on the other.

From the figure and motion of the berg, I come to describe the motive power, rather the explosive power, through which the delicate balance is destroyed, and motion made a necessity in order to gain again equilibrium

11*

and rest. Whatever may be the latent heat of ice, is a question for the professed naturalist. Two things are evident to the unlearned observer : an iceberg is as solid as ivory, or marble from the lowest depths of a quarry, and cold apparently as any substance on the earth can be made. This compact and perfectly frozen body, immersed in the warm seas of summer, and warmer atmosphere, finds its entire outside, and especially that portion of it which is exposed to the July sun, expanding under the influence of the penetrating heat. The scrutiny of science would, no doubt, find it certain that this heat, in some measure, darts in from all sides in converging rays to the very heart. The expanding power of heat becomes at length an explosive force, and throws off, with all the violence and suddenness of gunpowder, in successive flakes, portions of the surface. The berg, then, bursts from expansion, as when porcelain cracks with sharp report, suddenly and unequally heated on the winter stove. Judge of the report when the porcelain of a great cliff cracks and falls, or when the entire berg is blasted asunder by the subtle, internal fire of the summer sun ! If you would hear thunders, or whole broadsides and batteries of the heaviest ordnance, come to the iceberg then.

Speaking incidentally of noises, reminds me of the

hues and tints of the iceberg. Solomon in all his glory was not clothed like the flowers of the field. Would you behold this berg apparelled with a glory that eclipses all floral beauty, and makes you think, not only of the clouds of heaven at sunrise and sunset, but of heaven itself, you must come to it at sunrise and at sunset. Then, too, you would hear its voices and its melodies, the deep and mournful murmuring of the surf in its caverns. Hark! In fancy I hear them now, half thunder, and half the music of some mighty organ.

And this reminds me of the sea, which shares with the iceberg something of the glory and the power. In the first place, from the white brightness of the ice, the eye is tuned to such a high key, or so stimulated and bedazzled, that the ocean is not only dark by contrast, but dark in reality. It is purple, so deep as to amount almost to blackness—an evening violet I would call it, a complexion magnificent and rich exceedingly in the blaze of noon, and at late and early hours when the skies are full of brilliant colors. What heightens the effect of this dye of the ocean, is the pale emerald water around the berg, and in which it floats as in a vast bath, the loveliness, clarity and divine beauty of which no language can paint in a way to kindle the proper feeling and emotion. From ten to fifty feet in breadth, it encircles

the berg, a zone or girdle of sky-green, that most delicate tint of the sunset heavens, and lies, or plays with a
kind of serpent play, between the greenish white ice and
the violet water, as the bright deeps of air lie beyond the
edge of a blue-black cloud. There is no perceptible
blending, but a sharp line which follows, between the
bright and the dark, the windings of the berg, across
which you may, if you have the temerity, row the bow
of your whale-boat, and gaze down, down the fearfully
transparent abyss, until the dim ice-cliffs and the black
deeps are lost in each other's awful embrace.

I have spoken of the figure, motion, and the breaking
of the iceberg, incidentally mentioning its sounds, its
colors, and the surrounding waters. You are now ready
to go with us, and spend the afternoon about it. Early
in the morning, and for the last hour, all but its heights
and peaks has been wrapped in cloud-like fog. That,
you discover, is thinning off, and will presently all pass
away. The breeze is fresh from the north, and we will
sail down upon the north-eastern side, until we have it
between us and the 3 o'clock sun. We are upon sound-
ings, and, as we glide from the broad sunny tract into the
shadow of the berg, the ocean should be green, a deep
green. But we have been sailing with the white ice in
our eyes, and you see the ocean a dark purple. The

captain drops sail, and sets the men at their oars. As the current sets back from the berg—the reverse of the current below—you notice that they are pulling slowly, but steadily forward without any perceptible advance. We are distant a good hundred yards, as near again as we ought to be for safety. But this is the position for the painter, and it will be the care of the captain to keep it, the required time, as nearly as possible.

As the broad roller lifts us lightly and gracefully, and leaves us sinking on its after-slope, how majestic is the silent march of it, the noiseless flight of it! But look! —look!—as it flees in all its imposing breadth of darkness, see the great, green star upon its breast—a spangle green as grass, as the young spring grass in the sunshine, gleaming like some skylight of the deep, some emerald window in the dome of the sea-palace, letting up the splendor. What do you suppose that is? It is ice, a point of the berg pricking up into the illuminated surface and reflecting the light. You will understand that better, perhaps, by and by. But wait an instant. Now!—now!—Beauty strikes the billow with her magic rod, and, presto—change!—all is glittering green. A thousand feet of purple, cloud-like wave passes, in the twinkling of an eye, into the brightness of an emerald gem, and thus rolls up and smites the

iceberg. And thus, like night perpetually bursting into
the splendid noon, roll up the billows, and strike the
minutes of the hour. How beautiful is the transfigura-
tion! See them split upon this angle of the castle;
and as they run along the walls, with the whispery,
hissing sound of smoothly sliding waters, mark how high
they wash, and sweep them with their snowy banners,
here and there bending over, and curling into long scrolls
of molten glass, which burst in dazzling foam, and
plunge in many an avalanche of sparkling jewelry.
Into the great porch of yonder Parthenon they rush
in crowds, and thunder their applause upon the steps.

Is not all this very grand and beautiful? Have
you ever seen the like before? The like of it is not to
be seen upon the planet, apart from the icebergs. With
cold, fixed, white death, life—warm, elastic, palpitating,
glorious, powerful life—is wrestling, and will inevitably
throw. Do you see "the witchery of the shadows"?
Pray look aloft. Castle, temple, cliff, all built into one,
are draped with shadows softer than the tint of doves,
the morning's early gray, dappled with the warm pearly
blues of heaven, and edged with fire. The sun is behind
the ice, and the light is pouring over. A flood of light
is pouring over. All is edged with fire, streaming with
lightning; all its notched and flowing edges hemmed

with live, scintillating sunshine, ruby, golden, green, and blue. See you below that royal sepulchre through its crystal door ? Beauty hangs her lamp in there, and the sky-blue shadow looks like the fragrant smoke of it. Now tell me, was there ever any thing more lovely ? Have the poets dreamed of rarer loveliness ? The surf springs up like an angel from the tomb, and, with a shout of triumph, strikes it with its silvery wings. Ha ! you start. But do not be frightened. It was only the cracking of the iceberg. But was there ever such a blow ?—quick—tremulous—ringing—penetrating. Why, it jarred the sea, and thrilled the heart like an electric shock. One feels as if the berg had dropped, instantly dropped an inch, and cracked to the very core. Captain Knight, shall we not fall back a little ? we are surely getting too close under.

While I have been talking, the painter, who sits midship, with his thin, broad box upon his knees, making his easel of the open lid, has been dashing in the colors. The picture is finished, and so, at the word, the men pull heavily at their oars, and we come round upon the south-eastern, or the cathedral front, as I will call it, from the fact that the general appearance is architectural, and the prevailing style, the Gothic. A dome and minaret, curiously thrown in upon one wing of the berg, and some elaborately cut arches opening through the water-line into the cloister-like cavern, would suggest the Saracenic. But the pointed and the perpendicular prevail, springing up full of life and energy, vivid and flame-like in their forms.

As the berg faces, we are getting the last glances of the 4 o'clock sun, and have broad sheets of both light and shadow. You see how spirited the whole thing is. It is full of brilliant, strong effects. While the hollows and depressions harbor the soft, slaty shadows, points and prominences fairly blaze and sparkle with sunshine. The current now, you discover, sweeps us past the ice, and compels us to turn about and row up the stream. Here is the point where all is strong and picturesque, and here they hold on for the painter. Let us sit upon the little bow-deck, and look, and listen to the noises of the waves at play in the long, concealed, under-sea piazza. How they slap the hollow arches! Hisses, long-drawn sighs, booming thunder-sounds, mingle with low muttering, plunging, rattling, and popping—a bedlam of all the lunatic voices of the ocean. We appear to be at the edge of a shower, such a sprinkling and spattering of drops. All abroad, and all aloft, from every edge and gutter the iceberg spouts, and rains, and drips. Over the entire face of the ice is flowing swiftly down one noiseless river thin as glass, looking, for all the world, like the perpetual falling of a transparent veil over the richest satin. Here and there, the delicate stream cuts into the silvery enamel, and engraves, in high relief, brilliant shields of jewelry, diamonds, rubies, amethysts, emeralds and sapphires. But yonder is a rare touch of the enchanter. Pray, look at it carefully. It is a glistening blue line of ice, threading the whiteness from top to bottom, a good two hundred feet. It looks as if the berg were struck, not with lightning, but with sapphire. It is simply transparent ice, and may be compared to a fissure filled with pellucid spring-water, with depths of darkness beyond the visible, illuminated edge. Darkness below the pure light flowing in, and reflecting from the inner sides of the white ice, gives us the blue. You understand the process by which so beautiful a result is effected ? Well, the glacier of which this berg is a kind of spark, is mainly compacted snows, compressed to metallic hardness in the omnipotent grasp of nature. As it slides on the long, inland valley slope, it bends and cracks. The surface-water fills the crevice, and is frozen. Thus the glacier is mended, but marked forever with the splendid scar which you see before you. You fancy it has the hardness of a gem ; it is softer than the flinty masses between which it seems to have been run like a casting. On the opposite slope of the berg, you will find it the channel of a torrent, melting and wearing faster than the primitive ice.

How terribly startling is this explosion! It resounded like a field-piece. And yet you perceive only a small bank of ice floating out from below where it burst off. Small as it is, the whole berg has felt it, and is slightly rolling on its deep down centre. You perceive that it is a perfectly adjusted pair of scales, and weighs itself anew at the loss of every pound. At the loss of every *ounce*, the central point, around which millions of tons are balanced, darts aside a very little, and calls upon the entire bulk to make ready and balance all afresh. You see the process going on. There, the water-line is slowly rising ; and you peep into the long, greenish-white hollow, polished and winding as the interior of a sea-shell. Now it pauses, and returns. So will it rise and sink alternately until it stands like a headland of everlasting marble.

Again the painter wipes his brushes, puts away his second picture, and tacks a fresh pasteboard within the cover of his box, and gives the word to pull for the south-western side. How finely nature sculptures her decorations ! Would not Palmer, Powers, and others of that company, whose poetic language is in spotless stone, love to be with us ? Mark the high reliefs, and the deep, fine fluting of this angle, as we pass from the Temple front to the clifted. Here you see less to please, and more to terrify. A word or so describes it : It is a precipice of sparkling, white ice, freshly broken. The edge of newly broken china is nearest like it, with the suspicion of green for forty feet or more up, the reflection of that lovely pale green water. Now the currents recoil and roll in upon the huge wall in whirling eddies, requiring steady toil at the oars, to keep off a plump two hundred yards, the proper distance for sketching so large a perpendicular mass.

If we except the quality and texture of the fracture, there is little to paint in all this blaze of sunlight. The outline of the berg, though, is worth remembering. It cuts the blue vault like the edge of a bright sword, and pricks it with flashing spears. The eye darts from point to point along its lengthy, zig-zag and flowing thread, and sweeps from the sea upward and over to the sea again. How persistently the treacherous current labors to bear us in upon the cliff ! Let alone the oars five minutes, and we should be among the great rain-drops slipping from the overhanging crags.

Horrible ! The berg is burst. The whole upper front is coming. There it is—gone in the sea. Keep

still!—Keep still!—Don't be frightened! The captain
will manage it. Here come the big swells. Hurra!
Look out for the next! Here we go—splendid! Now
for the third and last. How she combs as she comes.
Hurra!—Hurra! Here we are—all safe—inside of them.
See them go!—racing over the ocean, circles of plumed
cavalry. Now for the berg. He'll make a magnificent
roll of it, if he don't go to pieces. Should he, then put
us half a mile away. See it rise!—The water-line—
rising—rising—up—up. It looks like a carriage-way.
Hark!—Crack—crack—crack. Quick!—quick! Look
at the black water here!—all spots and spangles of
green. Something is coming! There it comes! The
very witchcraft of the deep—Neptune's half-acre, bowers,
thrones, giants, eagles, elephants, vases spilling, fountains
pouring, torrents tumbling, glassy banks. Look at the
peaks slanting off into the blue air, and the great slant
precipice. Hah! Don't you see? It is coming again—
slowly coming! Crack—crack—crack. Down sinks the
garden—on roll the swells—down go bowers, thrones, stat-
nary—lost amid the tumult and thunder of the surf. Over
bends the precipice—this way over—frightfully over—in
roll the waves—roaring, thundering in—dashing, lashing
crag and chasm. Wonderful to see! Waterfalls bursting
into light above—plunging in snowy columns to the sea.

How terrible—terrible all this is ! But O, how beautiful ! Who, that does not witness it, knows any thing of the bursting of an iceberg ? It comes with the crash of a thunderbolt. But how can one tell the horrible, shocking noise ? A pine split by lightning has the point, but not the awful breadth and fulness of the sound. Air, ocean, and the berg, all fairly spring at the power of it. And then the ice-fall, with its ringing, rumbling, crashing roar, and the heavy, explosion-like voice of the final plunge, followed by the wild, frantic dashing of the waters. You see the whole upper face of the ice, yards deep, and scores of them in width, all gone. All was blasted off-instantly, and dropped at once, a stupendous cataract of brilliant ruins.

Here we are, at last, where the painter will revel—between the glories of sunset and the iceberg. What shall we call all this magnificence, clustered in a square quarter of a mile ? The Bernese Alps in miniature. A dark violet sea, and Alps in burnished silver, with the colors of the rainbow dissolving among them. Lofty ridges, of the shape of flames, have the tint of flame ; out of the purity of lilies bloom the pink and rose ; sky-blue shadows sleep in the defiles ; I will not say cloth of gold drapes, but water of gold washes—water of green, of orange, scarlet, crimson, purple, wash the crags and steeps ; strange metallic tints gleam in the shaggy caverns—copper, bronze, and gold. Endless grace of form and outline !—endless, endless beauty ! Its shining image is in the deep, hanging there as in a molten looking-glass. Look down and see it. Now the last rays of day strike the berg. How the hues and tints change and flit, flush and fade ! A very mirror for the fleeting glories of the sunset, or the fitful complexions of the northern light. Prodigal Nature ! Is she ever wasting splendors at this rate ? Watch them on this broad, slanting park of lily-white satin. White !—It has just a breath of pink. Pink ?—It is the richest rose—rose deepening into purple—purple trembling into blue, pearly blue, skirted with salmon-tints and lilac. Where are the train-bearers of this imperial robe ? There they are, the smooth, black swells, one, two, three, rolling up, and changing into green as they roll up—far up, and break in sparkling diamonds on the bosom of the lustrous alabaster.

Do you hear the music ? O what power in sound ! Clothed in green and silver, the royal bands of the great deep are playing at every portal of the iceberg. Hark ! Half thunder, and half the harmony of grand organs.

> " Waters, in the still magnificence,
>   Their solemn cymbals beat."

The painter's work is over. And now for harbor—all

sails spread—a downy pressure on them, and the twilight ocean. Indomitable pencil ! If the man is not at it again !—A last, flying sketch in lead. Let us take one more look at the berg—a farewell look. It is a beautiful creation—superlatively beautiful. It is more—sublime and beautiful—fold upon fold—spotless ermine—caught up from the billows, and suspended by the fingers of Omnipotence.

The Merciful One ! It is falling !—Cliffs and pinnacles bursting—crashing—tumbling with redoubling thunders.—Pillars and sheaves of foam leap aloft.—Wave chases wave, careering wild and high.—Columns and splintered fragments spring from the deep convulsively, toppling and plunging.—A multitude of small icebergs spot the dusky waters. One slender obelisk, slowly rocking to and fro, stands a monument among the scattered ruins.

CHAPTER XLIX.

DRIFTING IN THE STRAITS.—RETREAT TO TEMPLE BAY.—PICTU-
RESQUE SCENERY.—VOYAGERS' SATURDAY NIGHT.

WE are drifting to the north shore in spite of all that can be done, and positively have not been before in so great danger. Our anchor, with all the cable we have, would be swinging above the bottom, were we close to the rocks. A reckless skipper, not long ago in a similar predicament, let go his anchor with the expectation that it would catch in time to save him, but he went bows on, and lost his vessel. Our hope is that some one of the flaws of wind, now ruffling the water every little while in various directions, will catch our sails, and allow us to escape into Temple Bay, a land-locked harbor close by. My anxiety to return home makes this delay a little vexatious, and galls my thin-skinned patience. We had every reason to hope, this morning, that we should be through these perilous narrows and upon the broad gulf by midnight.

The breeze touches us at the last moment, and we are gliding through the narrow pass between high craggy banks, over a comparatively shallow bottom, visible from the deck, into what appears to be a lake surrounded by mountains not unlike those about West Point, barring their fine woods. Really Labrador can show us, at last, a little forest greenery. Without a point of grandeur, this is the most picturesque scenery we have found on the coast. The greenish waters, tinted by the verdure reflected from their surface, expand to the breadth of a mile by six or seven in length, with a depth of fifty fathoms or more. We glide past the village—a knot of fish-houses, flakes and dwellings, in the bight to the left or south, and drop anchor within pistol-shot of the spruces and a mountain brook. Here we are, till next week, like a lonely fly on this mirror of the mountains, and must make the most of our shadows and reflections, sunshine and solitude, and see what they will bring us.

I sit upon deck and look about upon the wild, noiseless scene, and say : What a lonely Saturday afternoon ! The weary week is just lying down to ruminate in these solemn shades. A few scattering sounds, the finishing strokes of the axe and hammer, and the low wail of the

12

surf beyond the coast-ridge break the rest of the cool, bracing air. The upper end of the lake, as I call the bay or fiord, is hidden behind a headland, reminding me of our Hudson Butter Hill. Nothing would be pleasanter than a small voyage of discovery by twilight. Below the stern of the schooner, which swings near the beach, are the timbers of a ship peeping above water, and full of story, no doubt, as so many old salts. We have had a most agreeable tea-time, the Captain entertaining us with incidents of his life upon these northern seas. My regret, not to say vexation, that we had to leave the strait and retreat to the safety of this lovely fold, provided by the Good Shepherd of the deep, is quite dissipated after a little sketch of the perils to which we should have been subjected among the currents, becalmed and immersed in fog, banks of which I see already peeping over the hills along the shore. Sunset and twilight and the dusk of evening have come and gone. The stars are out in multitudes, Arcturus among them high in the great arch, and the depths, above which we seem to hang suspended, are thickly sown with their trembling images.

CHAPTER L.

SUNDAY IN TEMPLE BAY.—RELIGIOUS SERVICES.—THE FISHERMAN'S
DINNER AND CONVERSATION.—CHATEAU.—THE WRECK.—WINTERS
IN LABRADOR.—ICEBERGS IN THE WINTER.—THE FRENCH OFFI-
CERS' FROLIC WITH AN ICEBERG.—THEORY OF ICEBERGS.—CUR-
RENTS OF THE STRAIT.—THE RED INDIANS.—THE RETURN TO
THE VESSEL.

MONDAY, *July* 19. Early yesterday morning, a boat
with tan-colored sails came off from the town, and found
that we were not traders from Newfoundland, as they
supposed, but visitors merely, and direct from Mr.
Hutchinson, their minister, of whose return they were
delighted to hear tidings. It was soon settled that I
should be their clergyman for the day, notice of which
was given very quickly upon their going back to the
village, by sending from house to house, and flying the
Sunday flag, a white banner with a red cross. Our men,
in holiday clothes, were prompt at their oars, and soon
placed us on the beach, where we were met by Mr.

Clark, one of the city fathers, who politely invited us to his house, and afterward attended us to the place of worship, a small rude building, which was crowded, the children gathering close about me. After the usual Church of England service, I preached extempore on our need of redemption, and the sufficiency and freeness of that which has been graciously provided. After a brief intermission, all returned to the evening service and sermon, which concluded the religious exercises of the day. We dined at Mr. Clark's, on fisherman's fare, garnished with salted duck, a new dish to us, and requiring the discipline of use and a rough life in order to relish very well.

While at dinner and after, our host entertained us in a simple, sketchy way with incidents and adventures illustrating the story of the place, and of his own life. Chateau, the name of the village, is more ancient than the old French and English war, during which it suffered pillage and burning. The wreck beneath our stern, of which I spoke, was that of an English vessel with a cargo of furs, fish and oil, and was there run aground and fired by the captain, to prevent her falling into the hands of the enemy. Even these remote rocks and waters have historic associations of thrilling interest.

According to the custom of those who live permanently in Labrador, Clark and a few of his neighbors remove, in autumn, to the evergreen woods along the streams at the head of the bay, and spend more than half of the year in hunting and sealing, and getting timber and firewood for the summer. In some respects, it is a holiday time, and compensates for the unremitting toil of the fishing season.

The experience of years with icebergs has not made them common things, like the waves and hills, but rather increased the sense of their terrible power and grandeur. They frequently arrive covered with earth and stones, an indication of their recent lapse from the land, and of the brevity of their time upon the sea. During the cold months they are deeply covered with snow, and have a rounded, heavy, and drowsy aspect. It is the warm weather that gives them their naked brilliancy, and melts them into picturesque forms, and rolls and explodes them in the magnificent style, I have attempted to describe. They are seen to move occasionally at the same rate of speed, whether through the densely packed ice or the open sea. Wind, current and tide, and the ocean crowded with ice as far as sight can reach, all frequently set in one direction, and the bergs in another. On they move, majestic and serene, tossing the crystal masses from their shaggy breasts, cracking, crashing, thundering along. There are spaces of dark water spotting the white expanse. It makes no difference ; all move on alike. None hastens in the open water ; none pauses at the heaped-up banks. All on the surface of the deep is only so much froth before the Alp whose foundations are immersed in the great submarine currents.

He told us a story illustrating the danger of icebergs, and the temerity of making familiar with them. A few years ago, while a French man-of-war was lying at anchor in Temple Bay, the younger officers resolved on amusing themselves with an iceberg, a mile or more distant in the straits. They made sumptuous preparations for a pic-nic upon the very top of it, the mysteries of which they were curious to see. All warnings of the brown and simple fishermen, in the ears of the smartly dressed gentlemen who had seen the world, were quite idle. It was a bright summer morning, and the jolly boat with a showy flag went off to the berg. By twelve o'clock the colors were flying from the icy turrets, and the wild midshipmen were shouting from its walls. For two hours or so they hacked, and clambered the crystal palace ; frolicked and feasted ; drank wine to the king and the ladies, and laughed at the thought of peril where all was so fixed and solid. As if in amazement at such rashness, the grim Alp of the sea made neither sound nor motion. A profound stillness watched on his shining pinnacles, and hearkened in the blue shadows of his caves. When, like thoughtless children, they had played themselves weary, the old alabaster of Greenland mercifully suffered them to gather up their toys, and go down to their cockle of a boat, and flee away. As if the time and the distance were measured, he waited until they could see it and live, when, as if his heart had been volcanic fire, he burst with awful thunders, and filled the surrounding waters with his ruins. A more astonished little party seldom comes home to tell the story of their panic. It was their first, and their last day of amusement with an iceberg.

It seems rather late in the day for persons of some experience in these regions, to be ignorant of the origin of icebergs. I asked our friend, as I had others, how he supposed that they were formed. He imagined that they were merely the accumulations of loose ice, snow and frozen spray, in the intensely cold regions of the arctic ocean. Piles of broken ice, driven together, and cemented by the heavy snows and the repeated dashing of the surf, would in time become the huge and solid islands that we see. Such is the theory of their formation with all whom I have heard express themselves on the subject, and I believe the one very generally received. When this explanation was objected to, and the facts stated that icebergs were glaciers, first formed on the land, and then launched into the sea, our kind host expressed his doubts more modestly than some others had done of less intelligence and experience.

Speaking of the currents in the straits, he said he could not well conceive any in the world more dangerous. While exceedingly powerful, they were shifting. What rendered this perilous to the last degree, was the excessively deep water and the boldness of the shores. One could toss a bullet into water frequently too deep for the anchorage of smaller vessels. In times of calm, and in connection with the dense fogs peculiar to those coasts, a vessel could not drift about in the straits without the risk of being thrown upon the rocks and lost. When we were lying becalmed off Temple Bay, on Saturday afternoon, he was watching us from a hill-top, and remarked to a neighbor, that he was sorry for the skipper out there, and feared, unless the wind came to his relief before dark, he would get ashore.

He remarked that fresh water may be dipped in winter, from small open spaces in the bay—a fact I do not remember to have read of in the pages of arctic voyagers. I concluded that this only is true, where the water is undisturbed below, and where the open spaces are small, and hemmed in with ice in a way to break off the wind. It is simply rain-water, I suppose, resting upon the surface of the heavier salt water. In the course of the conversation, he stated that there was, at some distance back in the interior, a remnant of the red Indians so called, once a savage and troublesome tribe in Newfoundland. Driven from thence on account of their hostile and untamable nature, they had finally taken refuge in the remote vales of Labrador, where they now live, as is commonly reported, nursing their ancient enmity, but too prudent to reappear among the whites, or let their exact habitation be known.

Pleased with the talk of the fisherman of Chateau, we bade him and his family good-by, and returned on board to a second dinner, a little more to our taste.

12*

CHAPTER LI.

EVENING WALK TO TEMPLE BAY MOUNTAIN.—THE LITTLE ICEBERG.
—TBOUBLES OF THE NIGHT AND PLEASURES OF THE MORNING.—
UP THE STRAITS.—THE PINNACLE OF THE LAST ICEBERG.—THE
GULF OF ST. LAWRENCE.

AFTER dinner and a pleasant conversation on deck, we found time to slip ashore, and thread our way through thickets of sweet-scented spruce to the mountain-top for a prospect. Once in my life, on the borders of a forest pond, in the lower St. Lawrence country, I experienced the plague of black flies to an extent that was quite frightful. I turned from the margin where, head and face covered with handkerchiefs, I was fishing, and ran to a woodman's hut. The same flies swarmed about us on the mountain of Temple Bay, and drove us down through its evergreens with all the speed it was prudent to make.

In the edge of the twilight, the Captain went across the bay to a little mouse of a berg, that had been all day creeping in from sea, to get a few cakes of ice ; and asked our company. Our mouse, as might be expected, turned out to be a lion. We rowed alongside, notwithstanding, and sprung upon his white, glassy back melted all over into a roughness that resembled the rippled surface of a pond. In attempting to walk to a fairy-like bowl, full of that lovely blue water, the painter slipped up, and came near sliding off altogether. But for the Captain, at whose legs he caught as he was going by, he would have had a fine plunge and a ducking. Our chick of a berg, only ten or twelve feet across with a few minute pieces of sculpture in the shape of vases and recumbent animals, lay in its pale green bath like a burr or star, its white points visible at quite a depth—a fact which served to corroborate some experiments we had been making with respect to the $_{.p}{}^{a}{}_{rts}$ of an iceberg under water. Here was a mass, with the exception of a few trifling spurs, only a little above the surface, but with a bulk, the extreme points of which were too far below to be discovered. To conclude several amusing liberties we were taking with it, the Captain proceeded to split off a kind of figure-head attached to the main body by a sort of horse-neck, which no sooner fell into the water than our bantling began to imitate the motions of the tallest giant of the icebergs. In making the grand swing, however, it rolled completely over, and came within an ace of catching us upon one of its horns. Anticipating the chance of danger from below, I looked over the side of the boat, when, sure enough, a prong was coming up in a way to give us a toss that would be no sport. A lucky push off saved us. Like the spoke of a big wheel it rolled up, giving us a blow in the ribs as it passed, and a good rocking on the swash. One would scarcely think that there was any excitement in so trifling an incident, but there was, and enough of it to make me resolve to meddle no more with a thing of the kind larger than a lamb. When it settled to rest, it was exactly upside down, and presented a curious specimen of the honey-comb work of the waters. It may occur to some that we were sporting upon the Lord's Day. Upon reflection I confess that we were, although we might plead the privilege of voyagers, and the long day which touches hard upon our midnight.

Upon our return we found the musquitoes, a peculiarly hungry and poisonous species, coming down from the woods in numbers. We determined to crush that mischief in the bud, and did it most effectually, by filling the cabin with the dense smoke of spruce boughs, and then, upon its escape, covering the entrance with a sheet. One only came feebly and timidly singing about my face before I got to sleep. About one o'clock, there were sounds above : shaking of blocks and cordage, now and then a thump with a creak of booms, and jerking of the rudder. I went·up ; there was no watch ; all were soundly sleeping. The ship's cat was out on the rail, running from place to place, and mewing mournfully. The sky looked ominous, and there was the roar of wind outside. The waters and the woods of the bay, so prettily named, were gloomy as the crypt of a temple. I crept to my dreams, out of which in no long time I was startled by the painter. He was getting up to have his look. He reported breezes, but in the wrong direction, and without comment felt his way back to bed. At two, the voice of the Captain put an end to slumbers, fore and aft. He was calling all hands to the deck, where presently all was noise and bustle, hoisting sail, and heaving at the anchor. The old motion was soon perceptible, and we knew that we were taking leave of Temple Bay—a fact of which we were assured by the Captain, who peeped in upon us, by lifting a corner of the musquito-sheet, and announced the good tidings that the wind, northeast, was blowing briskly, and that the straits would give us no further trouble.

No sooner were we clear of the " tickle," or narrows, than " Iceberg ahead ! "—" Ice on the lee bow ! " was cried by the man forward. It was no more to our purpose to go up and look at ices. It was a comfortable reflection that we were now bidding them farewell. By way of a parting salute, one of the bergs burst asunder with a great noise, before that we were out of the reach of its shells. But its thunder fell but faintly on our practised ears, and rather encouraged than disturbed our disposition to sleep. When daylight was broad upon the straits, we were over the worst, and the last iceberg, like the top of some solitary mausoleum of the desert, was sinking below the horizon. The high wind and sea were after us, and we ran with speed and comparative stillness. By noon we were fairly through ; with Forteau, the last of Labrador, on the north—to the south, the coast of Newfoundland, and the broad gulf of St. Lawrence expanding before us. We felt that we might then breathe freely. The breeze most surely did, and we sped on our way southward toward Cape Breton.

CHAPTER LII.

THE coast of Labrador was really fine, all the fore-noon, and sometimes strikingly grand. It has lost something of the desolate and savage character it has about the Capes St. Louis and St. Charles, and seems more like a habitable land. There are long and graceful slopes and outlines of pale green hills slanting down to the sea, along which is the craggy shore-line, black, brown and red. The last few miles, and which is near the Canadian border, the red sandstone shore is exceedingly picturesque. It has a right royal presence along the deep. Lofty, semicircular promontories descend in regular terraces nearly down, then sweep out gracefully with an ample lap to the margin. No art could produce better effect. The long, terraced galleries are touched with a tender green, and the well-hollowed vales, now and then occurring, and ascending to the distant horizon between ranks of rounded hills, look green and pasture-like. All, you must bear in mind, is treeless nearly, and utterly lonely. Here and there are small detachments of dwarf firs, looking as if they were either on their retreat to the woodlands of a warmer clime, or on their march from it, in order to get a foothold, and make a forest settlement remote from the woodman's axe. Anyway, in their lonesome and inhospitable halt, they darken the light greens and the gray greens with very lively effect.

The Battery, as sailors call it, is a wall of red sandstone, of some two or three miles in extent, with horizontal lines extending from one extreme to the other, and perpendicular fissures resembling embrasures and gateways. Swelling out with grand proportions toward the sea, it has a most military and picturesque appearance. At one point of this huge citadel of solitude, there is the resemblance of a giant portal, with stupendous piers two hundred feet or more in elevation. They are much broken by the yearly assaults of the frost, and the eye darts up the ruddy ruins with surprise. If there was anything to defend, here is a Gibraltar at hand, with comparatively small labor, whose guns could nearly cross the strait. Beneath its precipitous cliffs the debris slopes like a glacis to the beach, with both smooth and broken surfaces, and all very handsomely decorated with rank herbage. Above the great walls, there is a range of terraces ascending with marked regularity for quite a distance. Miles of ascending country, prairie-like, greet the eye along this edge of Labrador. "Arms of gold"— is it? Possibly these promontories, golden in the rising and the setting sun, may have suggested to Cabot or some other explorer, before or since, the propriety of christening this dead body of a country by some redeeming name.

Among the very pretty and refreshing features of the coast are its brooks, seen occasionally falling over the rocks in white cascades. Harbors are passed now and then with small fishing fleets and dwellings. Forteau has a church-spire pointing heavenward among its white buildings and brown masts, and is the most eastern place in the diocese of Newfoundland visited by Bishop Field. It is not unlikely that he is now there engaged in the sacred duties of his office, and certainly would have attracted us thither, could we have spared a day. On the point from which we took our final departure from the north shore, stands a high lighthouse, erected at great cost, and around its base are clustering the greens of a kitchen garden! Adieu, bleak Labrador! They tell me that the warmest of summers is now upon thy honeyless and milkless land.   If this is thy July—I say it under an overcoat of the deepest nap—spare me thy December.

But why, at parting, should I speak roughly unto thee, and whet the temper to talk ill of thee, in the presence of rich gardens, yellow fields, and ruddy orchards?   Hast not thou thy horned cariboo, the reindeer, thy fox of costly fur, and thy wild-fowl of wintry plumage?   Hast not thou thy bright-eyed salmon, graced with lines as delicate and lovely as those of beauty's arm, and complexioned like the marigold "damasked by the neighboring rose"?—thy whales and seals to fill with oil the lighthouse lamp, to fill with starry flame the lighthouse lantern?—thy pale green capelin, silvery-sided myriads that allure the "fish," calling their millions to the hooks and seines of thy toiling fishermen—hardy, hospitable people, whose kentles of white-fleshed cod buy the ruby wine and yellow fruits of Cuba and Oporto?   Hast thou not dealt kindly with us, and shown us these thy fat things, and all thy richer, nobler treasures?   Hast thou not uncurtained thy resplendent pictures of the sky, the ocean, and the land?   And have we not gazed delighted and awe-struck upon the grandeur of a great and terrible wilderness, upon the gloom of its shadowy atmosphere, upon the brilliancy of its sunlight?   Have we not heard the footsteps of the billows marching to their encampment in the grottoes of the cliffs ; and seen the silent, inshore deeps ; the imprisoned islands and grim headlands armed with impenetrable granite ; the vales and dells, and hill-sides with their mosses and their flowers, sweet odors, and sweet melodies ?—most beautiful, most wonderful of all, thine icebergs, and thy twilight heavens ? All these, and more, of thy greatness and thy glory, have we looked upon, and they will have their reflections, and their echoes in the memory forever. Beauty may watch, and supplicate, and weep sometimes upon the crags now receding from our view, but she is surely there, and native to the wildest pinnacle and cavern. And while to the careless eye and thoughtless heart thou art verily dark and bleak, yet art thou neither barren nor unfruitful. Old Labrador, farewell !

CHAPTER LIII.

WESTERN NEWFOUNDLAND.—THE BAY, THE ISLANDS, AND THE HIGHLANDS OF ST. JOHN.—INGORNACHOIX BAY.

NEWFOUNDLAND now lifts its blue summits along the southeast sky, a kind of Catskill heights, with here and there patches of snow, that recall to mind the White Mountain House. In the course of the afternoon, we pass them, and find that they are the highlands of St. John, the loftiest, I believe, in the island, and bound the bay called by the same lovely name.

What a region for romantic excursion! Yonder are wooded mountains with a sleepy atmosphere, and attractive vales, and a fine river, the river Castor, flowing from a country almost unexplored; and here are green isles spotting the sea—the islands of St. John. Behind them is an expanse of water, alive with fish and fowl, the extremes of which are lost in the deep, untroubled wilderness. A month would not suffice to find out and enjoy its manifold and picturesque beauties, through which wind the deserted trails of the Red Indian, now extinct or banished. Why they should have left, with all these unappropriated breadths of solitude for their inheritance, I do not precisely understand. There are mournful tales told of their wrongs and their revenges, the old story of contests between the civilized and the savage.

Yonder, at the termination of the highlands, is a cape, no matter what is its French name, since directly behind it is a bay with an Indian name tough enough to last one round a dozen capes—the Bay of Ingornachoix, noted for its harbors, inlets, and pretty streams, another fine region for the summer tourist. Beyond the woody distances rising in the east, there lies a lengthy lake, the centre of a little world of interest to the lovers of nature and the picturesque. It is no great distance across the island here to the shores of White Bay, a remote expanse of waters, to which few but fishermen have any occasion to penetrate.

As the evening advances the wind strengthens, and bears us rapidly along the coast. Thus we are encircling Newfoundland, and finding spots of beauty, to which, if we may not return ourselves, we can direct others of like taste and sentiment. We come down from the cold air,

and from looking at a fine aurora now playing in the
skies, and gleaming by reflection in the waves, and sit by
the cabin lights, and talk and write, inspect the sketches,
and listen to the roar of winds and surges—rather melancholy music.

CHAPTER LIV.

SLOW SAILING BY THE BAY OF ISLANDS.—THE RIVER HUMBER.—
ST. GEORGE'S RIVER, CAPE, AND BAY.—A BRILLIANT SUNSET.

TUESDAY, *July* 19. We have a brilliant morning
and a favoring breeze, but a vexatious current. What a
net of these currents has the tyrannous Neptune set
around his beloved Newfoundland! Like a web in a
dim cellar window, it is perpetually entangling some fly
of a craft in its subtle meshes. Buzz and struggle as
we will, he has got us by the foot, and, spider-like, may
look on, and enjoy our perplexity. We advance with
insufferable slowness, notwithstanding the considerable
speed of our rounded bows, through the water. "That is
the Bay of Islands," they said, early in the morning. It
is the Bay of Islands still. We are a long time sailing
by the Bay of Islands. But it gives us time to look,
and talk about it with the Captain. Beyond the forest-
covered hills which surround it, are lakes as beautiful,

and larger than Lake George, the cold, clear waters of which flow to the bay under the name of the river Humber. It has a valley like Wyoming, and more romantic scenery than the Susquehanna. The Bay of Islands is also a bay of streams and inlets, an endless labyrinth of cliffs and woods and waters, where the summer voyager would delight to wander, and which is worth a volume sparkling with pictures.

How fine a blue the waters of the gulf are in this light! We seem to be upon the broad Atlantic. What a realm of seas and shores, islands, bays and rivers, is this St. Lawrence world, in the midst of which we now are, and of which our people know so little! Where are our young men, who have the time and money to skip, from summer to summer, in the fashionable rounds of travel, that they do not seek this virgin scenery? One long, loud yell of the black loon, deep diver of these lakes and fiords, pealing through the silent evening, would ring in their recollection long after the music of city parks abroad had been forgotten.

Late in the day, and Cape St. George in view, a bold and clifted point pushed out from the mainland twenty miles or more, and commanding extensive prospects both inland and along the coast. A month would not suffice for all its many landscapes. St. George's River is a wild, rapid stream, and St. George's Bay is quite a little sea, deep, and darkened by the shadows of fine mountains, and broad woodlands. Like the Bay of Islands, it is a paradise for the huntsman, and the fisher. Awake, ye devotees of the fishing-rod and rifle, and the red camp-fire beneath the green-wood trees, and know that to visit St. George's cape and bay and river, and all that is St. George's, is better late than never.

The sun is in the waves, and yonder we have those wonderful heavens again. The west is all one bath of colors, colors of the rainbow. And clouds like piled-up fleeces, and like fleeces pulled apart and scattered, and fleeces spun into soft and woolly threads, and again those threads woven into downy fabrics, are weltering in the glory. The wind has fallen, and the waves have put out all their white, flashing lights, and now mould themselves into the flowing lines and the sweetest forms of beauty. We go down with glad hearts, and ask protection for the night.

13

CHAPTER LV.

FOUL WEATHER.—CAPE ANGUILLE.—THE CLEARING OFF.—THE
FROLIC OF THE PORPOISES.—THE NEW COOKS.—THE SHIP'S
CAT.

WEDNESDAY, *July* 20. We have a misty morning,
and a contrary wind. If there are any two words in
English, that early fell in love and married, and have a
numerous progeny, those words are Patience and Progress.
They do not walk hand in hand, but, like the red Indians, in single file. If Progress walk before, Patience is
close behind, which order of march now happens to prevail, and a good deal to our discomfort. In the mean time,
in company with this leisurely and quiet maid, we are
beating in and out from land, in long and tedious
stretches, with large gains upon one tack, and nearly as
large losses on the other.

Peeping through the rainy atmosphere is Cape Anguille, the neighboring heights of which are five hundred feet above the tide, and sweep off in dim and lengthy lines. The strong head-wind is blowing away the mists, the seas are up in arms, crested with snowy plumes, flashing and sparkling. Clouds, in white uniform, at quick-time march in long battalions, moving inland and leaving the defenceless shores to sunshine and the dashing surf. The sails mutter a deep, low bass. The " puffpigs," classic name for porpoise, are playing a thousand pranks about us, and we are partners in the frolic ; watching, laughing at, and pelting them, all of which they seem to regard as the merest nonsense of only a tubfull of helpless creatures in the upper air. They appear to be in the very highest glee, a party of fast young fellows, well bred and fed, and in holiday fin and skin. Like swallows round a barn, they play about our bows, wheeling, plunging, darting to the surface, spouting, splashing, every tail and rolling back of them full of fun and laughter. After a spell of this ground and lofty tumbling in the shadow of our jib, away they trip it, like so many frisky buffalo calves, side by side, in squads and couples, crossing and recrossing, kicking up their heels and turning summersets—a kind of rollicking good-by. Not a bit of it : round they come again, by tens and twenties, wild with merriment, on a perfect gallop, and dive below the vessel. Up they pop with puff and snort on all sides and ends, and dart away like shuttles, with a thread of light behind them, to go over and over again the gamesome round.

Sandy, whose coarse good nature has been dropping from his very finger ends in the way of stones thrown at the jolly fishes, has the smallest possible aptitude for the domestic art he is practising. Neither does his fancy take at all to the fair ways of neatness. Beyond frying pork and fish in one pan, and boiling potatoes in one pot, and making tea in one kettle, as a housewife steeps her simples, and every separate vessel, fakir-like, to sit from meal to meal in undisturbed repose, wrapped in the dingy mantle of its own defilement, Sandy has no ambition. Indignant, his superiors have read him several homilies to the point. But the lessons have fallen upon his attention like the first drops of a shower upon a duck's back. The painter even went so far as to indulge himself in a brief, emphatic charge, in the end of which there darted out a stinging threat, anent washing and scouring. Across the cloud of Sandy's unhappy brow a faint smile was, at length, seen to pass, and charge and threat dropped like pebbles into the muddy deeps of his forgetfulness. Sandy, therefore, has virtually been deposed, and now occupies the lowly position of a mere lackey to cooks of character. There are now, instead of one indifferent, three pre-eminent cooks : a painter, a captain, and a writer. They employ, divert, and frequently disappoint themselves in the several dishes they attempt. Not that the dishes in themselves are so bad, but that they fall so far short of the ideal of the excellent.

When I was a lad, spruce-beer and gingerbread were the nectar and ambrosia at general trainings. I wanted some ambrosia. The cooking-stove was instantly fired, and so was the painter, on the important occasion, who, from his skill in combining pigments on his pallet, had suspicions of ability in compounding ingredients for the pan and oven ; and therefore, nothing loth, was persuaded to undertake, with the secrecy of some hoar alchemist of old, in the dim retirement of the cabin, the conglomeration from flour and ginger, sugar, salt, soda and hot water, of a tremulous mass that should emanate, under his plastic hand, in a generous and tempting cake. To the large surprise of both mariner and author, order at length arose out of that chaos in a milk-pan, and appeared in upper day, when, with conscious but with a modest air of triumph, it was passed into the hands of the chief-baker, who roasted both it and himself, for a sultry and smoky hour, with entire success. Hot as metal from a furnace, and of a rich Potawatomie red, it was tasted, and found nearly as hot with ginger, and then prudently laid away to cool and petrify. The history of the decline and fall of that memorable loaf will probably never be written. It is enough to say, that, although the disintegrating process was at first a little difficult, owing to some doubt about the proper instrumentalities, yet it is now easily dissected with a saw. It is unnecessary to remark, that but one such batch of the ruddy bread is needed on a pleasure-voyage. The painter has fresh reason to congratulate himself that in all his works he succeeds in imparting an element of perpetuity.

Our great difficulty is the smallness of the caboose and the stove, which will not permit the carrying on of all operations at the same time—a circumstance which is apt to leave no more than a kindly warmth, if not a decided coolness, in all dishes but the last in hand. We, the landsmen of the culinary trio, have also a dreadful foe to fight, and, in any thing like a severe battle, are sure to fall. It is ever lurking near our outposts, and is sure to rush upon us in rough weather. They called it sea-sickness, I dare say, as early as when they voyaged for the golden fleece. Its effects are described in a language more venerable than that of Greece : " They reel to and fro, and stagger like a drunken man, and are at their wits' end." That describes our case exactly. It lays both dishes and ourselves completely on the shelf. Forthwith tea, cakes and coffee, meats, vegetables, fruits, and fish are allowed a play-spell, perhaps a long yellow holiday; and may go on a pic-nic, a bathing, or a fishing, or a shooting frolic under the table, among the baggage, or around the cabin floor, as the bend of things incline. The Captain, however, is apt to interpose in such disorders, and discipline the wild wares much to his own, and often to our relief.

We are amused, annoyed, and distressed at the ship's cat. She is an incorrigible thief and pick-shelf, and bent on making the most of us while we last. The painter is down upon her, and will not endure her for a moment. The cabin was recently the field of a bloodless battle, the din whereof was startling as far off as the caboose, in the smoke of which I was weeping over the remains of the late breakfast. Loud shouting, interspersed with shocks of irate bodies, boots, broom, cane, against barrels and amongst boxes came upon the peaceful ear, and warned me to hasten to the edge of things and look down. Tantæne animis celestibus iræ! There was no consciousness of a spectator of the militant manœuvres, but a mighty thrashing and furious thrusting, and whipping of a scraggy spruce-bough among tubs, jugs, and cans, and away behind. There was a steady fire in the face, and a pistol-shot sharpness in the " scat." Grimalkin answered with a terrible wauling, and finally with fixed tail made a dash past the enemy, escaping up the steps into my face and eyes almost, and retreating to the bowsprit. Puss is a bold sailor. She skips upon the taffrail, climbs the shrouds, sits with ease and dignity upon the boom, yawns and stretches among the rigging. Poor Pussy, she is not a silken-haired, daintily-fed cat, but a creature of backbone and ribs, coated with fur unlicked and scorched, indicative of kicks and a meagre cupboard. She treads no downy bed, and purs in no loved daughter's lap. As she comes mewing gingerly about my feet, and coils herself in a sunny twist of rope, I think of our own household tabby, and call her by all the feline names expressive of good-will and tenderness.

How the breeze pipes ! Hoarse music this, played upon the cordage of our light little schooner. Old Saint Laurent, thy winds and waves are not always symbols of a martyr's gentleness. A few seasons ago, just here in sight of yonder hills and valleys now dreaming under an atmosphere of quiet, Captain Knight experienced a most appalling sea. While there is nothing terrible in these now breaking over our barriers every few minutes, yet they effectually upset the stomach, and hence all comfort. We lie upon the slant deck in the sunshine, sheltered near the helm, and see the spray fly over us, and watch the idle flourishing of the topmast.

13*

CHAPTER LVI.

ST. PAUL'S ISLAND.—CAPE NORTH.—COAST OF CAPE BRETON.—SYD-
NEY LIGHT AND HARBOR.—THE END OF OUR VOYAGE TO LAB-
RADOR, AND AROUND NEWFOUNDLAND.

THURSDAY, *July* 21. After a boisterous night we
are on deck again, and find a pleasant change in the
wind. It is gray and rainy, but then our sails swell,
and we rush southward.

A dome of inhospitable rock peers through the mist,
one of nature's penitentiaries, which no living man would
own, and so has been deeded to St. Paul: Melita is
Eden to it. The saints, it appears to me, have been
gifted with the ruggedest odds and ends. Wherever, on
all these cast-iron shores, there is a flinty promontory,
upon which Prometheus himself would have shuddered
to be chained, there the name of an apostle has been
transfixed. Yonder is Cape North, the stony arrow-
head of Cape Breton, a headland, rather a multitudinous

group of mountain headlands, draped with gloomy grandeur, against the black cliffs of which the surf is now firing its snowy rockets. How is it they have not called it Cape St. Mary or St. John? All in all, this is a fine termination of the picturesque isle. Steep and lofty, its summits are darkened by steepled evergreens, and its many sides gashed with horrid fissures and ravines.

Here we part from the broad gulf, and enter the broader ocean, passing between the promontories of Cape Breton and the last capes of Newfoundland, Cape Anguille, and Cape Ray with its rocky domes and tables. Thus have we fairly encompassed this Ireland of America, in all but climate: White seabirds, with long wings tipped with black, sweep the air. We speed onward and homeward past the many-folded mountains. The eye slides along their graceful outlines, and follows their winding shores. Through the deep valleys we look upon the landscapes interior, softened by a purple atmosphere. Clouds are breaking around the woody summits, seas of forest-tops are smiling in the sunshine, and shadows are filling the rocky gorges with a kind of twilight. At last the sun is sinking behind the distant heights, and leaving his red footsteps on the clouds. C—— is painting his last picture, and these are the last pencillings of the voyage, We hail the cliffs of Sydney—

those remarkable cliffs that sat upon the horizon like tinted sea-shells, on the Sunday afternoon we were on our way to St. Johns. And yonder is the Sydney light twinkling through the dusk of evening. Our summer sail to Labrador and around Newfoundland is over. Where the anchor brings the vessel to a pause, there shall we leave the brave little pinkstern. May her wanderings in the future under the Union Jack be as happy as those of the present have been under the Stars and Stripes. Thankful for the Divine care, we will ask protection for the night, and guidance home, the final haven where we would be.

CHAPTER LVII.

FRIDAY, *July* 22. Sydney harbor. A bright morning, and the wind from the quarter where we should be happy to find it, were we going to sea. But, selfish souls! because it puts us to a small inconvenience, we now wish that it did not blow, and that we may have calm weather. We are to breakfast, to finish packing, and take our leave of Captain Knight, from whom we part with emotions of regret. He will depart in the next steamer for St. Johns, and we start for Halifax by an inland route.

Here we are, on our way across the Island of Cape Breton, bound for Nova Scotia. Our baggage—trunks, carpet-bags, reindeer-horns, snow-shoes, plants, and mosses—in a one-horse wagon, goes ahead; we follow

in another. We are delighted with the change from
rolling waves to rolling wheels. We are delighted with
our spirited nag. We are delighted with the scenery,
which, however, is in no way remarkable. I believe that
we should be delighted if we were riding through a
smoky tunnel. The truth is the delight is in us, and
will flow out, and would, be the world about us what it
might. Every thing amuses us, even the provoking trick
our pony has of slightly kicking up, every time the
breeching cuts into his hams upon going down hill. As
may be supposed, said pony is a creature of importance
to us, now that he is our motive power. We do not look
at the clouds now, and watch the temper of the atmosphere ; our eyes are upon the body and legs of the little
fellow wrapped in this brown skin. After the first effer-
vescence of spirit upon starting, with which, of course,
we were much delighted, he began to lag a trifle, and to
raise suspicions that he was not the horse good-natured
Mr. Dearing, his master, said he was. We are pleased
to find ourselves mistaken. Our very blunders are satisfactory. The longer he goes the smarter he grows, giving us symptoms of a disposition to run away, when ordinarily we might look for any thing else. Let him run.
We can ride as fast, and come in not a length behind, at
the end of our thirty-two miles, the distance to a tavern.

The ride along the shore of Sydney harbor, over a smooth, hard road, was really charming, and would have been to travellers of ill temper. Wild roses incensed the fresh air, and the sunshine was bright upon the clover-fields. On the steamer down from Halifax to Sydney, I became acquainted with a tradesman, an intelligent Scotch Presbyterian. Who should come running out of a little country store by the road-side, with a shout that brought our nag down upon his haunches, but our friend! He, too, was delighted, and shook us heartily by the hand, asking after " the Labrador," the icebergs, and our voyage in general. Set in the midst of our pleasure was one regret : our want of time to visit Louisburg, or the ruins of it. We talked it over, and then dismissed both the ruins and the regret.

From the bay of Sydney the way is wonderfully serpentine for a main road, winding about apparently for the mere love of winding, and when there seems no more real necessity for it than for a brook in a level meadow. We have liked it all the better, though, running, as it does, around the slightest hills, wooded with the perpetual spruce, intermingled with the birch and maple, crossing with a graceful twist little farms, and coming around garden fences, by the farmers' doors, under the willows and the apple trees. The native Indians, tricked out with cheap, showy finery, whose huts are seen lazily smoking among the bushes, were occasionally met, and chatted with. A young Mc. something, upon whose sleepy face was the moonshine of a smile, was found trotting his chestnut filly close behind our wagon. The persistence in the thing was becoming disagreeable, and we looked round several times with an expression which said plainly : "Please keep a little back." Mc. was in no humor to take the hint. When our pace quickened, the click of his horse's shoes, and the breath of his steed, which carried a high head, were close upon us ; a sudden slackening of our speed brought him, horse-head and all, as suddenly into our midst. Presently he changed his tactics, and dashed by, brushing the wheels with his stirrup, and so trotting on ahead, taking occasion to twist himself on the saddle, when a walk permitted, and look back. The fellow was a character, although of the softer kind, and we struck up an acquaintance, during which, in the effort to sustain his part of the conversation, he rode around us in all possible ways. A particularly favorite position was in the gutter at our side, where, in spite of our united care, he would now and then be literally run up a stump, or a bank. Whether on the lead, or following, we kept him frequently at break-neck speed, during which the conversation was mostly confined to monosyllables—loud and few—and, when forward, discharged now over one, and then over the other shoulder. Mc. was a farmer, and lived with "the old folks at home." He had been on a courting expedition, in which he considered himself successful. In fact, he made a clean breast of it, and told us the pleasant story of his love, and the fine qualities of the lass of whom he was enamored. Although she might not be thought handsome by a great many, yet she was handsome to him. Never errant knight rehearsed a softer tale in shorter periods, with a louder voice, or happier heart. He was full of it, and it mattered little to whom, or how he uttered it. For what distance he was intending to bear us company, I have no notion. The house of an acquaintance, at the gate of which were several persons, who seemed at once to understand him, and whose faces were so many open doors of curiosity, finally relieved us of him. It was evidently undesigned, and he pulled up, I thought, somewhat reluctantly.

CHAPTER LVIII.

EVENING RIDE TO MRS. KELLY'S TAVERN.—THE SUPPER, AND THE LODGING.

AT a sort of half-way house, the driver of the baggage-wagon stopped to feed and water, and I walked on alone, leaving the painter with his sketch-book. For a mile or more, the road wound its way through thick woods, mostly spruce, and " I whistled as I went," certainly not " for want of thought," and sang for the solitude, and was answered by the ringing echoes and the wood-thrush, whose sweet melody, sounding with a silvery, metallic ring, often made me pause and listen. Red raspberries, pendent from the slender bushes, tempted me frequently to spring up the broken, earthy bank, where, to my surprise I met the first strawberries coming on from the juicier climes. Ruby darlings, they had got only thus far along, and looked timid and disheartened, dropping wearily into the mossy turf, where they trembled like drops of blood. And so I loitered along the lonely highway, up which the sweetest of all the fruits were coming, and over which the wild birds were pouring forth their songs, and felt that I was only very, very happily going on toward heaven, taking home and loving, and beloved ones by the way. In the middle of the forest, I met a tall, thin Indian in ragged, English dress. He passed me by silently, and with an air of bashfulness. I was a little disappointed. When I saw him approaching, I proposed to myself a rest upon a log near by, and a talk with the man about his people. The wagons came up presently, and I resumed the reins, having, at the outset, been voted by a small majority much the better whip.

Late in the afternoon, we came upon the shores of Bras D'or, a fiord or inlet extending in from the ocean, and winding for many miles among hills, farms and woodlands in a manner exceedingly picturesque. The ride was lovely, too lovely for the merriment in which we had been freely indulging. Ebullitions of mirth gave way to thoughts and emotions arising from the beauty of the scenery and the hour. Clouds of dazzling flame, and a rosy sunset were reflected in the purple waters. As we came on at a rapid pace through the twilight and the succeeding darkness, rounding the hills abutting on the water, and thridding bits of wood, we settled into a stillness as unbroken as if we had been riding alone. It was nearly ten o'clock when we arrived at our inn, none the worse for our drive of thirty-two miles, good measure.

Our inn! Imagine, if you will, a long, low-roofed, dingy white house, with a front piazza, and hard by a sign swinging from the limb of a broad shade tree, creaking harsh plaints to the lazy breeze, and, in dark letters, asserting from year to year that this is the traveller's home. If it be your pleasure to indulge in such imaginings, let me at once assure you that in our Cape Breton Inn there is no corresponding reality. . Instantly extinguish from your mind said white house, tree and sign, and put in the place of them a log cabin of the old school, in the naked arms of the weather, backed by a stumpy field and weedy potato-patch, and fronted by a couple of rickety log sheds. That antique mensuration accomplished by the swinging of a cat would very nearly decide the whole extent of the interior, one side of which is a fire-place and fire, around which revolve, as primary orb, the hostess, Mrs. Kelly, and as satellites, a son and daughter and maid-servant. With all these powers, and with ample time, you may guess that we sat down at last to a savory and generous supper. There was tea, somewhat intimate, to be sure, with the waterpot, and there was bread, nice as the Queen herself ever gets at Balmoral. The butter, alas! was afflicted with that ailment which seems to be chronic throughout these her majesty's dominions, rancidity and salt. But the milk was creamy, and the eggs fresh as newly-cut marble, and the berry-pie, served at the hands of the daughter, a neat and modest girl with pretty face and figure, was a becoming finish to the meal.

Mrs. Kelly is a Highland widow, of whom a story may be told, not indeed of the tragic character of Sir Walter's Highland Widow, but sufficiently mournful. She walked back and forth before the door, and seemed to take a melancholy pleasure in relating it. Two fine boys had been tempted to leave her, of whom she had not heard a syllable for years, but for whom, even then, she was looking with the hope and yearning love of Margaret in Wordsworth's "Excursion." Her husband, kind man, was in the grave. Her two children and her little farm were much to be thankful for. But then it was not Scotland. A sad day for her when they were persuaded to leave "home." The land here was not productive, and the winters were so long and snowy. There was, however, a bright side to her fortunes, and I tried to make her see it. At the conclusion of the talk, she asked me in to read a chapter, and offer the evening prayer.

It was getting late, and I asked to retire. I found that we had retired. We were sitting in our private chamber, and the closely-curtained bed behind us, a match for one in an opposite corner, too long and too wide for a lad in his teens, was the appointed couch for two of us, and all ready. There were nine or ten of us, all told, and among them the daughter's lover, a good-looking and very well-appearing young man. Now that we were provided for, it was certainly no concern of ours how and where the others were to lodge, although I could not avoid feeling some interest in the matter. To hasten things to a conclusion, I rose, wound my watch, took off my boots, my coat and vest, demonstrations of my intention of going at once to bed that were not mistaken. Immediately all walked out of the house, and remained out, talking in the open air, until we were snugly packed away and pinned in behind the scant curtains, when they returned, and noiselessly went to rest in some order peculiar to the household, dividing between them the other bed, the floor, and the small chamber under the roof. When, in her native land, an ebony lady entertained Mungo Park, she and her maids lightened their nocturnal labors—spinning cotton—by singing plaintive songs, the burden of which was "the poor white man who came and sat under our tree." Thus our two maidens lightened both their labors and our slumbers, but by a less poetic process. While they busied themselves with sweeping the house, and washing dishes until after midnight, they kept a continual whispering, the subject of which was, in part, the poor sunburnt men who came to sleep under their curtains —but could not do it. Considering that the daughter had a sweetheart in the house, the sibilant disturbances of the girls were meekly suffered until they naturally whispered and swept their way to bed. After this we had a fair field, and did our best to improve it. The room being warm and smoky, I unpinned the curtain, and started for fresh air, stealing out as quietly as possible. Treacherous door! When I had succeeded in hitting upon the wooden latch, up it came with a jerk and a clack that went, it seemed to me, to the ears of every sleeper. I waited till I thought the effect of the noise had passed away, when I began slowly opening the door. It squealed like a bagpipe, startling the dreamers from their pillows, and arousing suspicions of a rogue creeping in, while it was only the restless traveller creeping out. There had been a kitten mewing at the door for some time. With tail erect, she whipped in between my feet. There was a puppy outside also, and some pigs; each in its way promising to keep up till daylight the serenade of barking and grunting, with which, from an earlier hour, they had entertained us. It was starlight, and I could see my ground, as I thought. I determined to have satisfaction by setting the dog upon the pigs, and then flogging the dog. Rapping one over the head with a bean-pole, by way of prelude to rapping the other, the puppy instantly joined in the assault, which, but for an unlucky stubbing of my naked toes, would have proved successful. I flung down my bean-pole with disgust, and beat, instead of the young rascal of a dog, an inglorious retreat. For the rest of the night, it was a triumph with the enemy, reinforced by some goslings and quacking ducks. If there was needed any more rosin on the bow that kept sawing across my tightly tuned nerves, two or three fleas supplied it at short intervals. The bite of the little villains made me jump like sparks of fire. There was, also, toward the chilly morning hours, a tide in our affairs, a regular ebb and flow of bed-clothes, and a final cataract of them, the entire sheet descending into some abyss, from which we never succeeded in recovering hardly any thing more than some scanty edges and corners of a blanket. It was a wonder to me how my companion in arms could sleep as he did, a pleasure he declares he did not enjoy ; but in his restlessness was surprised that I could slumber on so soundly, and snore through so many troubles—a dulness from which, of course, I tried stoutly to clear myself. Thus, as frequently happens, each imagined the other to have slept, and himself to have been wakeful all night. Undoubtedly, both waked and slumbered, and magnified the several small annoyances.

When we were ready to get up, which was disagreeably early, the household was stirring. But a peep through the crevice of the curtains, which had been carefully pinned together again by some fingers unknown, while we were dreaming, gave the needful hint, when out they went again among the ducks and goslings. We sprang out of bed, and dressed with all reasonable dispatch—an exercise in which we were slightly interrupted by a younger puppy, the pestilent animal persisting, in spite of a kick or two, in springing at and nibbling our feet.

14

CHAPTER LIX.

SATURDAY, *July* 23. We were off betimes, and trundling right merrily again along the hilly shores of Bras D'or, a much more expanded sheet of water than yesterday. At three o'clock, P. M., we arrived at David Murdoch's, the end of our journey with Dearing's conveyances, and where we remain until Monday morning.

I have just returned from a walk through wood and meadow, picking berries by the way, and now wait for dinner, which, from the linen on the table, the look of the landlady, and the general air of things, promises uncommonly well. From this frequent mention of the quality of our dinner, it may be thought that I think them of great importance. I do think them of very great importance ; not so much because good meals are necessary and the best on mere sanatory grounds, but because they are an allowable luxury, especially at a time when one is apt to have a sharp appetite and good digestion. A man is something of an animal, and likes excellent eating for the comfort of it, and the stomach's sake, and that *like* is defensible on good moral grounds. I need not add, that the indulgence of it should have upon it the bit and curb of moderation; in the application of which moral force consists temperance, a virtue that stands not in the scantiness, the meanness, or the entire absence of things drank and eaten, but in the strong, controlling will. After this brief apology for the hungry traveller's love of bountiful dinners well and neatly served, I will return to the sylvan nook where ours, for to-day and to-morrow, are to be cooked and eaten.

We are at the foot of a high, broad hill, verdant with meadows and pastures, and checkered with woods and orchards, around the lake-end of which the road comes gracefully winding down to the creek and the bridge close by. The expanse of water lying off to the west, as you might have guessed, is named St. Peter's Bay, and the buildings, a mile or more distant along the spruce and pine-covered shore, is St. Peter's itself, a village. The accommodations of Mr. Murdoch are ampler than those of the Widow Kelly; and the brown, wooden house stands backed into the thick evergreen forest, the front door dressing to the right and left, with its square-toed stone step in line with the trees along the street. We have each a neat room, softened under foot with a rag carpet, and dimmed by a small window and its clean white curtain. The narrow feather-beds are freshened with the cleanest linen. We have seen the last of our driver, who returns to-day as far as the Widow Kelly's.

With one horse attached to the hinder end of the forward wagon, he went over the bridge and up the hill, "an hour and a half ago."

SUNDAY, *July* 24. We rest according to the commandment, and have religious service in the family, the members of which, like most of the Scotch of Cape Breton, are Presbyterians. In the afternoon, we sauntered through the adjoining woods and fields, picking a few strawberries, and giving to ourselves a practical illustration of the ease with which people slip into the habit of Sabbath-breaking, who live in out-of-the-way places, distant from the parish church, and beyond the restraints of a well-ordered community. In the course of our walk, we came out upon the beach, and looked at the beautiful evening sky across the water. Bountiful Providence ! Where hast thou not sown the seeds of loveliness, and made the flowers of glory bloom ? Celestial colors are also beneath the foot. The swells that fretted, and left their froth along the sloping sand, were freighted with the jelly-fish, several of which were of the most exquisite purple.

CHAPTER LX.

MONDAY, *July* 25. We are out " by the dawn's early light," and assist in getting our baggage upon the coach, as David Murdoch calls his two-horse covered wagon, which is to carry us on to the Strait of Canso. We have breakfasted, and all is ready. As I pen these notes, here and there by the wayside, I keep them mainly in the present tense. David, a little fair-complexioned, sandy-whiskered farmer, innkeeper, stage-proprietor, and driver, all in one, is exactly the man for his vocation. Quick in his motions, intelligent and good-tempered, he is entirely to our purpose. He starts his Cape Bretons, a span of light, wiry animals, upon a canter, in our opinion an indiscreet pace. We pass St. Peter's, a superlative place—superlatively minute, the smallest city in the world. It

had, for several years, one house, but has of late been in
a more thriving condition. It has now a name on the
map, a population of some nine or ten souls, and two
houses, a large public work in the shape of a beach, and
a little shipping, not able to say how much exactly, as it
is all absent but a skiff and a bark canoe, and the wreck
of a schooner, in a poor and neglected condition. How
long, at this rate of progress, it will take for St. Peter's to
grow out of existence, is a fair question of arithmetic,
left for the statist of the island to cipher out. We
pause for a moment only, and that in front of a mer-
cantile establishment, if one may guess from a tin-foil-
covered paper of tobacco, and astride of it a couple of
pipes in the window, but dash· through its suburbs, a
pig-pen and a hen-roost, and pass the gates of a calf-pen
and a potato-patch, and gain the open country, a wild
and lonesome tract, half-wooded, and the other half
weeds, brush, and stumps of all calibre and colors,
from rotten-red and brown down to coal-black, and all
torn to pieces, and tangled into one briery wilderness,
just fit for the fires that occasionally scour through.

We were mistaken about the indiscretion of David, in
his driving, and add two more to the list of those impertinent travellers who hastily pass judgment upon persons
and things of which they are quite ignorant. David is

the Jehu of the road, and his steeds are chosen, and fitted to their master. Like locomotives, they work with the greater ease and spirit as they wax hotter. For three hours they trotted, galloped, ran, as if something more than horse was in them, and something worse than man was in their driver. There was ; as we knew by the flame in his face and about his nostrils, and by his breath that had spirit in it. Around the hills, and at their foot, over bridges, and through the bushy dales, the road described many a Hogarth's line of beauty, and many a full-blooded S. In whirling through these graceful sinuosities, now strongly on the right wheels, then heavily on the left, flirting the dust or mud into the air, we seemed to swim or fly on the oily brim of peril. Expostulation flashed out upon the lips in vain. A shake of the head, and a knowing smile, sharpened off by the crack of the whip, restored assurance, and fairly straightened all things out. But all went well, and passengers as well as driver became rash and brave, and foolishly came to like and applaud what at first they were disposed to protest against.

A change of horses has enabled David to persist in this extraordinary driving, which brings us to Plaster Cove at noon, where we part with both the mercurial little Scotchman, and Cape Breton. Thus have we coasted, and crossed this British Island, in which, with all that is repulsive and desolate, nature has done much, especially in the picturesque, and where agriculture and commerce have large fields for improvement. To the tourist that loves nature, and who, for the manifold beauties by hill and shore, by woods and waters, is happy to make small sacrifices of personal comfort, I would commend Cape Breton. Your fashionable, whose main object is company, dress, and frivolous pleasure with the gay, and whose only tolerable stopping-place is the grand hotel, had better content himself with reading of this Island.

14*

CHAPTER LXI.

PLASTER COVE, a small village, and our dining-place, is at the main point of departure for Nova Scotia on the Strait of Canso, a river to all appearance, and not unlike the Niagara, pouring its deep, green tides back and forth through its rocky channel, overlooked by cliffs and highlands. Directly opposite, the hills rise into quite a mountain, thickly wooded, down the sides of which is a broad clearing for the telegraphic wire connecting with the Atlantic cable. At first a very high tower of timber was erected on this, the Cape Breton side, in order to carry the wire above the highest mast, but it was soon abandoned and left to fall into ruin. The wire is now submerged, and enters the water in the form of a substantial iron rope strong enough for the anchor of a man-of-war.

Two o'clock, P. M., we crossed the strait in a small sail-boat, and encountered quite a disagreeable sea, enough so to give us a few dashes of salt water, and frighten the women that were in company. We have a two-horse post-coach, of queer shape and uncomfortable dimensions, being short and narrow in the body, but tall enough to serve for a canopy at the head of a procession. One could easily spread his umbrella overhead, and find some inconvenience in disposing of it closed down below. To Antigonish, the town for which we start in this—I am at a loss to determine whether antique, or an anticipation of the future—carriage, it is thirty-six miles, and not greatly different from as many miles lately passed over, if I may guess from what I can see for a mile ahead. Our fellow-sufferers in this strait jacket of a carriage are Scotchmen, and think in Gaelic before they speak, I imagine, as have many of them that we have met. They are much amused at the humour of the painter, of whose vocation and standing in the world they have not the remotest notion.

> "St. George, he was for England,
> St. Denis was for France ;
> Sing, Honi soit qui mal y pense,"

is the refrain of Master John Grubb, of Christ Church, Oxford, his ballad, rehearsed at the anniversary feast of

St. George's club, on St. George's Day, the 23d of April. And now for the reason that I have been humming this classic nonsense, or rather that I should have thought of it : To the north of us is a blue expanse, dotted and bordered by inlands, headlands, and the warm blue heights of Cape Breton. It is a kind of azure reticule, or pocket of the Gulf, and was early christened, by whom I cannot tell, St. George's Bay. This is the second Bay in honor of the martyr of Nicomedia, the patron Saint of England, to repeat a popish˚ fancy, that we have encountered within a few days. And truly, could the old religious hero revisit these earthly scenes, he would own that they had given his name to a very fine extent of water, whose purple hills to the northeast stand at the opening of the Strait of Canso. Due north, a vessel would touch, in a few hours' sail, the eastern cape of Prince Edward's Island, the garden of all the Gulf, another region for the summer traveller.

These landscapes of island, sky, and water are softly beautiful in the afternoon and sunset lights, but scarcely picturesque, and never grand. The country is dull and wearisome, gently diversified with hill and dale, woodlands and farms, in no very high state of culture, and thinly populated. There is some advantage, however, resulting from this dulness of scenery : it drives us to ourselves for entertainment.   A merrier time I do not remember than that lately passed on the driver's seat. The theme was scarecrows—a peculiar walk of art, in which the painter, during a recent stay in a remote part of the country, became sufficiently adept to frighten, not only the little creatures that pulled up the corn, but even the larger ones that planted it.   To such perfection did he finally carry old clothes and straw, that, like the statue of Pygmalion, his images became indued with life, and ended with running after the astonished rustics of the neighborhood.   We ride into Antigonish, a thriving village, with pretty white houses and spreading shade-trees, at dusk, and alight at a comfortable tavern, where we sup on salmon, and rest until after midnight.

CHAPTER LXII.

TUESDAY, *July* 26. New Glasgow. We halt here
for breakfast, after a sociable and merry ride of several
hours from Antigonish, where, after a refreshing sleep, we
were favored by a change of coaches, and the pleasant
company of an officer of the English army. Here is a
broad and fertile vale with a pretty river and town ; all
reminding us of New England. Across the river are
coal-mines, a railroad, and ther oar of cars, merely coal-
cars, however. Tide-water is close by, setting in from
the Strait of Northumberland, the lengthy water lying
between the mainland and Prince Edward's Island. We
are all ready for our ride to Truro, on Mines Bay, or a
spur of it, an eastern reach of the Bay of Fundy, and
distant forty miles, where we take the cars for Halifax,

or all the world. Those wonderful cars! Why, at Truro, I shall begin to feel at home, a point more remote than Europe, in the day of only sails and horse-power.

The ride is cheering, as we take it on the coach-top in the breezy, bright day. Broad farms, with barns and dwellings, grass and grain and orchards, cattle and bleating sheep spread out upon the hills, and stretch along the valleys. The plain of Truro has many of the features of a populous and well-cultivated county. Its groves and trees and wide meadows, waiting for the mower, form a pretty and extended landscape. The town itself, reached at three o'clock, with its central square and grass and shades, is too much like a village of New England to need further mention. While at dinner, the whistle of the locomotive indicated the direction of the station, a welcome call, which we obeyed with rather more than ordinary alacrity. The ride to Halifax, which occupied from four o'clock until dusk, was by no means at Yankee speed, and took us through a thinly inhabited country, somewhat broken, and interspersed with woods and waters—a region that makes no very definite or lasting impression, and yet one that the traveller looks out upon with some pleasure. The last few miles along the banks of the river flowing into Halifax Bay was a lovely valley ride. Rounded hills and bluffs green and bowery, and handsome residences looking out between pretty groves and down grassy lawns, never appeared more attractive. Had we been going the other way, perhaps they would not have seemed deserving of more than a passing look. In the weary hours, and along the torrid portions of the path of life, I am sure that I shall remember the quiet, refreshing scenery of that river, and wish myself among its graceful and placid beauties. From the noisy station we trundled in an ʻomnibus through the narrow streets of an old-fashioned, hill-side city, crowned with a fortress looking off south upon a bay and the distant ocean, and alighted at a hotel of stories and many windows, where we heard a gong, instrument of Pandemonium, and took tea with the relish of medicine, and talked over the conclusion of our journey. As haste was more requisite on my part, I resolved to post across the province to Windsor, that night, and leave the painter to wend his way homeward at his leisure.

CHAPTER LXIII.

COACH RIDE AT NIGHT FROM HALIFAX TO WINDSOR.—THE PRINCE
EDWARD'S MAN, AND THE GENTLEMAN FROM NEWFOUNDLAND.

IMMERSED in fog, and shut up in a small coach, three of us, a Prince Edward's man and a gentleman from Newfoundland, rode at a round trot, with but two or three brief intermissions, from ten o'clock in the evening until six next morning. The country, I conclude—if a man may have any conclusions, who rides with his eyes fast shut, and sleeps and nods—is a succession of hills and dales. From the bridges, over which we rumbled, and from the crowing of the cocks at midnight and at dawn, I argue that there were farms and streams. My companions were agreeable. Being partners in the enterprise, at the cost of twenty-two dollars and a half for an eight hours' drive, we had fellow-feelings on all things in general, and upon the expensiveness of night travelling in Nova Scotia in particular. The Prince Edward's man, a tradesman, was on his first visit to the States, in fact to the great world, and was a modest, thoughtful person, who talked as men of merely home experience are apt to talk, saying nothing to object to, nothing to startle, and some little to remember concerning the climate, the society, and products of his native isle. The gentleman from Newfoundland had seen the world to his soul's content, and now was a most passionate lover of wild nature. He had dined with nobility and gentry, and could talk of them and of cities, from the end of his tongue ; but of the pleasures of the sportsman in British America, out of his very heart. A more genial companion the lonely traveller could not easily light upon. I had seen him before, but forgot to mention it. It was at Murdoch's, on the last Sunday, which I was sorry to recollect of him. He drove up about noon, in woodman's dress partly ; washed, dined, and departed in great haste for Pictou, in order to reach Halifax in time for the very steamer that we were hoping to catch. With all his speed he missed it as well as we. Hinc illæ lachrymæ. In his conversation you heard the crack of the rifle, and the roar of the forest and the ocean. He was often reeling in the largest salmon and the finest trout, and bringing down with a crash in the brushwood the fattest of all bucks. The light of his nut-brown pipe, a costly article, flashing faintly on his well-marked face, reminded me of the red blaze of camp-fires in the woods, on the banks of mountain brooks, and the shores of solitary lakes. From one of a nature so companionable you part, on the road, after no longer than a day's acquaintance, with genuine regret. He was a character for the novelist, with a head and countenance both for painter and sculptor.

CHAPTER LXIV.

WINDSOR.—THE AVON AND THE TIDE.—THE STEAMER FOR ST. JOHN'S, NEW BRUNSWICK.—MINES BASIN.—COAST SCENERY.—THE SCENE OF EVANGELINE.—PARSBORO.—THE BAY OF FUNDY.—NOVA SCOTIA AND NEW BRUNSWICK SHORES.—ST. JOHNS.—THE MAINE COAST, AND GRAND MANAN.

WEDNESDAY, *July* 27. Windsor, N. S. Soon after our arrival, I walked down to the Avon, an arm of Mines Bay, itself an expanded inlet of the great Bay of Fundy, to view the wonderful tide. It was not coming in, as I had hoped, but quite out, leaving miles of black river-bottom entirely bare, with only a small stream coursing through in a serpentine manner. A line of blue water was visible on the northern horizon. After an absence of an hour or so, I loitered back, when, to my surprise, there was a river like the Hudson at Catskill, running up with a powerful current. The high wharf, upon which, but a short time before, I had stood and surveyed the black, unsightly fields of mud, was now up to its middle in the turbid and whirling stream, and very nearly in, the steamer from St. Johns, N. B.

In the course of an hour more I was on board, and waiting for the turn of the tide, upon which, of necessity, the boat takes her departure. I had missed, after all, seeing the first approach of the tidal wave, and had to content myself with what I have described, and with a short walk in the town, of late esteeming itself note-worthy on account of being the birthplace of General Williams, the hero of Kars, of whose fine personal appearance I have spoken.

We are now at the opening of the Avon into Mines Bay or Basin, as they call this small sea, and look upon scenes of which Longfellow speaks in the first pages of his Evangeline. It is simply a pleasant-looking farming country, checkered with fields of green, now of a yellow tint and then of a blue. Shores of reddish rocks and sand make a pretty foreground line along the west, and rise to the picturesque as they wind away northward. Headlands of gray and red rocks in slopes and precipices stand out in bold relief crowned with underwood and loftier trees. The clouds are clearing away before the breeze, and letting us have a sparkling sea, a fine blue sky, and landscapes dappled with light and shadow.

Parsboro, a village on the north shore of the Basin,

enjoys more than its share of broad, gravelly beach, overhung with clifted and woody bluffs. One fresh from the
dead walls of a great city would be delighted with the
sylvan shores of Parsboro. The beach, with all its
breadth, a miracle of pebbly beauty, slants steeply to the
surf, which is now rolling up in curling clouds of green
and white. Here we turn westward into the great bay
itself, going with a tide that rushes like a mighty river
toward a cataract, whirling, boiling, breaking in half
moons of crispy foam. Behind us is the blue reach of
Chignecto Bay, the northern of the two long and winding
horns of the main body of water, up which it would be
play for a fortnight to hunt romantic scenery, and witness the "bore," that most brilliant of all tidal displays.

Here is a broad sea, moving with strange velocity for
a sea. The prospect to the south is singularly fine.
Nova Scotia, sloping from the far-off sky gently down to
the shores, its fields and villages and country dwellings
gleaming in the warm noon-day, or darkening in the
shadow of a transient cloud—a contrast to the northern,
New Brunswick coast, iron-bound and covered with dark
forests. Drops from a coming shower are wasting their
sweet freshness upon the briny deep, an agreeable discord
in the common music of the day, and chime in, among
pleasant incidents, with the talk of the Prince Edward's

man, and the sparkling conversation of the Newfoundland gentleman. "And so sail we" into the harbor of St. Johns, the last of the waters of this divine apostle, in time for supper and a pleasant ramble about the city. You might call it the city of hills.

THURSDAY, *July* 28, 1859. St. Johns, N. B. This is my last date, and I write it out in full, in the light of a fine morning, on the deck of the steamer for Portland. The coast of Maine, truly picturesque as it is, with its rocky points, lake-like bays, and islands bristling in their dark evergreens like porcupines, and particularly Mount Desert Island and Frenchman's Bay, is the mildest form of Newfoundland scenery as you see it on the Atlantic side, with an additional dressing of forest and vegetation, sparsely studded with towns and habitations.

Speaking of Mount Desert Island, recalls Cole to memory, who was, I believe, the first landscape painter of our country that visited that picturesque region. I remember with what enthusiasm he spoke of the coast scenery—the fine surf upon Sand Beach—the play of the surge in the caverns of Great Head—the Ægean beauty of Frenchman's Bay—the forests, and the wild, rugged mountains, from the tops of which he could count a multitude of sails upon the blue ocean, and follow the rocky shores and sparkling breakers for many and many a mile. Familiar to me as all that has long since become, I shall not pass it to-day without emotion.

Grand Manan, a favorite summer haunt of the painter, is the very throne of the bold and romantic. The high, precipitous shores, but for the woods which beautify them, are quite in the style of Labrador. I look upon its grand old cliffs with double interest from the fact that he has made me familiar with its people and scenery. As it recedes from my view, and becomes a dot in the boundless waters, I will put the period to this record.

THE END.

Shakespeare's Works. Edited, with a Scrupulous Revision of the Text, by MARY COWDEN CLARKE, Author of the "Complete Concordance to Shakespeare." 1 vol. 8vo. 1064 pages. Illustrated with 49 Illustrations. Half mor., top gilt, $6; half calf, $7 50; mor., extra, $10.

—————— **2 vols. 1600 pages.** Illustrated with 49 Steel Plates. Half mor., top edges gilt, $8; half calf, $10; full mor., extra, $15.

Education; Intellectual, Moral, and Physical. By HERBERT SPENCER, Author of "Social Statics," the "Principles of Psychology," and "Essays; Scientific, Political, and Speculative." 1 vol. 12mo. $1.

A Christmas Dream. By JAMES T. BRADY. Illustrated by EDWARD S. HALL.

The Illustrated Horse Doctor: being an Accurate and Detailed Account, accompanied by more than 400 Pictorial Representations of the Various Diseases to which the Equine Race is subjected; together with the Latest Mode of Treatment, and all the Requisite Prescriptions, written in plain English. By EDWARD MAYHEW, M. R. C. V. S., Author of "The Horse's Mouth;" "Dogs: their Management;" Editor of "Blain's Veterinary Art," etc. (Nearly ready.)

The New American Cyclopædia: a Popular Dictionary of General Knowledge. Edited by GEORGE RIPLEY and CHAS. A. DANA. Vols. I. to X. To be completed in 16 vols. Price in cloth, $3; sheep, $3 50; half mor., $4; half russia, $4 50.

Abridgment of the Debates of Congress

from 1789 to 1856. From Gales and Seaton's Annals of Congress; from their Register of Debates; and from the Official Reported Debates, by John C. Rives. By THOMAS H. BENTON, Author of the "Thirty Years' View." Vols. I. to XIV. now ready. To be completed in 16 vols. Price in cloth, $3 per vol.; law sheep, $3 50; half mor., $4.

Villas on the Hudson: a Series of Thirty-

one Photo-Lithographs of Gentlemen's Seats on the Hudson. Oblong 4to. Cloth, $8; half mor., $10.

The Illustrated Byron. With upwards

of Two Hundred Engravings from Original Drawings, by Kenny Meadows, Birket Foster, Hallet K. Browne, Gustav Janet, and Edward Morin. (Nearly ready.)

Fables, Original and Selected; with an

Introductory Dissertation on the History of Fable, comprising Bibliographical Notices of Eminent Fabulists. By G. MOIR BUSSEY. Illustrated with Numerous Engravings from Designs by J. J. Granville. (Nearly ready.)

Adventures of Telemachus. Translated

by Dr. HAWKESWORTH. Embellished with upwards of 100 Engravings, by first-rate artists. 1 vol. 8vo. (Nearly ready.)

Adventures of Gil Blas, of Santillane.

Translated from the French of LE SAGE by T. SMOLLETT, M. D. Embellished with 500 Engravings after Designs by Gignoux. (Nearly ready.)

New Books and New Editions

PUBLISHED BY

D. APPLETON & COMPANY.

The Housekeeper's Encyclopedia of Useful Information for the Housekeeper in all Branches of Cooking and Domestic Economy; containing the first Scientific and Reliable Rules for putting up all kinds of Hermetically-sealed Fruits, with or without Sugar, in Tin Cans or Common Bottles. Also, Rules for Preserving Fruits in American and French Styles, with Tried Receipts for Making Domestic Wines, Catsups, Syrups, Cordials, etc.; and Practical Directions for the Cultivation of Vegetables. Fruits, and Flowers, Destruction of Insects, etc. By Mrs. E. F. HASKELL. 1 thick vol. 12mo. $1 25.

The Life and Writings of the Rt. Rev. GEO. WASHINGTON DOANE, D.D., LL.D., for Twenty-seven years Bishop of New Jersey. In 4 vols. 8vo. Containing his Poetical Works, Sermons, and Miscellaneous Writings; with a Memoir by his son, WM. CROSWELL DOANE. Vols. I. and II. now ready. Price, $2 50 each.

PUBLISHED BY D. APPTETON AND COMPANY.

On the Origin of Species by Means

of Natural Selection; or, the Preservation of favored Races in the Struggle for Life. By CHARLES DARWIN, M.A., F.R.S., F.G.S., &c., &c. 1 vol. 12mo. With copious Index. Cloth, $1 25.

After the Icebergs with a Painter. By

LOUIS L. NOBLE. 1 vol. 12mo. With Illustrations. (Nearly ready.)

The Manufacture of Photogenic or Hy-

dro-carbon Oils, from Coal and other Bituminous Substances, capable of supplying Burning Fluids. By THOMAS ANTISELL, M.D., Professor of Chemistry in the Medical Department of Georgetown College, D. C., &c., &c. 1 vol. 8vo. Beautifully printed. Cloth, $1 75.

Considerations on some of the Elements

and Conditions of Social Welfare and Human Progress. Being Academic and Occasional Discourses and other Pieces. By C. S. Henry, D.D. 1 vol. 12mo. $1.

Science Brought Down to the Year 1860.

Being a Supplement to Ure's Dictionary of Arts, Manufactures, and Mines. Taken from the English Edition. With additions by an American Editor. (Nearly ready.) 8vo.

Milledulcia: a Thousand Pleasant Things.

Selected from "Notes and Queries." 12mo. Cloth, top edge gilt, $1 50; in half calf, $3; morocco antique, $3 50.

Chambers's Encyclopædia : a Dictionary of Universal Knowledge for the People. Now publishing in Parts. Part 19 now ready. Price 15 cents each Part.

A Greek Grammar, for Schools and Colleges. By JAMES HADLEY, Professor in Yale College. 12mo. 366 pages. $1 25.

Virgil's Æneid; with Explanatory Notes. By HENRY S. FRIEZE, Professor of Latin in the State University of Michigan. 12mo. Eighty-five illustrations. 598 pages. $1 25.

Spanish Grammar. A New, Practical, and Easy Method of Learning the Spanish Language, after the system of A. F. AHN, Doctor of Philosophy, and Professor at the College of Neuss. First American edition, revised and enlarged. 12mo. 149 pages. 75 cents. Key, 15 cents.

An Elementary Grammar of the Italian Language. Progressively arranged for the use of Schools and Colleges. By G. B. FONTANA. 12mo. 236 pages. $1.

Plato's Apology and Crito ; with Notes. By W. S. TYLER, Graves Professor of Greek in Amherst College. 12mo. 180 pages. 75 cents.

French Syntax. A Course of Exercises in all parts of French Syntax, methodically arranged after Poitevin's " Syntaxe Française ;" to which are added ten appendices; designed for the use of Academies, Colleges, and Private Learners. By FREDERICK T. WINKELMANN, A.M. & Ph. D., Prof. of Latin, French, and German, in the Packer Collegiate Institute. 12mo. 366 pages. $1.

APPLETON'S RAILWAY GUIDE. Containing Time Tables of all the Railroads in the United States. Illustrated by Maps of the Principal Roads and Through Routes, and a large General Map. Published semi-monthly. Price 25 cts.

Appleton's Companion Handbook of Travel, containing a full Description of the Principal Cities, Towns, and Places of Interest, together with Hotels, and Routes of Travel through the United States and the Canadas. With colored Maps. Edited by T. ADDISON RICHARDS. Paper covers, 50 cts.; cloth, 75 cts.

Appleton's Illustrated Handbook of Travel. A Guide by Railway, Steamboat, and Stage, to the Cities, Towns, Waterfalls, Mountains, Rivers, Lakes, Hunting and Fishing Grounds, Watering Places, Summer Resorts, and all Scenes and Objects of Interest in the United States and British Provinces. By T. ADDISON RICHARDS. With careful Maps of all parts of the Country, and 200 Pictures of Famous Scenes and Places. From Original Drawings by the Author and other Artists. 1 vol. 12mo. 400 pages, double columns. Flexible cloth. Price $1 50. The Northern and Eastern States separately, $1. The Southern and Western States separately, $1.

Beaumont and Fletcher's Works. The Poetical and Dramatic Works of Beaumont and Fletcher. With an Introduction by GEORGE DARLEY, to which is added Notes and Glossary. 2 handsome vols. Royal 8vo. Well printed. Cloth, $6; in sheep, $7; half calf, extra, $9.

Moral Emblems, with Aphorisms, Adages, and Proverbs, of all Ages and Nations. From JACOB CATZ and ROBERT FAIRLIE. With 120 Illustrations truly rendered from Designs found in their Works, by JOHN LEIGHTON, F. S. A. The whole Translated and Edited, with Additions, by RICHARD PIGOT. 1 vol. Royal 8vo. Cloth gilt, $7 50; mor., $10; mor., extra, $12.

The Adventures of Brown, Jones, and Robinson. The Most Amusing Adventures of Three English Gentlemen bearing the above euphonious names. Each incident in their Travels on the Continent is Illustrated by a Spirited Design of a Laughable Character. 1 vol. 4to. (Nearly ready.)

Hopes and Fears; or, Scenes from the Life of a Spinster: a Novel. By the Author of "The Heir of Redclyffe." (Nearly ready.)

A History of Civilization. By Henry T. Buckle. Vol. I. Price, $2 50. Vol. II. (Nearly ready.)

The History of Herodotus. A new English version. Edited with copious Notes and Appendices, illustrating the History and Geography of Herodotus, from the most Ancient Sources of Information; and embodying the Chief Results, Historical and Ethnographical, which have been obtained in the progress of Cuneiform and Hieroglyphical Discovery. By GEORGE RAWLINSON, M. A., assisted by Col. Sir. Henry Rawlinson and Sir J. G. Wilkinson. With Maps and Illustrations. 4 vols. 8vo. Price $2 50 each.

Reminiscences of a General Officer of Zouaves. By Gen. CLER. Translated from the French. 1 vol. 12mo. Cloth, $1.

Life of William T. Porter. By FRANCIS BRINLEY. 1 vol. 12mo. $1.

The Ebony Idol. By a Lady of New England. 1 vol. 12mo. Illustrated. $1.

What may be Learned from a Tree. By HARLAND COULTAS. 1 vol. 8vo. $1.

The Physiology of Common Life. By GEO. HENRY LEWES. 2 vols. 12mo. $2.

Notes on Nursing ; What it Is, and What it is Not. By FLORENCE NIGHTINGALE. 1 vol. 12mo. Paper covers, 15 cents; cloth, 25 cents.

Dr. Oldham at Greystones, and his Talk there. 1 vol. 12mo. Price $1.

Voyage Down the Amoor ; with a Jour- ney through Siberia, and Incidental Notes of Manchoria, Kamschatka, and Japan. By PERRY MCDONOUGH COLLINS. 1 vol. 12mo. Cloth, $1 25.

A Run Through Europe. By ERASTUS C. BENEDICT. 1 vol. 12mo. Price $1 25.

The History of the State of Rhode Isl- and and Providence Plantations. By the Hon. SAMUEL GREENE ARNOLD. 2 vols. Price $5.

CPSIA information can be obtained
at www.ICGtesting.com
Printed in the USA
LVOW10s0133120717
541058LV00034B/1621/P

9 781330 876510